LP

Sefton Libraries Bookface   @seftonLibraries   Sefton Libraries

Your library Sefton

MK

Please return this item by the due date:

WITHDRAWN
FROM STOCK

- SEP 2008

Please return this item by the due date
or renew at **www.sefton.gov.uk/libraries**
or by telephone at **any** Sefton library:

Bootle Library   **0151 934 5781**
Crosby Library   **0151 257 6400**
Formby Library   **01704 874 177**
Meadows Library   **0151 288 6727**
Netherton Library   **0151 525 0607**
Southport Library   **0151 934 2118**

your Library Sefton   Sefton Council

A lover of fairy tales and history, **Lauri Robinson** can't imagine a better profession than penning happily-ever-after stories about men and women in days gone past. Her favourite settings include World War II, the Roaring Twenties and the Old West. Lauri and her husband raised three sons in their rural Minnesota home, and are now getting their just rewards by spoiling their grandchildren. Visit her at laurirobinson.blogspot.com, Facebook.com/lauri.robinson1 or Twitter.com/laurir.

Also by Lauri Robinson

Diary of a War Bride

**Brides of the Roaring Twenties
miniseries**

Baby on His Hollywood Doorstep
Stolen Kiss with the Hollywood Starlet

**Sisters of the Roaring Twenties
miniseries**

The Flapper's Fake Fiancé
The Flapper's Baby Scandal
The Flapper's Scandalous Elopement

Discover more at millsandboon.co.uk.

THE FLAPPER'S
SCANDALOUS
ELOPEMENT

Lauri Robinson

MILLS & BOON

First published in Great Britain 2020
by Mills & Boon, an imprint of HarperCollins*Publishers*
1 London Bridge Street, London, SE1 9GF

Large Print edition 2021

© 2020 Lauri Robinson

ISBN: 978-0-263-08996-7

MIX
Paper from
responsible sources
FSC
www.fsc.org
FSC™ C007454

This book is produced from independently certified FSC™ paper to ensure responsible forest management. For more information visit www.harpercollins.co.uk/green.

Printed and bound in Great Britain
by CPI Group (UK) Ltd, Croydon, CR0 4YY

To Kathy,
an amazing woman who loves to read.
Truly an author's best friend.
Thanks, Kathy, so very much!

Chapter One

1928

The Rooster's Nest was as dull as an old woman clicking knitting needles. There were no clusters of spiffily dressed men and women spewing chin music and laughing, blocking the way to the powder room. No groups of men wearing work clothes and standing near the bar, telling stories they'd told before but still tossing their heads back with laughter. No couples dancing cheek to cheek, filling the dance floor beneath the bright lights with their stained-glass shades.

Normally she'd be dancing, kicking up her heels and really cutting a rug; however, tonight Jane Dryer was sitting at the bar, tapping one foot to the beat of the music while sipping on a fruit juice cocktail. She let out a sigh while twirling her glass on the varnished wood of the long bar and scanned the room again, hoping the occupants had changed.

They hadn't. The same two couples sat at tables. One pair, the woman with red hair and the man with a tweed hat, looked like they were arguing, and the other couple, the one that kept leaning closer, whispering, looked shady enough they could be a gangster and his moll. The other tables and a couple of stools at the other end of the bar were occupied by men who, for the most part, were here for the drinking, not dancing or fun.

They might participate if she asked, but not a one of them, with their shirtsleeves rolled up past their elbows, revealing dirty arms, was one she wanted to dance with. She had her standards.

Actually, her sister Betty had set standards that they all three had to abide by during their nights out. Not just who they could dance with, but what they could drink so that none of them ended up blind, and which speakeasies they could visit so they didn't end up in a raid.

The trouble was, it wasn't *they* anymore. For months, she and her sisters, Betty and Patsy, had changed into the flapper outfits they'd sewn in secret, climbed out the bathroom window and visited speakeasies nearly every night.

It had been her idea several months ago for them to sneak out at night, escape the confines of their father's house. Despite the fact they were all grown women—she was twenty-one, Patsy twenty and Betty twenty-two—they'd been treated like they were all under five, complete with a seven-thirty bedtime every night. They'd found freedom in sneaking out, and Betty had set down the rules they had to follow to make sure they didn't get caught. They hadn't.

Gotten caught, that was, but her sisters were no longer with her on these nightly excursions. They were both married. Three months ago Patsy had married Lane Cox, the owner of the *Los Angeles Gazette* and the best reporter in the state. Patsy was a reporter now, too, and loving her new life.

A month later, Betty had married Henry Randall, an FBI agent. They were going to have a baby next year, around May, six months from now. Betty was in her glory. She'd always been a mother hen and was already sewing baby clothes.

Jane grinned. Betty would be a wonderful mother, and Jane was happy for her and for Patsy. She was just bored. And this place tonight made her even more bored.

"Dull night."

The long fringe around the hem of her dark

purple dress swished against her calf as she twisted her stool enough to glance over her shoulder at who'd spoken. She then glanced toward the piano and the empty seat behind it. So lost in boredom, she hadn't realized the music had stopped.

The piano player grasped ahold of the glass the bartender, who was as listless as the rest of the room tonight, slid across the bar.

Twisting her stool back around so she was facing away from him, she took a sip of her drink. In the past she'd talked to the piano players, even sat next to them on their piano bench, but no longer. They couldn't be trusted.

"No one's dancing," he said. "Not even you."

"No one to dance with," she said, without turning around. She knew what he looked like. He had a dimple in one cheek when he smiled, and he always rolled his sleeves up to the elbows when he played.

"What about that guy?"

Jane didn't need to look at him to know he was suggesting the fella at the table near the hallway. She shook her head.

"Why not?"

"He works at the docks." She'd never spoken to this piano player because, after the last one, she'd made herself a rule. No more piano players. No matter how nice looking or good smelling. This one wasn't here all that often—he only played a few nights a week—and had only been doing that for a couple of months.

"Why does it matter where he works? It's only a dance."

She lifted her glass, took a sip. "Go stand next to him."

He chuckled. "That bad?"

"It's like dancing with a dead rockfish." She shivered at the memory of the one time she had danced with that guy. The smell of rotten fish had been embedded in her nose for hours.

The piano player chuckled again as he set his glass on the bar with a thud. "I'm done for the night, Murray."

"All right, Dave," Murray, the bartender, answered. "See you tomorrow night."

"See you," he told Murray, then tapped on her shoulder. "Have a good night."

She still didn't face him but nodded.

"Will you be here tomorrow night?"

She shrugged. She never told anyone her plans, another one of Betty's rules that still stuck with her. Most of the rules she didn't mind, and with Betty's husband being an FBI agent, Jane was well aware of the dangers and consequences of not following several of them.

"Hopefully, it'll be more lively," he said.

Beneath the brim of her floppy black hat, she watched him leave. He was a real Joe Brooks—handsome, with his wavy brown hair and twinkling green eyes, and perfectly dressed from his white-and-black-striped shirt down to his black-and-white wing tip shoes. He really could make piano keys dance, too. She knew. She loved music and spent hours watching the musicians at each of the speakeasies. Piano music was her favorite, and she could listen to it all day, every day. Which was why she used to talk to the piano players, until one got to expecting her to talk to only him, and another one couldn't keep his hands to himself.

"Want another one?" Murray asked.

She shook her head while twisting her stool back around to face the bar. "No." There was no use hanging around here.

Murray tapped the varnished wood top of the bar twice with his hand. She didn't know why he did that, but he did; rather than nodding or answering, he'd just tap the bar. Even on nights when the place was hopping.

She should have left while the music was still

playing, providing a small amount of distraction. With so few people in the joint, someone might see her slip behind the curtain that hung along the back wall, hiding the door to the storeroom, which was also her exit route.

Having almost been caught once, she was very careful about not being seen slipping behind the curtain. It was a good ten minutes before Murray walked down the hall to the john. She stood, and after a quick scan to make sure no one was watching, she walked over to the piano and ran a hand over its smooth top as she casually strolled past it. After another quick glance around the room, she shot over to the wall and behind the curtain.

She opened the door to the storeroom and closed it just as quietly, then ran past boxes, crates and shelves full of bottles to the end wall, swung the shelf away from the wall and opened the hidden door behind it. As far as she knew, no one, not even Murray, knew about this door.

After pulling the shelf back in place first, she shut the door and clicked on her flashlight in order to see as she locked the door. She'd promised Betty and Henry she'd never leave it unlocked and wouldn't. The tunnel went all the way to their house. To their basement. A mob boss had built the house and tunnel several years ago, and when he'd been busted, the government had confiscated the house. Betty and Henry had purchased it after getting married. Father had tried to purchase it several times and questioned how Henry had managed to buy it. Because he worked for the government! He was an FBI agent. It didn't take much to figure that one out. But Father was still miffed that he hadn't been given the chance to buy it.

That's what her father cared about. Houses and money. Mostly money. He'd inherited a large amount of land from his grandfather and father, and created Hollywoodland, a place where only the rich and famous could afford to build a house. Father was obsessed with money, and with keeping it, to the point he'd made a list of rich men. Men he'd tried forcing Patsy and Betty to marry. Betty almost ended up marrying James Bauer, one of the men on Father's list. Up until Henry had walked into the church and objected to the marriage of Betty and James.

That had been amazing, and she'd been overjoyed for her sister, at how Betty had ended up marrying Henry instead of James that very day. Jane still was happy for her sister. She was also scared because she knew what had happened to

Betty—being forced to marry a stranger just because he was rich—would soon happen to her.

It was in the cards.

Lane had been on Father's list, but Patsy had already fallen in love with him by the time they got engaged. When that had happened Jane had hoped it meant things would be different, for her and Betty, but they hadn't been. Within hours of Patsy's wedding, Father was ordering Betty to marry James.

The sigh that left her echoed through the dark tunnel, and she instantly shone the beam of the flashlight on the walls and ceiling, making sure she hadn't stirred up any furry or winged inhabitants. She'd never seen any but always wondered if they were there, watching her with beady little eyes as she walked through the tunnel each night.

That was eerie; however, she would come back tomorrow night. It wasn't as if she had anything else to do. Now that her sisters were married, out of the house, she didn't have anyone to talk to, anyone to laugh with, anyone to just be there with her.

Not while she was cooking, cleaning, washing clothes or cleaning the newly built homes on the plots of land in the hills of the Santa Monica

Mountains, overlooking the fast-growing movie studios. That's how Father made his money. Money he wouldn't share with anyone.

She wasn't complaining, just frustrated. Father had provided well for his family. They had a very nice house, plenty to eat, clothes and everything else, but he wanted his daughters to marry money so that when they moved out, they'd no longer need any of his money. That was the truth of it. He cared more about money than his family, and there wasn't anything she could do about it. She'd end up marrying a man because of his money, and that curdled her stomach. Unlike Patsy, Jane hadn't met anyone who would ever compel those feelings in her, and she most certainly had never met anyone who would object to her wedding like Henry had Betty's.

How could she? She was never allowed to go anywhere.

She was doomed. Not only doomed—hopeless. Betty and Patsy were married, and though they were still her sisters and she loved them, she felt deserted.

The ceiling of the wood-lined tunnel shook, telling her she was walking beneath one of the streets between the Rooster's Nest and Betty's house. The tunnel was over ten city blocks long, and some nights it gave her the heebie-jeebies, afraid it might collapse on her. However, walking or taking the trolley by herself was just as scary.

None of that had been scary when it had been the three of them. They'd all three walked and taken the trolley to a variety of joints. She'd gone to a couple of other speakeasies since it had become just her sneaking out, but quickly discovered she didn't like walking the streets and alleys alone. Didn't like riding the trolley alone. She didn't even like walking alone down here in the tunnel all that much.

She ran the final few blocks and then locked the tunnel door once she was inside the basement of Betty's house. Taking a moment to catch her breath, she hung the keys on their hook and then walked upstairs and out the kitchen door. Henry had put a special lock on that door, one that locked from the inside, without a key, so all she had to do was pull it shut, because Betty and Henry were always asleep or at least upstairs in bed when she left their house.

Betty and Henry's property butted up to Hollywoodland and was only a short distance from her house, but the dark road was still lonely and the wind rustling the weeds and trees made her jumpy. The night air was also chilly, so she ran again, up the road, through the trees and across her backyard. Then she grabbed ahold of the boards of the ivy-covered trellis, climbed to the second floor of the house and slipped in through the bathroom window.

Once in her room, she quickly changed out of her flapper clothes, hid them in the trunk in her closet and climbed into bed before she dared let out a sigh of relief that she'd made it home once again without getting caught.

Staring at the shadows the moon was casting upon the ceiling, she wondered if marrying a stranger would be better than this. It was awfully lonely with both of her sisters gone. Married. Happy.

But she didn't want to get married.

She huffed out a breath.

Patsy had always wanted to be a reporter, and she was now. Betty had gotten what she wanted, too. To have her own family, her own house.

Jane rolled over on her side. She didn't know what she wanted because she didn't know what was out there. She read about all sorts of things in magazines, and wanted to see some of those things, do some of those things, and then she'd decide what she wanted.

Other than a weekly shopping trip, going to church on Sundays and sneaking out at night to speakeasies, she'd never been anywhere.

She didn't have anyone to talk to, either.

Maybe she'd talk to that piano player again tomorrow night. Dave. She'd know right away if he was like Allen, the one who couldn't keep his hands to himself. She'd been glad when Rodney had started playing there, instead. Until he'd come to expect her to sit next to him, picking out songs and bringing him drinks every night. Even told her she shouldn't be dancing with others.

He'd gotten grumpy when she'd told him to go sit on a goose egg. She'd avoided going to the Rooster's Nest on the nights when Rodney had been playing after that and had been glad when Dave had taken over, but she'd kept her distance because of Allen and Rodney.

That was one thing she didn't want. Another man controlling her.

Dave was nicer looking than either Allen or Rodney had been, and he'd never waved her over to sit by him like they had.

Maybe she wouldn't talk to him. If he got to

expecting too much she wouldn't have anywhere to sneak out to, and that would be awful.

David Albright stared at the ceiling above his bed, watching the glow of headlights that shone in above the heavy drapes whiz by as fast as the cars were speeding along the highway outside of the apartment building. He'd gotten used to the lights and the noise over the past few months, as he'd known he would when he'd rented this place four months ago.

Just like he'd gotten used to the hotel he'd stayed in for a couple of months. He'd had to leave there because Joshua kept calling and calling. For that reason alone, David hadn't installed a phone in this apartment. His brother wanted him to cut his research trip short, return home and get married.

David clamped his teeth together and breathed through the anger rising up inside him. He had no desire to get married. Ever. That want had died when Joshua had married Charlene.

Joshua. The older brother. The man who had everything. The brother, who had been groomed to take over the family business and had. Joshua had the chairman's seat in the family railroad business, more money than he could spend in his lifetime and a beautiful, loving wife.

David pushed aside thoughts of Charlene just as he had for the last four years—other than the sorrow he felt for her.

He'd felt a whole lot more for her at one time, right up until she'd turned down his marriage proposal because she was marrying Joshua. He'd accepted that.

What he couldn't accept was how hard Joshua was now pushing him to get married.

A knot formed in his stomach and David let out a huff. His time was almost up. Grandpa's birthday was a week and a half away. Which meant he needed to leave soon. Within days. Drive back to Chicago. No closer to figuring out how to get out of marrying Rebecca Stuart than when he'd left.

He'd left six months ago to explore the newly developed highway system for the stockholders, and his grandfather had told him to extend his trip. Take his time, stay in California awhile, sow his wild oats, and then return, report his findings and then decide if marrying Rebecca was not only right for the family, but right for him. Rebecca was the granddaughter of Grandpa's best friend, Orville Stuart. Orville had passed away a few years ago, and Grandpa claimed that upon her birth, he and Orville had discussed Rebecca marrying one of his grandsons. Now, twenty-five years later, that grandson turned out to be him. Joshua was already married.

Rebecca was a vamp. A gold digger who wanted to be an Albright and have all the prestige that went along with it.

He'd be the first one to tell her that the prestige she wanted wasn't all it was made out to be. As an Albright, your life wasn't your own.

David was used to that. His life had never been his own. He'd come to accept that. Especially four years ago, when Charlene had married Joshua instead of him.

David closed his eyes in order to stop his thoughts from going any further. He'd been down every path, trail and circle, trying to come up with a plan while he'd been here in Los Angeles. A plan that would not only prevent him from marrying Rebecca but one that would help Charlene. She'd changed so much the past couple of years, had become only a shadow of the person she'd used to be. He couldn't help but wonder if he wasn't the cause of some of that. If having him live in the same house as her and

Joshua reminded her of the past, of how he'd expected her to marry him.

He had expected that. Everyone had.

David released the air that was turning his chest hard. He'd arrived in Los Angeles without an agenda and would leave without one. Go back to Chicago. As he'd promised his grandfather he would. Odds were, he'd end up marrying Rebecca, too.

At times the weight on his chest of balancing his family duties with his own wants, his own visions, nearly suffocated him. At the same time, he thrived on the work he did with the railroad. Loved working on expanding the vast empire his grandfather had built. The country was still growing and new rail lines were still needed—as were other forms of transportation. Being a major player in areas where new lines were needed and overseeing them coming to fruition thrilled him, and he was good at it. Not even Joshua could deny that. The expansions he'd overseen the past several years had all been very profitable.

He'd continued to work on future possibilities while in California, additional lines and locomotives that could be considered once present projects were completed, but not even that—

working—had relieved the pressure on his shoulders while he'd been out here.

He'd found an escape from all the pressure during his time here by playing the piano at a speakeasy a few times a week. It was a hobby he'd always enjoyed, and most nights the speakeasy was hopping with people dancing and laughing and having a good time.

Not tonight.

He grinned. "Dancing with a dead rockfish," he said aloud. He'd never done that, danced with a rockfish, but could imagine it wouldn't be very pleasant. She was, though, pleasant. Cheery. The cute blonde flapper that was a regular at the Rooster's Nest nearly every night. She always had a smile on her face and enticed those around her to smile, too.

He'd never talked to her before tonight, but had noticed her right off when he'd first started playing there a couple of months ago. She always came alone.

Always left alone, too.

At least he assumed she did.

That was a very odd thing about her. How she just appeared and then disappeared.

From where the piano sat, with him behind it, he could see the door, and he never saw her walk out of it, or in it. She'd just all of a sudden be there dancing, laughing, having an all-in-all good time.

Murray didn't even know her name. That was odd because Murray knew most every customer by name. He just called her "doll." Which was fitting. She was a doll.

David rolled over and pulled the covers up to block the glow of lights on the ceiling so he could fall asleep, and a grin formed as he thought about her again. A flapper. Joshua would be fit to be tied if he knew about his piano-playing nights, him consorting with a flapper.

She was indeed there the following night, dancing, laughing, having a good time. Like usual, she'd suddenly appeared as if she'd dropped down through the ceiling a short time ago.

He'd waited for her to look his way, and when she finally had, he'd nodded at her.

She'd winked at him, laughed, and kept on dancing with some fella.

A different one than she was dancing with right now. She was something. Too bad she didn't live in Chicago. He'd haul her home just to irritate Joshua.

David was surprised when she left the dance

floor and plopped down on the seat beside him a moment later.

He finished playing the song, ended it on a high note that hung in the air and looked at her.

"Hey there, Joe," she said with a smile as bright as the overhead lights.

She was cute, with her round cheeks, twinkling blue eyes and little chin that had a tiny indent in the very tip. "Joe?"

She laughed. "Yes, you know, Joe Brooks. That's what the magazines call..." She paused as her blue eyes gave him a solid once-over. "A spiffily dressed fella."

"I did not know that," he admitted. "But my name's not Joe, it's David."

"Nice name."

She reached up and started flipping through the sheets of music above the keys. The sheets he had laid out in the order he was going to play them. They weren't in any order now, and he didn't mind. It wasn't as if anyone would notice.

"What is your name?" he asked.

A wide smile revealed her sparkling white teeth. "Oh, I'm just your average Jane."

He had heard that. Men called women Janes all the time. Men probably asked her for her name all the time. "Nice name, Average Jane."

Her joy-filled laugh hung in the air like the last piano note had. "What are you playing next?"

"What do you want to hear?"

"I was hoping you'd ask." She plucked out a song sheet and set it atop the rest.

"You want to dance to 'The Charleston'?" he asked.

She shrugged. "Or just hear the song."

He glanced around at the full tables, the full bar, looking for the man she had been dancing with a few moments ago. "What happened to your dance partners?"

She cringed. "The last one stepped on my toes one too many times."

"What about one of the others?"

"I'd already danced twice with each of them."

"I see," he said, just to have an answer.

"Why do people say that?" Frowning, she gave him a perplexed look. "I see? What do you see?"

He shrugged. "Why do they call men Joe Brooks or women Janes?"

"Because it's fun." The colorful ostrich feather poking out of her floppy white hat fluttered as she shook her head. "'I see' isn't fun."

He nodded. "I see."

They both laughed, and he struck the keys, playing the beginning of the song she'd chosen.

"Attaboy, Joe!" She swayed to the music as her feet danced while she remained seated beside him. "Ducky!"

He played faster, laughing at how she moved faster, bumping into him every now and again, and giggling with delight.

Other people had sat next to him while he played a song or two, which seemed to be the thing to do. He didn't mind. That was why he'd started playing here, to have fun.

As soon as that song ended, he flipped over the sheet and read the title of the one now sitting atop the stack. He pointed to a key. "Tap that one when I tell you."

Grinning, she held a trim finger over the key.

He began to play and then nodded at her.

She struck the key and tossed her head back as she laughed.

He kept playing and nodded at her again.

She struck the key and laughed again like it was the most fun she'd ever had.

They continued, him nodding, her striking, and laughing throughout the song.

When the song ended, she clapped her hands. "Elephant's eyebrows! That was fun!"

"Want to play another one?"

"You know I do, Joe!"

"David," he said.

"All right, Davie!"

He laughed and started playing another song, nodding at her when the time was right for her to strike a key.

She sat there beside him, striking keys, until shortly after midnight, when the crowd had dwindled down to those who were there for one thing—the alcohol.

He folded the cover down over the keys. "Looks like we're done."

She laid a hand on the piano. "That was fun. Thanks."

"You're welcome." He gathered the song sheets into a neat pile and acted upon a thought that entered his head. "Do you need a ride home? I could give you one."

"No." She flashed him a thoughtful grin, then said, "I don't trust piano players."

Considering some of the unsavory characters he'd seen in speakeasies, he could understand that. "What if I told you I'm not really a piano player."

"Then I'd trust you less." No longer grinning, she stood. "See you, Joe."

Curious, he watched her walk away, half-expecting her to disappear before his eyes.

She didn't. She didn't go out the door, either. Instead, she walked past it and down the hallway that led to the powder rooms.

The men's room was across the hall from the women's, and he walked down the same hallway, used the facilities.

He was washing his hands when he heard the women's door open and close. Turning off the water with one hand, he grabbed the towel with the other and, after a quick wipe, hung it back up and opened the door.

She wasn't in the hallway, nor was she in the main room of the speakeasy.

He dashed out the door and up the steps.

She wasn't on the sidewalk, either.

"How does she do that?" he said aloud, looking up and down the dark, quiet street.

Chapter Two

Jane locked the tunnel door behind her and walked down the short set of steps, disappointed. Not a piano player. Horsefeathers! Just when she'd thought she might have found a friend.

Sitting next to him, playing the piano, had been the most fun she'd had in a long time. Then he'd had to go and lie to her.

A heavy sigh emptied her lungs completely. She'd thought he might be different. He seemed nice and…sophisticated. Not just his neatly pressed clothes, but the way he sat with his back straight, his shoulders squared, his chin level. He looked like he could be in one of the magazines she'd snuck into the house, the ones filled with pictures of celebrities and stars.

He smelled good, too. Many of the men she'd danced with the past few months had smelled like cigarette smoke. Or fish. One or two had smelled like newly cut wood, and that had been all right, but David had smelled fresh, clean and a little spicy. Sophisticated.

Other things, like how his bow tie had been perfectly straight beneath his chin, how the dimple had been in his cheek every time he'd looked at her, how a teasing glint had shone in his eyes when he'd called her Average Jane, filled her thoughts as she traversed the tunnel, crept though Betty's house, ran to her house and slipped in through the upstairs window.

She was no longer glad she'd talked to him tonight. He'd disappointed her, just like the other piano players. She wouldn't talk to him again. Or play the piano with him. Remembering that made her smile. That truly had been fun.

She smiled again the next morning, remembering that. Playing the piano. She might have to learn how to do that someday. After climbing out of bed and getting dressed in a red-and-white-plaid dress that hung to her ankles, she tucked thoughts of playing the piano again deep inside, where only she knew where it was hidden and went downstairs. Her flapper life was miles away from her real life. This was where she really was Average Jane.

The Dryer home, her home, was a somber

place. Always had been, always would be. Her father had a lot of money, but it was all for show. Inside the walls of this big fancy house, there was a pauper attitude that drove her crazy. What was the use of having money if you just let it pile up? There had to be so much more to life than that.

Father was at the table in the dining room, reading the newspaper. She wished him a good morning and didn't react one way or the other at his reply that was little more than a grunt.

In the kitchen, she said good morning to her mother while walking to the cupboard to collect dishes to set the table. There was already a pan of caramel rolls that smelled delicious sitting on the counter. They were her favorite, and Mother usually only made them on special occasions.

Mother was the best cook. The kitchen was where she could always be found, with an apron tied around her trim waist and her long blond hair tucked up in a bun. Other than on baking day, she never requested assistance with cooking. Cleaning, though, and other such tasks, were all on Jane's shoulders now that her sisters were gone.

She carried the dishes into the dining room, set the table, returned to the kitchen and filled serving dishes to carry back to the table. All this, as well as the entire meal, was completed in silence. That was one of Father's rules. Silence. The only time the radio could be on was to hear the news. That's how she and her sisters had lived since birth. Seen, but not heard.

The silence was just one of the things that had always driven her crazy. Her list had grown considerably since Patsy and Betty had gotten married, including how, now that it was just her, there was no one to distract Mother while shopping so a tube of lipstick or a magazine could be secretly purchased and snuck into the house.

She and her sisters had always pooled the money that their father had paid them to clean houses and used that to purchase such things, which they also shared. They'd used that same pool of funds on their nights out to buy fruit drinks. Now that it was just her, she'd had to limit her spending considerably. Even though it was just her doing the work the three of them used to complete, the money she received was still the same as it had been. The same amount of work being completed for one third of the cost didn't seem fair to her, but right now nothing seemed fair.

As soon as the meal was over, Father stood.

"Jane, your presence is requested in my office." He turned and left the room.

Her entire being quivered. This was it. Her fate was about to be destined. She didn't want to marry a stranger. Truly, truly didn't. She didn't want to get married at all. Her entire life she'd been told what to do, when, how. She wanted time to live, time to see all the things she read about in magazines. Time to decide what she wanted to do with her life. Since her sisters had moved out, she'd felt empty. Like there was a hole in her that needed to be filled.

A ripple of rebelliousness rose up in her. She wasn't going to marry a man just because he was wealthy. Because her father wanted her to. That was disgusting, marrying for money. Furthermore, this was her life, and she should have some say in it, some control.

Mother patted her arm before she stood and walked into the kitchen.

Jane's shoulders fell as if she no longer had bones to hold them up. Mother was just one of the reasons she and her sisters hadn't wanted to marry a man of Father's choosing. They, including her, believed they would end up just like Mother. Obeying every rule Father laid down.

It was hard to understand how Mother could

always appear so happy, content. Like everything was just fine when it wasn't.

Marriage must do that to a person, but turning a blind eye, as Mother appeared to do, was not something Jane could do. Not now. Not ever.

No one should have to marry someone they didn't want to. Her sisters had found a way to defy Father's demands, and there had to be a way that she could, too. She just couldn't think of one other than running away, which was what she'd always said she would do, but when it came right down to it, she wasn't brave enough to do that.

"Jane!"

She jolted so hard at her father's bark that her knee struck the underside of the table, shooting pain up and down her leg.

Delaying would make things worse, so she stood and, ignoring how her knee stung, walked out of the dining room, down the hall and into his office.

There, she perched herself on the edge of the burgundy velvet sofa, hands folded in her lap. Just like she had every time her presence had been requested for as long as she could remember.

Tall, with short gray hair and permanent frown wrinkles on his forehead and around his eyes,

Father sat behind his big wooden desk that glistened in the sunlight shining in through the windows because of how she'd polished all the furniture yesterday.

Head up, sitting stiff and straight, he said, "I will not be securing a husband for you."

Blood rushed to her head so fast it pounded in her ears, and for a moment she wondered if the echoing had been there before, making her incapable of hearing. He couldn't possibly have said, *not securing a husband.*

The silence made the echoing in her ears louder. She swallowed. "Oh?" Her voice came out in a squeak. That was all she could think to say. Her mind was as blank as a white sheet hanging on the line. Her heart was still pounding, though, and she had to tell herself to breathe for fear she might faint. "Why?"

"Due to your sisters both being married, I've determined that you will remain here," he replied.

Her hearing was still muffled, her heart still pounding, her mouth still dry, and her mind was trying hard to process what he'd just said. "Here?"

"Yes, here with your mother and I. She can't complete all the cooking and cleaning by herself.

This house is too big. We needed all this room when I built it because of you girls, and it's only fair that you help take care of it."

She shook her head, trying to understand. *Fair? Help take care of it?*

"And I still need someone to clean the houses once they're built."

Her stomach clenched. Cleaning those houses had been somewhat fun with her sisters, but now it was just boring. "For how long?"

He frowned. "Forever. There's no reason for you to get married. You'll inherit all this." A slight smile formed as he gave a quick nod. "You're excused."

Excused? She hadn't asked to be excused. She hadn't asked to inherit anything, either. She didn't want to inherit anything. And she most certainly didn't want to go on living here, like this, forever.

Too stunned to speak, to think of anything to say, she stood and walked out of the room, down the hall, into the dining room.

Mother, clearing dishes off the table, looked up, smiling. "Your father told you the news?"

"Yes," Jane answered, shocked that Mother would be happy about it.

Mother frowned. "I thought you'd be happy

that he's realized his mistake in trying to force you girls to marry men of his choosing."

Jane's entire body started to tremble, to shake. Anger, fear and a plethora of anxiety stirred and boiled inside her like a pot of stew. That was only a part of it. He was using that as an excuse to have a maid for the rest of his life.

No one wanted to remain at home forever with their parents.

She certainly didn't.

She should have known something was about to happen when she saw those caramel rolls this morning!

Two hours later, she was supposed to be up-stairs, cleaning, but she wasn't. She'd climbed out the bathroom window and was at Betty's house. So was Patsy. Upon hearing the news, Betty had called their youngest sister who had immediately driven over.

Jane's temper was still boiling as she told them exactly what their father had said to her. How she would remain at home, being a maid, a ser-vant, for the rest of her life.

"Oh, dear." Betty had one hand pressed against her breastbone and the other to her stomach. "I can't believe it. I truly can't. Father has changed the past few months. We've all seen that."

"You only see him at Sunday dinners!" Jane paced the floor in front of the blue upholstered couch where both of her sisters sat. Father had changed in some ways. He had become friendlier, nicer, even happy at times, but she wasn't. She wasn't happy at all! "Forever! That's what he'd said. Forever!" She threw her hands in the air. "I won't do it! I can't! I want to see things! Do things!" They had, too, and that was why they'd gone along with her plans of sneaking out.

"Father has changed," Patsy said. "We just have to think about this for a minute. He may not have said what you think he did."

Jane blinked back the tears. She didn't cry. Not ever. And wouldn't now. But she couldn't believe her sisters were standing up for Father. He had been nicer since they'd both gotten married, but not that much! "I'll run away!" She'd said for years that she would run away and was completely serious right now. She'd find the courage to do it.

"Running away won't solve anything," Betty said. "But we will think of something. The three of us. One for all and all for one."

That had been their motto for years, just like they'd called themselves Rapunzels because of their long blond hair and their father's rules, but none of that was true now for Patsy and Betty. They were married, would soon have families. She wouldn't. She'd be an old maid. Her sisters didn't understand what that meant because they'd never experienced the loneliness that she had the past couple of months. It was awful and she couldn't do it any longer.

Running away was her only option.

David opened the solid wooden door of his apartment, took the telegram, tipped the young man and closed the door. On his way past the table, he tossed the yellow envelope on top of the stack of identical ones. He didn't need a reminder from his brother to know he was due home next week.

His suitcase was packed. He'd leave tomorrow to start the six-day drive, regretting every mile.

That was already happening. His regret. If he had the choice, he wouldn't go back to Chicago. He'd stay right here in California. But he couldn't do that. He had commitments. Not only to his family, but to the family business. The shareholders. The employees. The customers.

Others, too. Friends, charities, all the things he did like about his life.

He released the air that was so hot it nearly

charred his lungs. What he didn't want was a wife. He may have at one time. Charlene. Ever since they'd been young. Very young. She'd been his first friend, his best friend for years. He'd grown up planning on marrying her. Planned it so thoroughly he'd never thought about marrying any other woman.

But that had changed.

He shook his head, refusing to go down the path again. He'd gotten over the fact that Charlene and Joshua were married.

He was frustrated because those old memories had resurfaced when Joshua started pushing for him to marry Rebecca—do his family duty.

Being forced into a loveless marriage shouldn't be anyone's family duty.

Flustered, he left his apartment and drove to the automobile shop, where he purchased two additional spare tires, an extra gas can and water bag. All needed for his trip home. There were parts of the trip where towns were few and far between. The condition of the roads in some sections on his way here had eaten away tires the way a dog eats a bone, and he assumed it would be the same back to Chicago.

Then he drove to the beach for one final look at the Pacific Ocean. The water was sky blue today, with only a few white-tipped waves rolling into shore, leaving the sand smooth and glistening.

He'd seen the ocean before, many times. Not just since coming out here several months ago, but during his years of growing up. His parents had traveled substantially while he'd been growing up, and he and Joshua had often joined them. Not only in the States, but across both the Atlantic and Pacific oceans. His parents had talked about buying tickets on the *Titanic*, before it sank. Not even that tragedy had stopped them from traveling.

He missed them, his parents. They'd been gone eight years now and were a major part as to why he didn't want to marry Rebecca. His parents had been in love. They'd loved each other and him and Joshua. He'd been eighteen, a freshman in college, when they'd died in a late-night fire in a hotel in New York where they had been staying while attending a railroad convention, and he still missed them. Missed the family they'd been while his parents had been alive.

The house had always been full of life then; now it was like a tomb. He hated having to go back.

Which, in part, was why he had to. He walked

back to his car and then drove back to his apartment, to get ready to go play piano one last time.

By the time ten o'clock rolled around, David figured Jane wouldn't be there tonight. She hadn't been last night, either. Which was just as well. If she was a flapper on the hunt for a sugar daddy, she needed to find a higher-class establishment than this place.

As soon as the thought crossed his mind, he chided himself. That was something Joshua would say.

He let out a sigh. Maybe he wasn't so different from his brother.

"Want another one?" Murray asked.

David looked down, spun his empty glass in a circle and contemplated leaving. Then, because it was his last night, he nodded. "Yes, I'll have another one."

"Another dull night, I see."

He twisted and grinned at how she'd emphasized *I see.* "Hello, Average Jane."

She sat on the stool next to his.

"The usual?" Murray asked her.

She drew in a deep breath, and as she let it out, she slapped the bar with one hand. "No, Murray, tonight I want wine, and don't tell me you don't have any. I know you do."

Murray's eyes widened. "I'll have to get it out of the storeroom."

"That's fine," she replied. "It's not like you're pouring drinks with both hands right now."

The gray-haired bartender cast her a frown as he walked away, toward the far end of the bar.

"Are you celebrating something tonight?" David asked.

Her eyes weren't sparkling, nor were her cheeks shimmering. "I wish."

Fine tendrils of blond hair framed her face beneath her hat, and once again he noted just how pretty she was. Exquisite, and yet sad. "What's wrong?"

She shrugged while casting a gaze around the room. "What's not wrong?"

Nothing in his life, but in the world overall, there had to be some good things. He managed to come up with a few. "Well, we aren't at war, the economy is doing good, the Yankees won the World Series."

She grinned, then frowned. "Have you ever been to a baseball game?"

He'd been to Wrigley Field more times than he could count. "Yes. Have you?"

"No."

She was wearing a bright yellow dress, with a

matching cloche hat that had a silk flower pinned on the side, but tonight the luster of her outfit didn't match her. There was no glow about her. There normally was, and it normally floated in her wake like the tail of a comet shooting across the sky. Secretly, he'd hoped to see that shine and sparkle one last time before going back to his darkly shrouded life.

Murray was back and poured dark-colored wine into a short glass, setting it down in front of her.

David stopped her from reaching into her pocket with one hand and gave Murray a five-dollar bill with his other hand.

"You want the bottle?" Murray asked.

David glanced at her, then replied, "Sure." He picked up the bottle and his glass and stood. "Let's go sit over there."

She glanced at the table he'd gestured to, then shrugged one shoulder and picked up her glass.

As they walked toward the table, which was behind the piano and isolated from the other people in the room, she asked, "Do you drink wine?"

Prohibition hadn't stopped, or even slowed, his family from serving wine at every evening meal. "Sometimes."

"Me, too. Sometimes. Most joints keep it locked

up as tight as churches do." She sat down and pointed at his drink. "They make more money selling that stuff."

He set his glass and the bottle of wine on the table and sat down. "Do they?"

She took a sip of her wine. "Yes."

Picking up his glass, he said, "Or maybe men prefer whiskey."

"Probably," she said, sighing. Then, looking at his glass, she asked, "Is that Minnesota 13?"

Considering the only place he'd seen her was a speakeasy, he wasn't surprised she knew the name of the whiskey in his glass. "Yes."

"Good. That other stuff can blind you. Even kill you."

"I've heard that." He leaned back in his chair. "Do you visit a lot of speakeasies?"

She shrugged. "Some." Taking a sip of wine, she added, "I was hoping this place would be hopping tonight."

"Are you going to visit another, instead?"

"No."

Something was clearly not right with her. "Well, then, why don't you tell me why you are so sad?"

"Why do you think I'm sad?"

"You're drinking wine, for one. I've never seen you drink anything except fruit juice."

She narrowed her eyes. "You were watching what I drink?"

"Not watching. I merely noticed," he clarified.

"Why?"

"No reason. I notice a lot of things. Just like I noticed you look sad tonight."

She took a long drink from her glass, downing half of it. "I'm not sad. I'm mad."

The way she set her glass down demonstrated that. "Why?" he asked.

"Because I don't want to be a maid the rest of my life."

Maybe his earlier thought had been right, that she was looking for a sugar daddy. "Perhaps you could look for a different job."

"No, I'll be a maid forever. An old maid."

She sounded despondent, almost like she held no hope. He knew the sound, because he'd echoed it himself more than once. "You certainly aren't old."

"I'm not right now, but I will be someday, and I'll still be a maid. I don't have any other choice."

She certainly was convinced of that. He wasn't. She was too young. "How old are you?"

"Twenty-one. How old are you?"

"Twenty-six."

She planted one elbow on the table and propped her chin on her palm. "How long have you been playing the piano? Not just here, but at other joints."

He shrugged. "I told you the other night that I'm not a piano player. The Rooster's Nest is the only place I've ever played."

"Baloney!"

Due to his love of music, he'd learned to play the piano as a child, but had only ever played at his home and at a few parties while in college. "No, it's true, and it was fun."

"Was?"

He nodded. "Tonight was my last night."

Her chin dropped even while propped up in her palm. "Why?" She snapped her head upright and stared at the bar. "Did Murray fire you? I'll go tell him—"

"No," he interrupted, convinced she was about to jump to her feet and head to the bar. "I wasn't fired. I'm leaving town tomorrow."

"Where are you going?"

The heaviness of being an Albright weighed down on him harder than ever. "Chicago."

"Why?"

He emptied his glass and let the whiskey settle

in his stomach before answering, "Because that's where I live, and it's time for me to go home."

She stared at him for a lengthy moment. "Now, you are the one who looks sad."

He probably did. He was sad.

"Don't go," she said as if it was as simple as that. "Don't go if it makes you sad."

He put that back on her. "Don't be a maid if it makes you mad."

Her entire posture seemed to shrink, not just her shoulders. "If only it was that simple."

He agreed wholeheartedly. Picking up the bottle of wine, he filled his glass, then topped up hers. He set the bottle down and picked up his glass.

As they both took a drink and set their glasses down, he considered if he should give her some money, to tide her over until she found a new job. Which, in a sense, would make him a sugar daddy. He didn't want that any more than he wanted to be married.

"So, why do you have to go back to Chicago?" she asked.

He nearly laughed as his thoughts were an exact answer to her question. "To get married."

Her eyes grew wide and she leaned back in her chair. "Oh."

He shrugged. "I didn't mean to shock you, but that's what is expected to happen. It's what some might consider an arranged marriage. She's..." There were a lot of ways he could describe Rebecca, but he held back his opinions. "What you might call a friend of the family, and I'm the one obligated to fulfil a promise my family made to hers."

She still appeared stunned, but leaned closer to the table again. "Obligated? You don't want to marry her?"

"No. I'm not interested in getting married. Not to her or anyone else." He didn't add that he wasn't interested in being a sugar daddy, either. Those were his assumptions only, and not very kind ones.

She lifted her glass and took her time taking a drink and swallowing. "I—I—" She glanced around as if cautious before quietly stating, "I knew a woman, and her father was making her marry a man she didn't want to marry. They were at the church, the ceremony had just started, and then the man she *did* want to marry walked into the church and objected to the wedding. She and that man got married instead. Right then at that church."

He picked up his glass and drank down the

wine and refilled his glass. Her eyes had taken on a slight shine, and that alone was enough to make him glad that things had worked out for whoever those people had been. However, ultimately, he'd never be that lucky. "Good for her, for them, but there isn't anyone who will object to my marriage."

She nodded as he held the bottle over her glass, silently asking if she wanted more. He refilled her glass and set down the bottle. There wasn't a single person who would object to his marriage. Other than him.

"Maybe you could find someone to object," she said.

He probably could find someone, yet he shook his head. "Objecting wouldn't do any good."

"Oh." She let out a sigh. "I was going to offer to do that for you."

Despite the solemnness of the conversation and the defeat filling him, he had to grin. "That's kind of you, but the wedding will be in Chicago."

She shrugged. "I've never been to Chicago."

Astonished, he leaned back in his chair and crossed his arms. "You'd be willing to go to Chicago to object to my wedding?"

She nodded.

"Why?"

"Why not?"

His spine tingled and he shook his head. "I'm not interested in becoming a sugar daddy."

She grabbed her glass, drank all of her wine. "A sugar daddy? You think I want a sugar daddy?" She set the glass down firmly and stood. "I knew I couldn't trust you."

"Wait." He grabbed her arm. "I'm sorry. That was rude of me. I apologize."

She stared at him with narrowed eyes.

"Please, sit back down. Your offer just surprised me. In all honesty, if I thought it would help, I'd be tempted to take you up on it."

Maybe it was the wine, mixed with the whiskey, but his mind went down that road for a moment, then he quickly concluded it wouldn't be enough. He'd have to be married to get out of marrying Rebecca.

He wasn't about to do that.

He was trying to get *out* of a marriage, not into one.

Chapter Three

Jane sat down and chided herself for getting mad at him so quickly. She had made the offer. It was just that, for a moment, she'd thought she'd found the answer to her woes. Not a solution as her sisters claimed they'd find. There was no solution. Furthermore, any solution Patsy and Betty came up with would be based on them, on what they now had. Husbands. She was happy for them, but that's not what she wanted. Her sisters no longer went out at night. They were home in bed by eight thirty, just like her parents.

She didn't want a sugar daddy, either. That would be the same thing as a husband, which she didn't want any more than she wanted to be a maid forever.

Her plan was all she had. Run away. The problem with her plan was that she'd visited speakeasies, heard the chin music, the gossip. Los

Angeles was not a safe place to run away. She could end up shanghaied. Patsy almost had been, and Henry had been shanghaied. There were other dangers, too. She didn't want to go on living the rest of her life as a maid to her parents, but she didn't want to die, either.

She'd spent last night upstairs in her room, weighing the risks of running away and had concluded that because of Lane and Henry, and their ability to find people, if she was serious about it, she had to run far away. Trouble was, she didn't have the money to get far away.

She'd also concluded she couldn't run away alone. That would be too dangerous.

"Why wouldn't it help? Having someone object?" she asked.

"Because it wouldn't be enough," he answered.

She frowned.

"You said your friend married the person who objected," he said.

"She did."

"That's why it worked." He took another drink of wine.

She nodded. He was right. Henry had married Betty after objecting. "Sorry," she said.

"Don't be. It was kind of you to offer." He grinned. "It was a good idea."

Still disappointed, she said, "Not if it won't work."

While staring at his glass of wine, he asked, "Would you really consider going to Chicago with me?"

"Yes," she answered without hesitation. "I wouldn't have said it if I didn't mean it."

"What about your job?"

It wasn't a job. It was an imprisonment and she was willing to do anything to be released from it. She shrugged. "They'll get along without me."

"Do you have family? Commitments here?"

The commitments she had weren't ones she'd made. They'd been imposed upon her since the day she'd been born, and would be forever. For the rest of her life. If she didn't do something now, she would be stuck fulfilling those commitments until she was an old woman living in a big house all alone. That was her father's plan, not hers.

She took a drink of wine and resolved that this could be the only chance she'd get. "No."

He nodded and scratched his head. "I need to think about this for a minute, Jane."

"Think about what?" she asked cautiously, afraid to wonder on her own.

"What you said about objecting to my marriage to Rebecca." He rubbed the back of his neck. "Objecting won't be enough, but if I was already married to someone else, I wouldn't be able to marry Rebecca."

She was nodding because that was true, but stopped mid-nod to ask, "Married to whom?"

"You."

Her breath stalled so hard and fast, she coughed. Coughed until her eyes started to water. "Me?" she finally managed to ask. What had she gotten herself into?

"Yes, you," he said.

Marrying someone and running away were not the same things. They weren't even close. Not in her mind. She wanted freedom, not another form of confinement. "No, it won't be. I don't want to get married."

He rubbed his forehead, squeezed his temples. "I don't, either."

She pressed a hand to her stomach, which had started to churn. The aftertaste of wine, too much wine, burned in her throat. Oh, dear. She wasn't pickled, and she didn't want to be in a pickle, either.

"How about if I paid you?" he asked.

She opened her mouth to say no but closed it

as he held up his hand, stopping her from answering.

"Hear me out, I'm…well, I'm thinking this through as I speak. What if I was to pay you to be my wife? We'd have to get married. Truly married. We'd need a marriage license to prove it was real. But it would only be for a week or so, until my grandfather's birthday, then we could return here, by Thanksgiving." He was now rubbing his chin, hard. "Get a divorce, and…" He huffed out a breath. "It could work. My family would be upset, but bottom line, I'd have a reason to never get married again." He nodded. "This could really work for me."

Jane quivered, in part because what he said could work for her, too. The paying-her part. The being married for only a week or so. She truly didn't want to get married, but more, she didn't want to live the rest of her life being a maid. Returning here would work, too. She didn't want to run away forever. Never see her sisters again. Never meet the baby Betty would have in May. Never meet her other nieces or nephews when they came about. She just wanted to be gone long enough that her father would know she had a mind of her own. A life of her own. It was her way of standing up to him, like Patsy had about being a reporter, and how Betty had about not marrying James Bauer.

Her mind was racing through all sorts of channels until one hit a dead end. "You said you're leaving tomorrow."

"I am. I have to be home for my grandfather's birthday. I promised him I would be."

She sighed. Even if she agreed, it wouldn't work. "There is a five-day waiting period to get a marriage license in California." She knew that from Betty's wedding.

He nodded, then lifted a brow. "There's not in Arizona. You can get married at the same time you get your license. By the judge, right then and there at the courthouse. I saw billboards about it on the way out here."

She'd never seen a billboard like that, but she'd never been anywhere outside of Los Angeles. "You did?"

"Yes, and Nevada has quickie divorces. People go there from around the world to get divorced."

She had read about celebrities going to Nevada to get divorced and remarried. Those stories were often in the magazines. They even had quickie divorce ranches, where people stayed while waiting for their divorce case to be heard.

A very famous actress had done just that. She'd read about that not long ago.

"What do you think, Jane?" His face was serious. Especially his eyes. "I'll pay you whatever you think it's worth, and I have an apartment here. On Venice Boulevard. You can live there upon your return. I'll continue to pay the rent until you find a different job and get established."

Her heart was racing, her stomach bubbling with excitement. This really could work for her. And him. If she had her own place to live, her own money, her father wouldn't have control over her ever again. There wouldn't be anything he could do. "We'll be back here by Thanksgiving?" That was important because she'd have to let her sisters know something; otherwise, Henry might come looking for her and, knowing Betty, she'd convince Henry to call in the entire bureau.

"Yes. I promise. I'll drive you back myself."

"What will you do then?"

"I'll return to Chicago, that's where I live." He shook his head and patted the table. "But I'll still pay for the apartment, for as long as needed. You name the price. Whatever price you need to do this for me."

Her hands were trembling, she was jittery all over. She'd found her answer. A plan that would work. It was foolproof. Except for one thing. She didn't know how much an apartment cost or how much she'd need to live on until she found another job. Other than the cost of cosmetics, magazines, drinks, she'd never had that much experience with money. "I—I don't know how much. I don't know what I'll need."

"That's all right. I'll—I'll give you allotments. Whatever you need until you're resettled." He shook his head as if a bit flustered, but his eyes were sparkling. "The money isn't the issue, Jane. It's if you'll do it or not. Elope with me."

Elope! She pressed a hand to her breastbone, heaved in and out several breaths. That meant marriage. The very thing she didn't want. Yet, at the same time, it was her only chance to get what she did want.

She had to say yes. Had to. This was her chance! "Yes, David, I'll elope with you."

He seemed shocked. "You will?"

She paused for a moment, wondering if she should be shocked, too, or change her mind, but then she picked up her glass and held it up. "To us."

He picked up his glass, held it up to hers and as their glasses clinked, said, "To us."

He took a drink, set down his glass. "This is crazy."

She emptied her glass and set it down. "Yes, it is." It was also her only solution.

"I just have to go home and get my suitcase," he said. "Where do you live? I can pick you up in, say, an hour?"

A moment of dread washed over her. It took her half an hour to walk from here to home. Home. She couldn't tell him where she lived, just in case he'd heard of Hollywoodland, heard of her father. Horsefeathers! She didn't even own a suitcase. She cringed at how hard she was thinking, how she could make this work. Then it struck. An epiphany of sorts. Betty had a suitcase. Mother had bought her one for her wedding night and it was in her basement. Excitement renewed itself. "Two hours?" she asked. "And do you know where Star's Studio is?" That was only a block away from Betty's house, yet far enough away from her father's house that he wouldn't make the connection.

"Yes."

"I'll meet you there. On that corner, by the streetlight." There was a big awning she could hide under. "In two hours."

"Two hours." He nodded. "All right. My car is a red-and-black Cadillac."

She nodded. "Red and black."

His dimple was showing as he ran a hand over his lips as if trying to hide his smile. "We are really going to do this."

"Yes," she said, smiling even as her stomach churned. "We are."

He stood. "I take it you don't need a ride home?"

She couldn't leave the hidden door unlocked and she shook her head as she stood. "No, I have a way home." Not wanting him to know about that, she glanced around. The curtain was only two steps behind her, but she couldn't let him see her, and... Oh, it was her lucky night. Everything was working out. "Don't forget your jacket. It's on the stool by the bar."

"Thanks for the reminder." He held his hand out to her, and she shook it.

"See you in two hours."

"I'll be there," she replied. Then, as soon as he'd turned his back, walked toward the bar, she shot behind the curtain and into the storeroom.

Once she'd locked the hidden door, she ran the entire ten blocks of the tunnel. It wasn't until she grabbed Betty's suitcase off the shelf near the basement door that she paused.

Heart racing, she gulped for air and forced herself to not second-guess her decision. It was made. Period.

She hurried to the shelf and scrounged through a box of items she kept in the basement. Cosmetics and jewelry and such. After filling her pockets, she spun around, scanning the room.

She couldn't leave without telling her sisters something. Waking Betty wouldn't work; she'd try to talk her out of this.

This. The perfect, foolproof plan.

Foolproof was confirmed when she spied a notepad on the stairs. Four steps up so she couldn't miss it. There was a pen, too!

And a note.

From Betty.

Jane,
I was so worried when I didn't hear from you today. I was afraid you had run away until I heard you sneak through the house earlier.
Patsy and I have been talking on the phone. We are coming over to see you tomorrow morning after breakfast.
Love,
Betty

Jane picked up the pen but refrained from pressing it against the paper right away. She had to pen this note carefully. Between her sisters and their husbands, one being a newspaper reporter and the other an FBI agent, she couldn't leave any clues that they could use to find her. Yet, she had to say enough that her sisters wouldn't worry. And it had to be believable.

Being paid to marry someone wasn't believable. She was still in shock herself. Stunned that everything had fallen into place so perfectly. Not the marriage part, but other than that, she was going to come out of this smelling like a rose. Being a divorcée wouldn't bother her. That wouldn't be nearly as constricting as being one of William Dryer's daughters.

That was it. She knew what to write.

I'm eloping. With the piano player who used to work at the Rooster's Nest.

This was working perfectly because in the past she'd said that she would elope, run away with a piano player! She truly hadn't been planning to do that, but her sisters would believe she had been all along! She'd specifically penned *used to* because both Patsy and Betty knew she'd flirted with several past piano players—only because it was fun, not because she liked any of them that much, but her sisters didn't know that. Nor did they know David. He'd started playing there after they'd both gotten married.

I'll be home by Thanksgiving. Father's temper may have calmed down by then.

She doubted that, but she wanted to let them know she was coming back. They just didn't need to know why. She'd tell them all the details in person. Afterward.

I'm so happy.

She was.

Please don't tell anyone! Except Patsy, of course.
Love,
Jane

She laid the pen on the paper and hopped over that step. Then more carefully than usual just in case Betty was listening for her, she snuck up the stairs and out the kitchen door.

With the suitcase swinging on her arm, she ran all the way home.

Deciding what to pack did present a dilemma. Flapper clothes? Or regular clothes? In the end, it didn't matter because not much would fit in the suitcase. She chose a couple of her favorite flapper outfits and the pale green dress she'd worn to Patsy's wedding and the peach one she'd worn to Betty's.

By the time she got her underclothes, night-clothes, and other essentials in the suitcase, she had to sit on it to try to force the latches together, but it was too full. Finally, after removing several items and while sitting on it again, the case latched shut.

She wouldn't need a nightgown. She could sleep in her underclothes. The black shoes she was wearing did match most of the outfits some-what, and she wouldn't have to wear hats while being gone.

Next, she filled her black purse—it matched her shoes and was the largest one she owned—with jewelry, makeup and other such essentials, and all the money she had to her name.

With her hand on the light switch, she gave the room a quick once-over, making sure it was as neat and tidy as when she'd entered. Satisfied, and with her heart pounding, she clicked off the light, slipped out the door, and hurried into the bathroom.

She didn't take a breath until her feet touched the ground. Climbing down the trellis with the suitcase and her purse had been harder than climbing up had been. They were both heavy, and the fingers on her right hand were cramped from having to hold on to the suitcase handle and grasp the trellis at the same time. Her purse handle was large enough to hook over her fore-arm, and though it was stuffed full, it hadn't been nearly as cumbersome as the suitcase. She transferred her purse to her right arm and picked up the suitcase with her left hand, then ran across the yard.

Not daring to sneak through Betty's yard, just in case her sister had found her note already, she stayed on the road, crossed the intersecting street and continued another block to the street that Star's Studio was on, running the entire way because without a watch she feared she only had minutes before David would arrive.

She ran the entire block in front of the studio, not stopping until she was beneath the big red canvas awning over the front doors of the studio.

It cast a shadow for her to hide in while watching the street corner for a red-and-black Cadillac.

There, she set the suitcase down and planted her hands on her knees, gulping air into her burning lungs.

Her breathing returned to normal as the seconds turned into minutes.

Long minutes as she stood there, staring at the corner.

Waiting.

Watching.

And waiting some more.

David was certain if it had only been what *he* wanted, he'd have changed his mind, but he couldn't do that to Jane. He'd been the one to talk her into it, so couldn't back out now.

He'd talked her into eloping!

Wine or whiskey had never affected his thinking before. Nothing had ever made him even consider doing something like this. Paying a woman to elope with him. He was desperate not to marry Rebecca, but he barely knew Jane. He could be putting himself in an even worse predicament.

No, his gut said that wasn't true. She didn't want to get married, either, but would uphold her end of the bargain. He would, too. He'd pay her until the end of time if this worked out the way he hoped it would.

She'd earn the money. He had no doubts about that.

She was a virtual stranger, but he'd have time to learn all he'd need to know about her during their drive to Chicago.

He'd also have to warn her about that. His family. Joshua. Rebecca. Grandpa… Actually, he could see Grandpa liking Jane. She was very, very likable. Adorable, too, which was really going to make Rebecca mad. Rebecca could be Snow White's stepmother from Grimms' fairy tales. He'd studied the writing style of those works in college, had a professor who was nearly obsessed with the Brothers Grimm and their fairy tales. From the first time he'd read about the mirror, mirror on the wall, he'd related the witch character to Rebecca. How she thought her beauty—her black hair and icy blue eyes—surpassed all others.

It didn't. Her blue eyes were nothing like Jane's blue eyes. Jane's were like the ocean, a sparkling blue, that squinted when she laughed. Jane's eyes could also be big and round, and when she blinked, those long lashes looked like butterfly wings.

Oh, yes, Rebecca was going to be jealous of Jane. He'd have to be extra vigilant about keeping Jane away from Rebecca.

But it wouldn't be for long. The shareholders meeting was scheduled for the Monday after Grandpa's birthday. As long as he was there, gave his report, signed where he needed to sign, he and Jane could leave the following day. Stop in Nevada for a quickie divorce, and then drive back to Los Angeles well before Thanksgiving.

He owed Jane for coming up with the idea, as well as participating in it.

A knot formed behind his rib cage as he approached Star's Studio, saw the corner empty. He told himself not to worry, that he was early, on purpose, so she wouldn't need to wait for him. He'd have much rather picked her up at her place of residence, because he didn't like the idea of her waiting on a street corner in the middle of the night. She hadn't wanted that, for him to see where she lived. The look on her face when he'd offered her a ride the other night had told him that.

There was an exclusive neighborhood up the

hill from the studio, and he assumed she must work at one of those houses.

A maid's salary wasn't much; therefore, if she didn't live in the house where she worked, she was probably ashamed of where she did live. He'd pay her well enough that she'd never have to worry about that again and consider it an investment well made. He believed in that—good wages. It was yet another thing he and Joshua had clashed about over the years.

He steered the car to the side of the road and pushed up his jacket sleeve to read his watch. His gaze hadn't yet fallen to the dial when the passenger door opened.

"Hello there, Davie," she said, so bright and cheerful that a corpse would have had to smile.

He wasn't a corpse, so he did more than smile. He laughed. If nothing else, this was going to be a good time. She lit up the darkness inside his car far more than the streetlight could.

"Let me get that for you," he said, referring to her suitcase while grasping hold of his door handle.

"No need, I already got it." She opened the back door and set her suitcase next to his on the seat. After closing that door, she jumped into the front seat, pulled her door shut and dropped her purse on the floor by her feet. With a clap of her hands, she said, "Let's get a wiggle on."

The soft floral scent of her perfume instantly filled the car, making his smile grow. It reminded him of the large flower garden his mother used to take pride in. This trip back to Chicago would be nothing like the long boring drive he'd completed on the way out here months ago, and a part of him wasn't sure if he should be happy about that or not.

He pulled the car away from the sidewalk and turned it around in the middle of the street so he could head south, then west to the road that would take them all the way to Chicago. He'd never done anything like this before—this spontaneous, this outrageous—and questioned turning back for a few blocks. "Have you heard about the Mother Road?"

"No."

He glanced down at the stack of maps on the seat between them. It was too dark for her to read them right now. "It's the road that we will take all the way to Chicago. You can read the maps when it gets light out, but we'll drive through California, Arizona, New Mexico, Texas, Oklahoma, Kansas, Missouri, and Illinois. The Mother Road is the name some have given one of the major roadways of the highway system the government established a few years ago. It's actually named Highway 66 and it is the major roadway west of the Mississippi. Some claim the gangsters had a lot to do with it being established."

"Gangsters? You aren't involved with the Mob, are you?"

He chuckled at her gasp and assured her, "No. Just the opposite, in some ways."

"What do you mean? Are you with…?"

He heard her swallow.

"The FBI or something?"

"No." He was going to have to tell her everything sooner or later, so might as well start now. "My family owns the A and R Railroad. A for Albright, R for Roberts. My grandfather started the Albright Railroad, back in 1879. Ten years before that, the first transcontinental rail line had been completed, connecting the west coast to the east coast, through the central part of the nation. My grandfather envisioned another route, one that went down into Texas and then over to California in order to capitalize on the cattle markets. He wasn't the only one. There were too many railroad companies to even name back then."

"So, you're rich," she said peculiarly.

"My family is well-off," he answered cautiously, wondering why she'd sounded as if the idea of him being rich disgusted her. "There's no need to worry if you'll get paid or not. I assure you, you will."

She sat quiet for so long he glanced over to see if she'd fallen asleep.

She hadn't, and a moment later, she asked, "Did he build it? Your grandfather? A route that went to Texas?"

"Yes, and no. He built a large section of it, and over the years, through partnerships, mergers, acquisitions, the Albright Railroad became the Albright and Roberts Railroad and traveled on the completed routes. My grandfather and Charles Roberts were instrumental in getting smaller lines to collaborate with one another, share tracks, cars, switchbacks." If there was one man he admired, was truly proud of, it was his grandfather, and he was proud of being the one to follow in his grandfather's footsteps when it came to acquiring more lines, more mergers. "Every type of business has its own set of rivals, but the railroads, they actually had wars. Many disputes were settled by the courts, but some were actual violent confrontations. My grandfather and Charles brought a lot of the owners together and explained that they all would be more successful working together than feuding and working separately."

"Did it work?" she asked.

"Yes, it did. The A and R Railroad continues to transport cargo and passengers, not only along the southern routes, but other routes as well, from Chicago to all points west, including California, on a daily basis. And it has just as many routes to the east."

"If I'm understanding this right, and your family owns the A and R Railroad, why aren't you just taking a train home to Chicago?"

"That brings us back to your question about the FBI. Some railroad men feel that the government is going to run them out of business by building the highway system, that soon trains won't be needed. They feel that the mobs are paying off the politicians to build the highway system for them to be able to transport their own goods and people by automobile. Maybe some are. But for the most part, mobsters don't like to ride on trains because they could be recognized and arrested. Our lines of passenger cars have contracts with the government that allow law enforcement and intelligence agents to board and transport detainees without having to purchase a ticket in advance."

"Oh, that's what you meant."

He wished it wasn't so dark so he could see her face. She no longer sounded disgusted. She actually sounded interested. "Yes, and the reason I'm driving and not traveling on the train is so I can report back to the stockholders of the A and R."

"Report what?"

"My experience in driving the Mother Road. Highway 66. Assure them that the highway system will not impede upon the railroads. It's a big country. There's room for highways and railways. There's even room for airplanes. They have been flying airmail for years, but that hasn't impacted the amount of mail the railroads still carry. Even the passenger planes and airports being built. There's room for them, too. People deserve options."

She twisted, looked at him—he could feel her gaze.

"This is all very interesting. I never knew any of that. Can you tell me more?"

He was glad she wasn't bored. Not this early in the trip. "Sure, what do you want to know?" He loved the family business and could talk about it nonstop. It's what kept him going. He'd never give up his place in the railroad. It was the one thing about his life that he loved.

"I don't know," she said. "All of it, anything you can tell me."

He stuck to the facts as he filled her in on the history of railroads, their present-day workings and on the family business. He did mention his grandfather and Joshua, and that his parents had died, as they talked and he drove. She offered sincere condolences for his loss, even reached over and patted his hand. So sincere he wondered about her family, her parents, but refrained from asking when she changed the subject, asked about how he'd learned to play the piano. He explained that it was just a hobby, something he'd always enjoyed.

They talked about music, songs and other little things up until she started yawning.

"We won't get to Kingman until noon," he said. "There are pillows and blankets in the back seat if you want to sleep for a while."

She smothered another yawn. "What about you? You have to be tired, too."

They had long ago left the city, along with any sort of paved roads. "This road is rough enough it'll keep me fully awake. We won't hit pavement again until Oklahoma. For a short distance. But

Kansas is paved the entire way, with bricks in some places, wood in others. Same with Illinois, but Missouri is like Oklahoma, paved in places, but not all the way through the state."

"How long will it take us to get all the way to Chicago?"

"About six days."

"Hmm…" She yawned again. "I might as well take a nap. Can't see anything anyway. Not even you."

"I'll pull over and—"

"No sense in doing that. I don't need a pillow or blanket. I'll just lean my head back and sleep right here." She let out a loud sigh. "Sitting up."

Within a matter of seconds, she was sleeping, and in a matter of minutes she slid sideways, her head landing on his shoulder. As the yellow cloche hat tickled his cheek, he started questioning this whole elopement idea. It could cause trouble. Was sure to cause trouble. He contemplated that long and hard as he drove. He contemplated something else, too, that he hadn't up until now.

Jane. And why she'd so quickly agreed to help him.

Chapter Four

Disoriented for a moment, Jane wondered what sort of dream she was dreaming when she opened one eye and was nearly blinded by sunlight. She shut the lid again and covered both eyes with one hand.

"Sorry. We need to stop here for gas."

Both eyes popped open and she sat up, stared at David for a moment, while blinking to clear her vision. It all came back to her like a splash of water in the face. She'd run away. Eloped. With David Albright.

A shiver rippled over her and she shot upright and scooted across the seat. Away from him. A rich man. She'd eloped with the exact type of man her father had wanted her to marry.

"I didn't mean to startle you."

"You—you didn't. I was asleep. Fell asleep."

He opened his car door. "I know this fueling

station has a powder room. I stopped here on my trip west." He smiled at her as he climbed out. "I stopped other places, too. We'll avoid some of those ones."

She pulled up an answering smile and nodded, and as soon as he shut the car door she rubbed her arms as memories came shooting back into her mind. She couldn't marry him. Not even for three weeks.

Her hat slid down over one eye, and she reached up to straighten it, but then plucked it off her head instead and tossed it into the back seat. No one was going to recognize her here. That was the reason she had to wear hats while going out at night back home, so no one would recognize her. That felt good, to know that she didn't have to wear a hat—unless she wanted to, of course, because there were some hats she really liked.

How could she be thinking about hats right now? She'd considered telling him to turn around last night, when she'd discovered he was wealthy, but had decided this was still her only chance. She flipped her head forward and plucked out the pins holding her hair up. Her sister Patsy had despised not being able to cut her hair short in one of the short, bobbed styles—Father wouldn't permit any of them to do that.

Jane thought those haircuts looked nice on some women, but she preferred her hair as it was. All she had to do was wash it a couple times a week and let it dry. All on its own it formed ringlets she could pin up to make it look short, or pull it back in a chignon and give herself finger waves on both sides of the center part. The one style she would never wear was earphones, where women created two buns right over their ears. She'd tried that once. It had looked like she had elephant ears—round fuzzy ones!

Hair? She was thinking about her hair right now, when his wealth added another layer to all of this! If Father discovered… But he wouldn't. They'd be divorced before anyone even learned who David Albright was. Furthermore, there wasn't anything she could do about it right now.

She opened the door and stuck her legs out, to stretch out the kinks before climbing all the way out. She hadn't ridden so long in a car, ever, and stretching felt amazing. Standing next to the car, she arched her back to get the kinks out of it, and seeing David on the other side, said, "I'm going to use that powder room you mentioned."

He nodded, but when he turned and looked at her, he kept staring. And staring.

So did the man who was putting the gas in the car.

Slightly confused by their stares, she asked, "Is that all right?"

"Yes. Yes, that's fine," David said, nodding oddly.

"Powder room's around back, ma'am," the other man said slowly, oddly.

"Thank you," she told him, while glancing at David, wondering if he too was having second thoughts this morning.

She certainly was, and wasn't sure what to do about that. Stretching her arms over her head to get rid of more kinks while walking around the car, she tried convincing herself this was still a good plan and continued to do so all the way to the side of the white stucco building, where she found the powder room and entered it.

There, she took time to think while using the facilities and washing her face. Not that thinking did any good. She couldn't just walk home.

David was standing outside the door when she opened it. "Oh, I'm sorry. I wouldn't have taken so long if I'd known you were waiting."

"I already used the men's room. I was just waiting for you."

"Why?"

He held up a black box. "To take a picture."

Excitement overrode her other thoughts. "You have a camera?" Patsy had a camera, now that she was married and a reporter. Jane had always dreamed of having one, even begged her mother for one for Christmas one year, but Father said they were a waste of money.

"Yes, I do." He took two steps back and looked down inside the camera. "Smile."

Tilting her head, she put both hands beneath her chin and stuck her elbows out because she'd seen all sorts of movie stars do that in pictures in magazines.

He laughed. "One more."

She twisted and struck another pose. This time with one arm up, bent at the elbow and her wrist cocked.

He laughed again and clicked the camera.

She rushed forward. "My si—friend has a camera." She still hadn't mentioned her family. Last night, while he'd been talking about his, she considered it, but had been worried he'd turn around and take her back home if he knew she'd run away from home. She hadn't wanted that, and didn't right now, either. "I've always wanted a camera. When will we see the pictures?"

"When we get to Chicago, we'll turn in the rolls of film and have them developed."

"Elephant's eyebrows! This is so darb!" Hardly able to contain herself, she asked, "Can I take a picture of you? Please?"

"Sure." He handed her the camera.

This was so exciting. He was so handsome, wearing his white-and-green-striped shirt and black suspenders, she could imagine the picture she was about to take on the cover of a magazine. To ease her shaking, she took a deep breath and looked into the box, but her excitement was making her tremble so hard she could barely make out his tiny image.

"You have to hold still," he said.

"I'm trying." She was, but the harder she tried, the more the camera shook, and then she started laughing at herself. "Oh, horse feathers!"

He was laughing, too, and draped an arm around her shoulder. "You can take one later."

"I'm just so excited that you have a camera," she admitted, while being very disappointed. She wanted to take a picture of him. "Later will be better. I won't be so nervous then."

"There's nothing to be nervous about."

"I know, but I just am," she admitted. "What if I break it?"

"You won't."

As they rounded the corner of the building, she noticed the man washing the windshield of David's car. "Excuse me!" she shouted, and then hurried toward him. "Will you take a picture for me?"

The man tucked his rag in his back pocket. "Sure."

She handed him the camera. "Of David." A thought struck. "And his car. That will be a perfect picture!"

David draped his arm around her again and pulled her near the front of the car beside him. "Of us," he told the man. Then, looking down at her, he added, "And the car."

She clasped her hands over her heart while smiling up at him. "Perfect."

"Smile!"

Standing sideways in front of David, she turned just her head to face the camera, and smiled, thinking about how she couldn't wait to see the pictures. Just couldn't wait.

Her excitement collided with something in her mind. The part that said she'd never be able to show anyone the pictures because no one could ever know who he was. That hung heavy as she walked around the car and climbed in.

David drove only a couple of blocks before stopping again. "We'll eat here," he said, nodding toward a small café he'd parked in front of. "There's not another town until we get to Kingman, and that's still several hours away."

Nodding, she picked up her purse, opened it and started pulling out strings of beads that looked like pearls but weren't, gloves, a couple of brooches, bracelets, earbobs, headbands, barrettes, a hairbrush…

"What are you doing?" he asked.

"Looking for my coin purse," she answered, still pulling items out and growing concerned because she'd put all her money in the small red sequined pouch and was sure she'd put it in her purse.

"Why?"

"To pay for food."

He took the purse and set it back down on the floor. "I'll pay for your meal. I'll pay for whatever you need on this trip as part of our bargain."

Once again, questioning if she should have agreed to this bargain, she dropped her handful of jewelry back in the purse by her feet.

"What is all that stuff?"

Her cheeks grew flushed. "Things that wouldn't fit in my suitcase."

He glanced into the back seat and his eyes grew wide. She twisted in order to see what he was looking at, and her eyes grew wide, too. She hadn't noticed, probably because she'd worked so hard to finally make it shut, but there were clothes, just pieces of them, sticking out around the edges of the suitcase.

Grimacing, she looked at him. "I was in a hurry."

He laughed. "And I don't want to be near when you unlatch that." Opening his door, he added, "It looks like it's about to blow apart at the seams."

The suitcase did, and she hoped it wouldn't pop open while they were driving. Some parts of the road had been rough, very bumpy, and she didn't want a sudden rainstorm of her clothes in the back seat. Or the front seat, where some might end up if the latches let loose.

He opened her door. "Come on, Goldilocks, time to eat some porridge."

"I don't like porridge," she said, taking his hand. "But I do like caramel rolls."

He helped her out of the car, closed the door and winked at her. "Then you can have caramel rolls."

She would have a caramel roll, and she would see this through—marry him. If she went home now, it would be like giving up. Or giving in to her father, and she couldn't do that. This was what she wanted. Freedom. No matter what she had to do to get it, including marrying David.

As David opened the door of the small wooden building and held it for Jane to walk inside the café, he knew he'd made a mistake. He'd underestimated Jane. She was cute, adorable in all the little hats he'd seen her wear over the past couple of months, but when she'd stepped out of his car in the light of day, and arched her back, stretched, he'd been thunderstruck.

So had the guy pouring fuel into his car.

Her blond hair hung almost to her waist, an array of tumbling corkscrews that caught on the breeze as they fell over her shoulders, down her back. He hadn't been able to look away. Neither had the station attendant until he'd realized he was dumping fuel on the ground.

The attendant apologized for the wasted fuel and said he wouldn't charge him. David paid for the fuel. If he'd been that attendant, he wouldn't have noticed the fuel until he'd been waist deep in it. He'd instantly dug his camera out because, at that moment, he'd known at some point in his life he'd want to remember this day.

He'd understood that this ploy could be more trouble than marrying Rebecca, but this morning, seeing Jane's beauty, the full weight of what he'd done hit, and again while taking her pictures. She was a charmer, without even opening her mouth, and he didn't need the troubles that could create.

They sat at a table. He told the waitress they wanted two of the specials written on the chalkboard hanging on the wall, and a caramel roll. He didn't even know what he'd ordered other than the caramel roll, because he still couldn't pull his eyes off her long enough to read the specials written on the chalkboard. It was as if her hats had been hiding a masterpiece of art. A masterpiece of rare, priceless beauty.

"Why did you agree to do this?" he asked as the question formed in his mind.

She shrugged. "Because no one should have to marry someone they don't want to."

"But you don't want to marry me, you said so."

"And you don't want to marry me," she replied.

He didn't want to marry anyone, yet that's what he was about to do.

"You're questioning this plan, aren't you?" she asked.

"Yes. Are you?" he asked.

"Yes."

"So, what do we do?" he asked, fully prepared to return her to Los Angeles. He'd been the one to pull her into this idea, but now it was her choice to call it off.

Her smile was soft and timid as she shook her head. "What do you think?"

His conscience battled with his brain as the waitress set down two cups of coffee and walked away.

He took a sip of coffee before saying, "To be honest, Jane, I don't know what we should do."

She shrugged. "Have you changed your mind about marrying the woman your family wants you to marry?"

"No."

She picked up her coffee cup. "Then, I guess we go forward."

He nodded and leaned back in order to give the waitress room to set their plates of food on the table.

They ate, left the restaurant and drove across land largely uninhabited by man or beast, an awkward silence echoing between them.

By the time they pulled into Kingman and found the courthouse, which wasn't hard with all the billboards, David was full of doubt. That wasn't like him. Doing something like this wasn't like him.

"This is where we get married?" she asked, somewhat demure.

"Yes." They were both staring at the brick building. "Now's your chance to say no."

"I thought we settled that at the restaurant," she said. "Or is that why you haven't spoken since we had breakfast? You've been trying to figure out how to get rid of me."

"No, I haven't. I do want to make sure you know what you're getting into."

She laughed softly. "I don't have a clue, but I'm banking on it being better than what I left."

He turned, took in her profile as she continued to stare out the windshield. "It was that bad?"

She nodded, turned and cast him a serious gaze. "To me it was. I felt isolated. Alone. Locked up. I can't go back there. Not yet."

Looking into those blue eyes, the sadness in them, told him he didn't have a choice. He had to marry her, and when this was over he'd give her enough money to make sure she never had to return to her previous employer.

He opened his door. "All right then, let's do this."

"Wait." She grasped his arm. "I don't want you doing this for me."

A chuckle bubbled in his throat at how cute she looked—and sincere. "Well, then, how about we decide that we are doing it for each other, and ourselves?"

She frowned slightly.

"You won't have to return to being a maid, and I won't have to marry Rebecca."

Releasing his arm, she said, "And it's only for three weeks."

"It is," he agreed, hoping to convince himself as much as her.

Grinning at him, she twisted and opened her door. "Let's get a wiggle on."

The little courthouse knew what they were doing. They probably made more money from marrying people than they did in collecting taxes from the entire population of the county.

He'd never asked what her full name was, and watched as she wrote "Jane Marie Bauer" on the application. Her hand trembled as she wrote, and as she handed him the pen. He wrapped his fingers around hers and gave them a gentle squeeze before taking the pen and writing his name. David Augustus Albright.

Smiling at both of them, a short redheaded clerk with thick glasses took the application to type the information onto a marriage license. While that was happening, another woman, plump with round pink cheeks, took them into a room across the hall. The walls were lined with shelves and the center of the room held tables. It looked like an old-fashioned general store.

There was everything from three-piece suits and bridal gowns to oversize bibles, pillows and blankets, picnic baskets and bottles of wine, which were hidden inside those oversized bibles.

On one table there was also a glass display case hosting rows of rings on a blanket of thin black velvet. He hadn't thought about rings. They were all simple bands, not one was real gold. When he asked if Jane had a preference, she offered a timid smile and shook her head.

He bought two. One for her and one for himself, hoping they wouldn't turn their fingers green before this fake marriage was over.

He'd just completed his purchase, paying the pink-cheeked woman, when the redheaded clerk opened the door.

"It's time!" she said cheerfully.

He took hold of Jane's hand firmly. "Ready?"

She smiled and nodded as her lashes fluttered.

They followed the woman into the judge's chamber. The judge sat behind his desk as he asked them to face each other and hold hands. Then he asked David to repeat the vows first.

Jane's fingers were trembling, and David rubbed the top of her hands with his thumbs, hoping that would help ease her nerves.

His own nerves were bouncing around as if they couldn't believe he was doing this. He wasn't a deceitful person. He despised deceit, yet here he was, creating a huge deception. This was one he could live with though, because in the grand scheme of things it wasn't just for him. Others would benefit by it, including Jane.

He listened carefully as the judge spoke, so he could repeat each word. "I, David Augustus Albright, in the presence of these witnesses, take you, Jane, to be my lawful wedded wife, to have and to hold, from this day forward, for better, for worse, for richer, for poorer, in sickness, and in health, to love and to cherish, till death do us part."

The judge then asked her to repeat the same lines, and she did, fumbling slightly on her own name. David smiled, letting her know that everything was going to be fine.

After the judge quoted his authority, given by the state, to perform marriages, he announced them man and wife. Of course, his next line was, "You may kiss your bride."

David took a deep breath, leaned down and briefly brushed his lips against her cheek. He had to bite his lips together at how the simple touch of her skin made his lips sting.

The wedding had been a quick, simple event that couldn't have lasted five minutes, and they were back in the Cadillac in less than half an hour from when they'd climbed out of it. "That wasn't so bad," he said, "was it?"

"No. No, it wasn't."

David drove out of the parking lot, and like the billboards had promised, there were three hotels on the main street. All announcing vacancies. He pressed his foot firmly on the gas pedal and didn't let up until the town was no longer visible in the rearview mirror and the rutted road threatened to rattle the car into pieces, or at least cause a tire that still had a good couple of hundred miles left in it to blow out.

"Why don't you want to get married," she asked.

Refraining from the fact that the only woman he'd ever considered marrying was already married—to his brother—he said, "I have other things I want to do."

"What?"

"Continue to expand the railroad, but also investigate other transportation options. Airplanes are the mode of the future. Commercially. I'd like to be a part of that."

"Have you ever flown in one?"

"Yes, several times."

"You're lucky. That must be amazing. This is the first time I've ever been outside of Los Angeles."

"Why don't you want to get married?" It was odd how they were talking as if they *weren't* married, considering they'd just left their wedding.

She held a thoughtful silence for several moments before saying, "Because, like you, I have other things I want to do."

Repeating what she'd asked him, he asked, "What?"

She grimaced slightly and then sat straight, looked at him. "I'm not sure, but I know there has to be more to life than what I've experienced so far, and getting married wouldn't let that happen."

"How do you know that?"

Frowning, she shrugged. "Well, because, getting married means you just move from one house to another. Live there. Nothing else really changes."

She sounded so despondent. So hopeless. That surprised him because she was full of life. "Why do you say that?"

Leaning her head back against the seat, she said, "Because I've seen it. I know people who have gotten married. They just stay home now. When they do go out, it's with each other."

"Maybe that's because they like being together. That is part of the reason people get married, don't you think?"

She shrugged. "Maybe."

"My parents loved spending time together. They were rarely apart. They traveled extensively together, and when they were at home they were still together, supporting each other in their endeavors."

"Didn't your father work?" she asked.

It was his father's shoes he was following in and he was proud of that. It was also why he wasn't interested in getting married. Actually, it was having children that he wasn't interested in, because he knew what it was like to have a mother and father who were gone all the time. "Yes, he worked for the A and R. Furthered its expansion greatly."

"So your mother was home every day, cooking and cleaning and washing clothes?"

Again, despondency filled her voice. Perhaps her job as a maid was the reason. "When my mother was home, because she often traveled with my father, she was busy with other aspects of the family business."

"What do you mean?"

"Events, parties. She was always working on something. Raising money for the less fortunate, hosting holiday parties for friends and families, putting on social events for employees of the railroad." It had been a long time since he'd thought about all that. His mother had always been orchestrating some type of event. Charlene had taken over some of those events, but they didn't have the same flair as when his mother had been alive. When she'd died, and his father, both in that fire, the house itself seemed to have died.

"You sound like you miss her."

"I do." Oddly enough, because they hadn't been home that often. But when they had been, life had been wonderful. That's how he remembered it. He remembered looking forward to when school was out of session, too, because that had meant he was able to travel with his parents.

He glanced at the road maps of the states along Highway 66, which were sitting on the seat between them, the ones she'd read earlier and had folded each one of them perfectly flat again before picking up the next one. An idea formed and he decided to act upon it. The slight detour wouldn't delay their journey by more than a few hours.

"What kind of parties did your mother host?" she asked.

He laughed, now enjoying the memories that were floating in his head. "All kinds. Holidays, birthdays, fundraisers. If she could think of a reason, there was a party."

Time flowed as they talked, and it was late afternoon by the time he turned north.

"Why are you turning? The map showed Flagstaff is straight ahead."

"I know," he answered. "But there's a small town just up the road where we'll get gas."

"Oh. All right."

He stopped at the fueling station, where they both got out, used the facilities, and then he stopped again at a small grocery store at the edge of town.

"It doesn't look like there is a café, but we can buy a few things at the grocery store," he said.

She agreed with a nod and helped him pick out pickled eggs, cheese, crackers, soda pops and a couple of chocolate and peanut candy bars.

He set the bag of groceries in the back seat before climbing in the driver's seat. It was a two-hour drive on a rough dirt road, and he wanted to get there while it was still daylight.

"Shouldn't we be going the other direction?" she asked.

He had pulled away from the store and had continued heading north. "Yes, but there is a place I want you to see. It's a little bit of a distance, but I think you'll like it."

"Did you stop there on your way to California?"

"Yes, but I'd seen it before then." Keeping his eyes on the road in order to dodge some of the larger ruts and wash outs, he said, "My parents brought my brother and I here when we were young."

"How old is your brother?"

"He's thirty-four. Eight years older than me." Thus lay the reason Joshua had resented him since the day he'd been born. He'd had all of their parents' attention for eight years, and then along came a little brother. That resentment had gotten worse after their parents had died.

"I bet you've missed him while you've been in California," she said.

Despite the conflicts between him and his brother, he'd never stooped to belittling or disrespecting Joshua. "I've missed my grandfather the most. Augustus Percival Albright."

"You were named after him. Your middle name."

"I was."

"I never met either one of my grandfathers," she said. "They both had died before I was born."

That was the first time she'd mentioned her family. "I'm sorry." Curious, he asked, "What about your parents?"

She shrugged. "My father works, my mother cooks. Tell me about your grandfather. What's he like?"

Understanding she didn't want to talk about her family, he said, "A grumpy old man, but he's the best. I don't know what I would have done without him after my parents died. Even before then. He's, well, he's Gus."

"Gus." She giggled. "Tell me more."

They talked while he drove, mostly about his grandfather and somewhat about him, until he topped the final hill. For most of the trip, the view had been trees, brush and small hills, and a whole lot of dusty clay dirt, but here... He sighed. Here, it was glorious.

"David," she whispered, staring out the windshield. "It—it's the Grand Canyon."

"It is." His heart nearly flipped at the shine in her eyes. "Surprised?"

"Yes! I saw it on the map, but it looked so far away from the road we were on."

"Not that far." He pulled the car as close as possible, then shut off the engine. They had met a few cars along the way, but no one was here now other than them.

She opened her door and climbed out, pressed both hands to her breastbone while walking closer to the edge. "I can't believe I'm here! I truly can't!"

"Don't get too close," he warned.

"It's so beautiful, so much more beautiful than the pictures I've seen." She held her arms out wide and lifted her face to the sky. "It makes me feel like I'm on top of the world." She looked at him. "Thank you! This is amazing!"

"You're welcome." He took her hand and

walked with her along a foot trail to an over-
look, where they both stood, gazing over the
massive canyon walls and the pure vastness of
it that went on and on.

"I've seen pictures of it, but..." She shook her
head. "This...this... I wish your camera could
capture the colors we are seeing right now. There
are so many shades of browns, of yellow, and or-
ange and red. It's so beautiful it's breathtaking."

The sun was already setting, and it was beautiful, but he was looking at her, not the canyon,
yet felt the same way. He wished his camera
could capture the colors he saw, but he'd add
in the blue of her eyes, the creamy peach of her
skin, and the spun-honey-gold of her hair. She
was truly breathtaking.

Chapter Five

Jane couldn't pull her eyes off the Grand Canyon. It was not only beautiful, it was surreal, dreamlike that she was actually here. David had spread a blanket on the ground for her to sit on as she stared at the sun slowly setting behind the massive cliffs.

"I never thought I'd see it."

"Why?"

She turned toward David and grimaced. "I didn't know I'd said that aloud."

"You did, so why would you have thought that?"

"I don't know." She shifted her gaze back to the canyon. "I wanted to see it, but I want to see a lot of things and it all seemed impossible. Like it would never happen." A shiver rippled over her arms, but it felt good and made her smile because she indeed was here, looking at the Grand

Canyon. Curious, because she hadn't mentioned that she'd wanted to see it, she asked, "Why did you bring me here?"

"Because I thought you'd like to see it." He grinned. "And nothing should seem impossible. If you want to do it, do it."

As she watched him walk toward the car, she felt a sinking feeling in the pit of her stomach. The same sensation she'd felt when they'd been at the courthouse.

She didn't know why she'd done it, but she had. As soon as her eyes had seen the word *marriage* on that application, her stomach had fallen clear to the floor, and for some crazy, unknown reason she couldn't fathom, she hadn't written her name, her real name on that application.

Jane Marie was correct, but she'd written Bauer instead of Dryer. Why? And what reason would ever have made her use Bauer? As in James Bauer, the man Betty had almost been forced to marry. None of them liked him. Betty, Patsy or her. Well, Betty had insisted that he wasn't that bad, just dull and boring. Jane had called him a worm. But one that talked. His monotone voice used to make her shiver.

Why on earth would she have chosen his name? Why would she have not used her own name?

Was she truly that afraid of getting married?

She looked at the canyon again. When David had asked her why she didn't want to get married, she'd answered honestly. Both of her sisters had gotten married, and yes, they were happy, but the only difference was that they'd moved into different houses and now lived with their husbands instead of her. They no longer went out. She had to do that by herself.

Was she jealous? Was that what why she hated the idea of marriage? Because her sisters were happy and she wasn't? Patsy had always wanted to be a reporter. She'd even convinced her father to let her go to secretarial school, and now she was a reporter.

And Betty, she had her own house and was pregnant. That's what she'd always wanted. To be a wife and mother.

Jane pushed the air that had grown heavy out of her lungs. She'd never had a dream like her sisters had—of something she'd wanted. She'd just wanted to live. Live outside of the boundaries of her life. Like seeing the Grand Canyon and so many other things that she read in magazines. She wanted to see what was out there before deciding what she wanted.

Including getting married.

Yet, she was married.

She hadn't even been forced into it.

She'd chosen to marry David.

Of her own free will.

He'd even given her the option to say no right before they'd walked into the building.

She hadn't wanted to say no, so why hadn't she used her real name?

Her insides sank a little deeper.

She must be demented.

A click had her twisting, looking back over her shoulder. David stood there with his camera.

"Did you just take my picture?" she asked.

He grinned. "Yes, I did."

He was such a good person, so kind and generous, and she'd lied to him, made this whole fake marriage even more of a farce. It wasn't even legal now. It might not work, might not help him after all, and he'd already helped her. Had given her the escape she'd needed, and he'd shown her the Grand Canyon.

Oh, what had she done?

She'd wanted this, agreed to this, so why had she messed it all up?

He walked over, lowered onto his knees and set the camera and bag of groceries on the blanket before sitting down beside her. "We need to talk."

Horsefeathers! He knew. He knew she'd put the wrong name on the marriage application. "All right." Her voice sounded high-pitched. Scared.

She was scared, and ashamed of what she'd done.

"I owe you an apology," he said.

A tiny whimper formed in her throat. She was the one who needed to apologize. Finding an ounce of courage, she turned, looked at him. At his handsome, sophisticated face, which she really liked. She liked him. Would consider him a friend. A good friend. She hadn't truly had a friend before. Other than her sisters. She'd known other people in school, but once she'd graduated she'd never really seen any of them again.

He laid a hand on top of hers. "I should have told you before the ceremony as to exactly what you are getting into. I apologize that I didn't."

Her heart started thudding. "What are you talking about?"

"My family. Certain members are not going to be happy when I bring home a wife."

Relieved, she said, "I figured that. They were expecting you to marry someone else." She had figured that, but hadn't really thought about it. She'd been too busy thinking about herself.

"Yes, and they know that I didn't want to get married to anyone—I've said that numerous times."

"Don't want to marry anyone," she corrected. "We aren't really married."

"Yes, we are. I have the license in my suitcase." He winked. "But I know what you mean. We will get a divorce in Nevada on our way back to California."

That wasn't completely what she meant.

"We'll keep everything between us platonic," he continued, "so there won't be any problem getting a divorce. However, during the time we are with my family, we'll have to act married."

"Act married?"

He nodded.

There were so many aspects of this that she truly hadn't considered before making her decision to elope with him.

"It'll only be for a couple of days," he said. "We'll arrive the day before my grandfather's birthday and leave the following Tuesday. I have a meeting I need to attend on Monday for the Railroad."

"So six days?"

"Yes."

She could do anything for six days.

He held several bills out to her. "Here's your first installment of payment."

She shook her head. "This is for my benefit, too." That's why she'd agreed to elope, so she could get away, and she had. "We'll wait until it's over. You can pay then."

He looked at her for a long time, until she was almost uncomfortable.

"Be honest with me, Jane, fully honest," he finally said. "Was someone hurting you? Where you worked, was someone hurting you? Is that why you wanted to get away?"

"No." She swallowed the bitterness on her tongue because that was the truth. "It was me. I felt like I was cooped up. A bird locked in a cage. I'd never been anywhere outside of Los Angeles and I wanted to get away. See what else is out there."

"I'm glad no one was hurting you, and I can see why you would feel that way. You are too vibrant, too alive, to be locked up anywhere." He patted her hand. "For the next three weeks, you can be as free as a bird. If you want to see something, do something, just tell me, and we will." He held up the money. "All expenses paid."

She had to smile at how his eyes twinkled, but guilt over what she'd done—used the wrong name on the marriage license—grew inside her. She still wanted to help him. Still liked the idea of saving him like Henry had saved Betty from marrying James, but this was so different. Very different from what she'd first imagined.

Her mind twisted down another trail. No one would ever know she'd put down a false last name because she'd use the same one on the divorce as she had the marriage. The whole thing was fake, so surely that little piece wouldn't matter.

What mattered was that David didn't have to marry someone else. Because of her. She was helping him just like Henry had saved Betty.

It was like a weight was suddenly lifted off her shoulders. The smile that pulled on her lips felt real, justified. She could do this.

As her justification settled, she nodded. "Caramel rolls."

"What?"

"Caramel rolls for breakfast," she said. "That's what you can buy me. That's what I want. Caramel rolls every day."

"Done! Caramel rolls it is."

She laughed. "Good."

"But right now." He dug into the grocery bag, started lifting things out. "You have pickled eggs, cheese, crackers, soda pop." His eyes shimmered with optimism as he pulled out the last items. "And candy bars."

"That all sounds delicious. And perfect." It was perfect. Right now, her life was perfect.

They ate and watched the sun fall lower, and lower and lower, changing the sky like the scenes of a motion picture changed on the big screen of the theater. She and her sisters had gone to the theater instead of a speakeasy once, and it had been nice, but this, this was in full color, and truly spectacular.

Once the sun disappeared, dusk settled in fast, David put everything back in the grocery bag. "It's a long trip back down the road, and I'm not sure how far away the closest hotel is."

He had to be exhausted after driving all night and all day. "Can't we just stay here?" she asked. "We have blankets and pillows." Shrugging, she added, "If we get too cold, we can sleep in the car."

"You want to sleep here?"

She looked up at the sky, at the stars that were starting to appear. They looked so close. So bright. "Yes, I do. If you don't mind."

"I don't mind. I'm so tired I could sleep anywhere."

"Then lie down." She picked up the grocery sack. "I'll put this in the car and get the pillows and the other blanket."

He reclined onto his back and put his hands beneath his head, arms akimbo. "Be careful of your suitcase."

She giggled. "I will."

With his head on a pillow and his feet free from his shoes, David stared up at the stars. He'd pointed out every constellation he could remember to Jane, but was still searching the sky, waiting to see if another one would let itself be released from the far recesses of his mind.

He hadn't been home for almost six months. Things could have changed, though he doubted it. Joshua's onslaught of calls and telegrams were focused on setting a date for the wedding. A wedding that wouldn't happen now, because Jane had agreed to go along with his half-baked impulsive idea.

A deceitful solution, which didn't bode well, and he was still having a hard time justifying it. If Jane hadn't been so intent upon seeing it through, he'd have put a stop to it.

And what?

Married Rebecca?

No, that went against what his goals were. He didn't want to be tied down in Chicago by a wife. There were too many opportunities to grow transportation right now, and he wanted to be a major player in it. He wanted the A and R to expand beyond the rails. Now, while the opportunities were ripe. The military and government were investing more and more in airplanes and the public wanted to have that mode of transportation, too.

However, that didn't justify what he was doing. He'd never been so torn.

Despite the heaviness in his mind, a grin formed.

Caramel rolls.

That's all she'd asked for in form of payment.

He'd buy her caramel rolls and pay her when this was over. He'd never met anyone like her, and she did deserve the opportunity to see what was out there.

"David?"

"Yes?" he answered, smiling at her whisper.

"Have you ever slept outside before?"

"Yes. Have you?"

"No."

She was still whispering as if they were in hiding and their seekers were nearby. Concerned she was scared, he asked, "Do you want to leave? Or sleep in the car?"

"No. I'm fine, but I am glad you're here with me."

"I'm glad, too," he answered, even as a new concern entered his mind. They had a long way to go yet, and even though it would all be over in three weeks, he needed to be diligent about not coming to care for her too much. She was charming and fun and beautiful, but didn't fit in his life any more than Rebecca did.

"Good night," she whispered.

"Good night." He closed his eyes and willed sleep to come so he could stop thinking about how close she was lying next to him and how easy it would be to wrap an arm around her and pull her even closer.

At some point, after he'd fallen asleep, he must have pulled the other blanket over the top of them. Or she had, because when he awoke, he was on his side and her back was snuggled up against his chest. His arm was around her waist, holding her close and the blanket was covering both of them.

He froze, recognizing the effect her closeness, her warmth, had on his body. The desires that created. The exact things he'd been afraid of happening when he'd fought to fall asleep last night.

"Are you awake?" she asked as quietly as she'd whispered good-night hours ago.

"Yes," he replied, and started to pull his hand off her stomach.

She grabbed his wrist. "Don't move."

He had to move. This was not a good position for them to be in.

Holding on to his wrist tighter, she whispered, "Look over there. By that big pine tree."

Her head was beneath his chin, the golden curls soft, silky and fragrant. He pulled his focus off them, how they were warming his blood even more, and looked in the direction she'd suggested.

A large deer stood next to the tree. A buck, with a ten-point rack and its nose in the air, sniffing for a female and poised to pounce in pursuit of the first whiff.

David did not need that comparison right now.

"Isn't he magnificent?" she asked. "He looks so regal."

The buck was clearly in rut, and David knew anything between him and a doe right now would be in danger. David threw off the blanket and sat up, shouting at the animal.

It shot off through the trees.

"Why did you do that?" She rolled over on her back, looked up at him.

Her golden hair was strewn about the pillow, her eyes sleepy. The sight of that was far more magnificent than the buck. She took his breath away.

"David?" Her brows knit together above the bridge of her nose. "Why did you scare him away?"

He grabbed his shoes. "Because I didn't want us to get trampled. He's a wild animal and we are in his territory." Both shoes were on and he stood.

"I hadn't thought about that." She stretched, arching her back.

His pulse increased and specific body parts throbbed, and he had to look away.

"Look at that sunrise," she said. "It's as beautiful as the sunset was."

"It is," he said, although, like last night, he was looking at her instead of the sky. Couldn't help himself. She'd sat up and was twisted at her waist, looking over one shoulder at the sky.

He considered getting his camera to snap a

picture, but he didn't need to. The image was already embedded in his mind.

The wind was tugging at her curls, the blanket pooled around her waist and the pillows still had indents from being slept on. It was her, though, the way her head was tilted and her smile so natural that was so memorable.

As if she could read his mind, she asked, "Could I use the camera this morning to take a few pictures?"

"Sure. I'll get it." He walked to the car, taking a few much needed deep breaths.

While she snapped pictures, he collected the pillows and blankets and loaded them into the car. She was still at the canyon rim, camera in hand, when another car rumbled over the hill and into the parking area.

David joined Jane as a young couple climbed out of the car and held each other's hands while they walked toward the rim of the canyon.

"Hello," Jane greeted.

"Hello," the young woman replied. "We were hoping to see the sunrise, but we didn't get here in time."

Jane looked up at David and smiled before replying, "It was beautiful."

The young man, wearing brown work overalls and a homespun cotton shirt, made their introduction. "I'm Sam Wallis, this is my wife, Sarah."

Sarah tucked her shoulder-length brown hair behind her ear as she snuggled closer to her husband. Laying a hand on his chest and beaming, she said, "We are on our honeymoon."

Once again, Jane smiled up at David while answering, "We are, too."

David hadn't thought of it that way, but it was their honeymoon. Of sorts. He nodded at the couple. "I'm David Albright, and this is Jane."

"That's wonderful," Sarah said. "Would you take our picture? I have a camera, and I'll take one for you, too."

"Of course!" Jane handed him his camera and took the one from Sarah.

For the next several minutes, she snapped a variety of pictures of Sam and Sarah. Her nervousness over using the camera had completely disappeared. David chuckled to himself as she instructed the couple where to stand and how to pose as if she'd taken hundreds of pictures.

She even had them kiss for one.

"Do you want us to take one of you?" Sarah asked as Jane gave her back their camera.

"Yes, please," Jane answered. "With the canyon behind us."

David had already anticipated that happening and handed Sarah his camera. Unbeknownst to Jane, he'd taken a couple pictures of her taking pictures. She'd been so engrossed she hadn't even noticed.

Sarah snapped a couple of pictures, then said, "Now one of you two kissing. I know that's going to be the favorite one that you took of us."

Jane's expression was wary and a bit shy when she looked up at him. David's instincts said it wasn't a good idea, but since accepting it was all part of the ruse they'd created, he gave her a nod.

Placing a hand beneath her chin, he looked her in the eyes, saw the apprehension, the unease. Slowly, he leaned down, angling his face to align his lips with hers. She stiffened as their lips touched and he momentarily considered pulling back, but then she cupped his face with both hands and pressed her lips firmly against his.

He kissed her once, twice, and then, unable to stop, he pressed his lips against hers again, longer, harder, while grasping her waist, pulling her up against him.

Moments before becoming completely lost in kissing her, he broke away, breathing hard.

Her eyelids fluttered open and she instantly averted her gaze, though he saw how she was breathing heavily too. Sarah handed him back his camera with a smile, gushing about how beautiful the photographs would be.

They left shortly afterward, and he was still internally shaken by that kiss. He'd tried to shake it off, but it was still there. It was as if her lips had opened something inside him. Something bright and warm and unhindered. He wasn't sure what that meant, but he couldn't stop it from lingering.

"I saw what you did," she said after they'd been driving for a short time.

He glanced at her, knowing what she was referring to.

"The money you put in their car," she said with a soft smile. "Sarah and Sam."

He nodded. The couple had looked young. Nineteen or twenty at the oldest if he'd had to guess. Their car had been old, scratched and battered in places, so had their shoes. But they had looked happy, in love. He wasn't exactly sure why, other than a part of him truly hoped the best for the young couple. While the couple had been taking a stroll hand in hand along the trail, and Jane had been climbing into the car, he'd taken out his wallet and tucked several bills into the crease of their car's seat, where they would easily spot the money but the wind wouldn't blow it away. Enough money to make their honeymoon and the beginning of their life together more carefree financially.

"I'm sure they'll be surprised," she said.

"I figured they could use a wedding present."

Nodding, she said, "That was very nice of you. You are a nice person, but…" She bit her lip and glanced away.

"But?"

Huffing out a breath, she said, "I don't think we should kiss again."

"I agree," he replied without thought.

"You do?"

"Yes." Refraining from explaining it any further, he asked, "Are there any other sites you want to see on the maps?"

"I haven't looked."

He nodded toward the pile of maps. "Open the New Mexico map—we'll be there in a couple of hours."

She opened the map, and luckily the next several hours were taken up with discussions over upcoming towns and the scenery they drove through, from mountain scenery at the tallest point in Arizona, to the enormous pine forests, before the land grew flat again near Flagstaff.

They ate there and he bought her an additional suitcase before they climbed back in the car and drove until the sun was setting.

Finding a hotel in a small New Mexico town, he rented two rooms and upon delivering Jane her suitcases and instructing her to lock her door, he entered his room and leaned against his closed door as relief flooded him.

A sense of disappointment also hit him, a form of separation.

She was right next door, not miles away, yet, after having her at his side for nearly forty-eight hours straight, it felt as if something was missing.

Jane lay in bed, on her side, staring at the wall that David was on the other side of, listening to the muffled sounds that must be him getting ready for bed. She didn't dare close her eyes, not until she knew she'd instantly fall asleep, because if she did close them one thing would come to mind.

Kissing him.

Her heart thudded.

Bee's knees, but she'd never experienced anything like that ever before. Not in her entire life. She couldn't quit thinking about it. All day. Not even with all the other things she'd seen. She'd tried taking pictures, hoping that would help. It hadn't. Neither had reading the maps.

When they'd climbed into the car at the Grand Canyon, her knees had been weak and she'd still been gulping for air. She'd never imagined a kiss could do that. Then he'd put that money in Sam and Sarah's car as a wedding gift. He was so kind and caring.

She'd never known anyone like him, and that scared her. That's why she told him they shouldn't kiss again. As soon as his lips had touched hers, something happened. Like when a light was switched on. It filled her and made her want more. She'd actually grabbed hold of him and kissed him!

Furthermore, she had wanted him to kiss her before then. While taking pictures of Sam and Sarah kissing, she'd been wondering what it would be like to kiss David, and then next thing she knew, it had been happening.

Although she'd said they shouldn't do that again, kiss, she wanted to. He was making her wonder about being married. Not him and her, but her sisters. Why they'd been so excited, and why they were so happy now.

She missed them. Wished she could talk to them. But this was a choice she'd made, and once she was back home she'd tell them everything.

After she and David were divorced.

At that thought, she flipped over and pulled the blanket up to her chin, telling her mind to stop. Just stop thinking and go to sleep.

That finally happened, and the next morning she dressed in a green-and-black-plaid dress and tied a white silk scarf around her neck, leaving the ends long so they hung over the front and the back of one shoulder. She was ready when David knocked on the door, and when she opened it, saw him standing there, the idea of kissing him hit her all over again.

She huffed out a sigh.

"Are you all right?"

"Yes," she answered, unable to hold back another sigh. "I'm fine."

"Not looking forward to another day on the road?" he asked while stepping in and picking up both of her suitcases—the one she'd stolen from Betty and the one he'd bought her.

She picked up her purse and hooked it on her forearm. "You really shouldn't be so nice."

"Oh?" He carried her bags into the hallway. "So you don't want me to stop at the restaurant up the road that has caramel rolls?"

She followed and closed the door behind her, trying very hard to find a reason to not like him so much. "How do you know they have caramel rolls?"

He waited for her to walk in front of him. "I asked the hotel clerk."

She scrunched up her face, knowing he couldn't see it and knowing he would have asked. That was him. "Maybe I don't want a caramel roll this morning."

"Then you don't have to eat one."

No, she didn't have to, but she would, because she did like them. She liked him, too.

She considered that throughout the day and the next, as they drove and drove, stopped at small attractions, fueled the car, changed tires, bought more tires and rented hotel rooms. She also ate caramel rolls, snapped pictures and tried to find a flaw in David. Just one. She wasn't exactly sure why she wanted him to have a flaw, something that she didn't like, but she figured if she could find one, then she wouldn't like him so much.

It was hard though, because he was so nice and likable. Not only had he given those newlyweds a wedding gift, he pulled over every time they saw someone with a flat tire and offered to help them.

Still searching, she asked if she could drive once they'd hit the paved section of road in Oklahoma.

"Sure," he answered, and pulled the car to the side of the road.

She'd half expected him to say no. Nervous at first, she carefully eased the car back on the road and held it at a slow pace.

"It'll be Christmas by the time we get to Chicago if this is as fast as you're going to drive," he said with a laugh.

"I was just getting used to the car," she justified, but wasn't miffed. His teasing wasn't a flaw. It was just part of who he was. Another part she liked.

"Are you used to it?"

"Yes."

"Then hit the gas."

She glanced at him, gripped the wheel tighter and pressed her foot harder against the gas pedal.

"That's my girl," he said. "You're doing great. You really are a good driver, Jane."

Pride filled her. "Thank you." He did that, too, all the time—complimented her. No one had done that before. She was usually told what she was doing wrong, not right.

She drove while he read the maps and they discussed things along the road and things they would see later on during their trip to Chicago. There wasn't a thing along the way so far that she hadn't liked, that she couldn't wait to tell her sisters about. She missed them, but in all honesty she didn't have a lot of time to think about them. Not with the way her mind was focused on David, and the things he was showing her. Every state was new and different. From the landscape to the cities they drove through, no two places were alike. It was all so wonderful. Every day was like she'd bought a new magazine, and driving along the roads was like flipping the pages, reading about something new. Instead of reading, she was seeing and doing!

All because of David.

Her thoughts were interrupted when the steering wheel began to shake beneath her hands and a loud bang sounded. She screamed, even though she instantly knew they'd blown a tire. That had already happened several times along the way.

"It's all right," David said. "Just pull to the side of the road."

"I know." She'd already slowed the car and

eased it to the edge of the paved area. "It just startled me. It happened so suddenly."

"I should have warned you," he said. "And checked the tires before you started driving, but you're doing great. Just let it roll to a stop and then shut off the engine."

As soon as the engine went silent, she let the air out of her lungs and then laughed at herself for screaming. "I don't know why that startled me so."

"Because you didn't expect it," he answered, opening his door. With a wink, he added, "That's why it's called unexpected!"

She laughed again and shouted, "I see!" because he'd already shut the door. Then, untying the white silk scarf from around her neck, she used it to tie her hair back so it wouldn't blow in her face when she opened her door and climbed out.

The white scarf matched the red-and-white-striped dress and the white gloves that she took off and tossed on the car seat so they wouldn't get dirty. David was already sliding the jack beneath the car, and having helped before, she knelt down beside him to hold the nuts that he'd take off and need again once he put the new tire back on. He'd insisted that she didn't need to help when the first tire had blown back in New Mexico, but she'd said she wanted to help, so he let her.

He hadn't yet gotten the tire off when a car pulled alongside them and stopped.

"Need any help?" the man asked.

Chapter Six

By the time the fourth car stopped to ask if they needed help, David's endurance was wearing thin.

He assured this driver, just as he had each and every one of all the others that had stopped to ask if they needed help during each and every tire change, that they didn't need any help. And once again listened to Jane gush about how nice it had been for them to stop and then wave goodbye as if she'd known this Good Samaritan as personally as all the others.

"You really should stop doing that," he said while pulling the jack out from beneath the car.

"Doing what?"

He sighed. It wasn't her fault that she caught the eye of every man driving past. Dressed in her cute, fashionable way—he hadn't known a woman could tie a scarf in so many different ways—she was more than eye-catching.

Who would ever have thought that a beautiful woman could wear a man out? He hadn't. But Jane… She was…well…different from other women. She didn't even realize that every man, young and old, who drove away had two things in their eyes. Admiration for her and envy of him.

He couldn't hold that against the men, or her. She was just that way, friendly. Happy.

So happy. Always. Even while helping change a tire in the November wind. Which was getting colder and colder.

"Get in the car," he shouted over the wind. "It looks like it's going to rain soon."

She walked around to the passenger side and climbed in. A wave of guilt struck him. He hadn't meant to sound so harsh, but she did have to be getting cold.

Once he had everything put away, he pulled open the driver's door. "Did you want to drive some more?"

"No, thanks." She nodded toward the map where she was noting the flat tire with a pen. She'd started doing that after they'd left the

Grand Canyon. Marking each of the places they'd stopped on the maps and noting why.

It starting raining shortly thereafter, and the temperature continued to drop. He stopped several times, searching for a motel room, but each place only had one room, with one bed. Finally, when the rain turned to ice and he knew it was too dangerous to continue, he ended up renting a single room with a single bed, and was lucky to have been able to. The people behind him, as well as those who drove in while he was carrying in their suitcases, were told the hotel was full.

Jane was shivering and, shortly upon entering their room, she left it again, to use the bathing facilities at the end of the hall.

He copied her actions upon seeing her walk back into their room with her freshly washed hair and sparkling clean skin. Grabbing his suitcase, he shot down the hall to the bathing room. Those men who had been envious of him earlier today wouldn't be now. Now, they'd think he was crazy. He was wondering that himself.

While bathing, he used the time to convince himself that they'd slept side by side at the Grand Canyon and he could do it again. It was only eight hours.

She was in the bed when he entered the room, curled in a ball near the wall.

He set his suitcase on the floor and locked the door. "Are you still cold?"

"Yes."

"I thought your bath would have warmed you up."

"It did, but now my hair is wet and these sheets are as cold as the rain outside." Her teeth chattered as she spoke.

He clicked off the light and crossed the room, sat on the bed and removed his shoes and shirt, but kept on his undershirt and pants. He hadn't considered some of the consequences of this plan. Being with her all day every day was tempting parts of him that had never been pushed so far to their limits.

The sheets were cold, and she was shivering so hard the bed was shaking. Although he knew it would test him further, he slid an arm under her neck and pulled her close. She was chilled to the bone.

Wrapping his other arm around her, he rubbed her cold shoulders and upper arms left bare by the sleeveless dress she was wearing. "Maybe you should put on a nightgown."

"No, I'll warm up in a minute."

That was the problem, she would warm him up, too. Hot in specific places.

"Will it be this cold in Chicago?"

"Colder," he answered.

"Colder?" She snuggled closer.

He drew in what he hoped was a fortifying breath. "Yes."

"How much colder?"

"There could be snow."

She shot upright and stared down at him. "Snow? Like on-the-top-of-the-mountains snow?"

"Yes." November was one of those months where it could snow regularly, or not at all.

"Bee's knees! How much?"

She laid her hand on his undershirt, and he wondered if she could feel how fast his heart was racing right now. He certainly could.

She had her other hand pressed below her throat. "I saw a picture in a magazine of kids throwing snow at each other. It looked so fun!"

The light from the hotel sign shone in the window, cascading her with a yellow glow, and he grinned at how enthralled she looked. "It's called a snowball fight."

"Have you ever done that?"

"Yes, many times."

Sighing, she lay back down and put her head on his shoulder as she pulled the covers up under her chin. "I want to have a snowball fight."

"If there's enough snow, we will." Rubbing her upper arm again, he added, "But you'll need a warm coat." She smelled so good—soap and water, and her—that the sweet smell that reminded him of honeysuckle in bloom.

"I don't have a warm coat. I've never needed one."

"We'll buy you one tomorrow. The trip is only going to get colder from here." He rubbed her shoulder again. "We'll get you a long-sleeved nightgown, too."

"I won't need them when I get back to California."

He didn't want to think about that. Actually, he didn't want to think right now. He needed to close his eyes and go to sleep while there was still a chance of that happening. "Go to sleep, Jane."

"Night," she whispered, and then let out a long sigh.

He did, too, and stared at the ceiling, willing the desires that had been building for days to quell.

* * *

True to what David had said, the following day was colder than the previous one and he stopped at a store in Missouri, where Jane was unable to do anything but stare at the array of coats with fur collars and made of soft, thick wool. He'd told her to pick out whatever coat she wanted, but there were so many to choose from.

It might be easier if her mind was on coats. It wasn't. It was still on last night, on sleeping next to him. He'd been so warm and smelled so good she could have stayed right there forever.

She shook her head to dispel the thought and told herself to be sensible and focus on a coat. That's when she caught sight of the most beautiful cape she'd ever seen. A deep burgundy velvet one with hand slits on each side. The thick, soft black fur trimming the hood and the hem was heavenly, as was the black silk lining.

"How about this one?"

She spun around, away from the cape. David was holding up a long, brilliant blue coat with a brown fur collar that extended to the waistline, where it buttoned with two big gold buttons.

"That's very pretty." She stepped closer to examine the coat. The cuffs had the same soft brown fur around them as the collar, and the back had two long columns of the same big decorative buttons as the front.

"Here, try it on," he said.

She turned around and slid her arms in as he held the coat for her. It was fur lined and made of wool and instantly made her feel toasty and snug.

"There is a mirror over here," said the black-haired saleslady who had shown them to the coats.

Jane walked over and looked at herself. The coat was very becoming, and very pretty. It extended well past her knees, which would provide added warmth, and the back had a slit to making walking and sitting easier.

"You make that coat look very lovely," the saleslady said.

"Do you like it?" David asked.

"Yes, I do. Very much," Jane answered, rubbing the soft fur. She did like it. It was the prettiest coat she had ever seen. "It's very warm."

"Good," he said. "We'll take that one."

The saleslady stepped up behind her and lifted the coat off. "Excellent choice."

As the lady stepped away, David appeared in the mirror's reflection, directly behind her.

Jane smiled at his reflection. Had to. He was so very handsome. "It's a lovely coat. Thank you."

"Now, try on this one," he said, and draped the burgundy cape over her shoulders.

She gasped as the silk slid over her arms. The cape was weightless compared to the coat. She held back a sense of disappointment, knowing the cape would not be warm enough even if it was the prettiest thing she'd ever seen.

"It looks as if that cape was made specifically for you," the saleslady said.

David, still standing behind her, reached around her and buttoned the one large black button under her chin, then he flipped up the hood.

She nearly gasped again, at her own image. She looked almost as sophisticated as he did. Her heart tumbled as she saw his face in the mirror looking over her shoulder.

His smile was so big, and his eyes had that little mischievous gleam she'd come to recognize.

The fur hem brushed across her calves as she turned around. "You saw me admiring this one, didn't you?"

"Do you like it?" he asked in return.

"Yes, but it won't be as warm as the blue one."

He pushed the hood off her head and lifted her hair out from beneath the cape so it hung over her shoulders. "We'll buy both of them. One for cold days, and one for not-so-cold days."

"But I don't need them both. Once I return to Califor—"

He pressed a finger to her lips. "You need them now."

She shook her head.

He nodded. "As my wife, you'll be expected to look the part."

Guilt once again made her feel sick. The only person she could be mad at was herself. She'd chosen to do this and chosen to use the wrong name.

Once in the car, where she wore the cape to ward off the chill, she asked, "What else will be expected of me, as your wife?"

He started the engine and pulled the car away from the curb. "We won't be there that long, so there is nothing for you to worry about."

She swallowed, but the lump in her throat wouldn't go away. There was plenty for her to worry about.

"We'll need to buy you some other clothes, too. Dresses and such."

"Why?" she asked.

"Because it will be colder there, and as my wife there is a certain wardrobe you should have."

She frowned. "You don't like my dresses?"

He sighed. "I like your dresses—you look just fine in them—but they won't be appropriate."

A snap of anger filled her. "Appropriate?"

"Yes. For the weather," he said.

She didn't believe he was truly talking about only the weather, and this, being told what to wear, was one of the reasons she hadn't wanted to get married. She'd been told what to do, what to wear, forever. She'd run away from that. "What else about me won't be appropriate?"

"Nothing. All I'm saying is that you'll need long sleeves."

No, he was saying more than that, he just wouldn't say it.

"We'll buy them once we get to Chicago," he said. "You can pick them out. Whatever you want. There's nothing to be concerned about." He glanced at her. "I'd think you'd like the idea of new clothes."

She did, usually. Right now it was the principle of all this. "I like the clothes I have."

"I do, too, and I'll like the new ones you pick out."

She bit her lips together, fully understanding that was his polite way of saying she had no say in the matter. She thought about that as they drove, realizing she hadn't had a lot of say in anything since the beginning.

They spent two more days, and nights, traveling and sleeping in hotels. Luckily, they didn't need to share a room again, because she was trying hard to keep her distance from him, and the only time she could truly do that was at night. Except that, even when he wasn't right next to her, he was in her mind, front and center.

She couldn't find a reason not to like him or to be mad at him, but she felt as if she needed to because all her thinking had led her to believe one thing—she wasn't any more in charge of her life here than she'd been at home.

In some ways.

The trip had been fun, and she liked the way David explained things along the way, and how she could ask questions. Ultimately, she was destined to be thwarted no matter what she did.

It was late in the afternoon when they arrived in Chicago. The traffic, buildings and people filling the sidewalks reminded her of Los Angeles. But the weather didn't. The sky was gray and snowflakes were falling. Tiny ones, but they were snowflakes. She rolled down her window and caught one on her finger, examined the tiny crystal as it melted.

The flakes melted as soon as they touched the hood of their car, but not on the ones that were parked along the streets. The flakes weren't melting on other places, either, building awnings and rooftops. The thin white coating the flakes created grew thicker as they drove.

"Will it keep snowing all day?" she asked. It was gray and gloomy. Not at all like the pictures she'd seen of children having a snowball fight, laughing with their knitted scarves and hats full of white snow.

"From the looks of the sky, yes, but we'll make it home before it starts piling up."

Home. That word made her stomach bubble. She was trying not to, but couldn't help growing more nervous with each minute that ticked past. He'd told her about his family. His grandfather, brother and sister-in-law. How they all lived in the same house. A tiny shiver rippled over her and she rubbed her arms to ward off a second shiver that was quickly following the first.

"Do you want me to stop so you can get your other coat?"

"No, I'm fine." The cape was perfect in the car. The blue coat had gotten too warm yesterday. Furthermore, she wasn't chilled because of the weather. She had a sense of dread, much like when she'd climb up the trellis at night, knowing the fun was over and she was back in her real life. That's what scared her. For the most part, traveling with him had been like reading a magazine, where everything was perfect, but that wasn't real life. Now she had to put the magazine away, and unlike when she snuck into the bathroom back home, she didn't know what to expect upon arriving at his house.

"There's nothing to worry about."

She swallowed. "They aren't going to like me." Why would they? He'd married her instead of someone they wanted him to marry. Rebecca Stuart.

"I like you," he said.

She couldn't even smile at that, because she liked him too and didn't want to. She hadn't expected that. Her reason for agreeing to help him had been because no one should have to marry someone they didn't want to marry. She still felt that way, but it went deeper when it came to him. She didn't want him marrying anyone. The thought of that made her feel odd. Dark and tangled inside. She wished she could talk to her sisters.

That was a wish she'd had every day. She missed them. She missed her parents, too, and was beginning to think she'd been wrong about some things. Maybe her father hadn't been just being mean with all the rules he'd made them live by, but had been trying to protect them. He had changed the past few months, even in saying he wouldn't force her to marry someone. But she hadn't wanted to remain at home forever. Inherit everything. Maybe she should have told him that instead of running away. That's what her sisters had done. Stood up to him. She hadn't. She'd run away.

They were probably worried about her, too, and that bothered her, but there wasn't anything she could do about that. Just like there wasn't anything she could do about David's family not liking her. She'd just have to grin and bear it. Which was exactly what she had been doing her entire life.

Grinning and bearing.

"It's only for seven days," David said as he steered around a street corner.

"Seven? I thought it was only going to be six."

"We arrived a day early." He turned onto another street.

With each turn he made, her stomach fell just a little more. Everything had sounded so simple when she'd agreed to this, but it wasn't simple, and she was certain that pretending to be his wife was not going to be simple, either. Nor easy.

"We're here," he said as he turned the car onto a brick driveway.

She gasped so hard she choked and coughed. "That's your house?"

Made of tan stone, it was four stories tall, with steep gables, multiple brick chimneys and two large pillars connecting an archway over the front door. The front two corners of the house had huge round turrets with cone-shaped shingled roofs, making it look like a castle in a fairytale book.

"That's not a house, it's a mansion. A castle." She couldn't help but compare it to her home, and the other homes in Hollywoodland. They were small compared to this house. Actually, there was no comparison. Her father, with his love of money and houses, would be jealous of this house.

Her heart sank as she turned, looked at David. "How wealthy is your family?"

"Wealthy enough."

Her father was wealthy, too, but they didn't live in a castle. Proof again that she'd done exactly what she hadn't wanted to do. Marry a wealthy man. Albeit a fake marriage, which she'd made even more fake.

Her stomach rolled as he drove the car up to the side of the house, stopped, turned the engine off.

"And along with that wealth come some very specific responsibilities."

He sounded so serious the hair on her arms stood. "Wh-what do you mean?"

"This isn't going to be easy, Jane. We are going to have to pretend to be in love, very much in love." His smile was strained as he turned, looked at her. "In order to make this work, everyone is going to have to believe that."

It was as if her fears were inching upward, like when she'd climbed up the trellis, getting higher and higher, but this time, when she got to the top, there wouldn't be a window she could climb through.

"You just have to be yourself," David said.

Be herself? When a moment ago he'd just said they had to pretend to be very much in love? That didn't go hand in hand. She didn't want to be married. Especially not to a rich man that her father would approve of. She didn't want to be in love, either. When her sisters had fallen in love, they'd changed, and she hadn't liked that.

She wrung her hands together beneath her cape, her hands icy, as the air seeped out of her lungs.

She was in a worse pickle now than she'd been at the Rooster's Nest, when she'd thought all this was such a grand idea. Except now she had a husband, one she had to pretend to be in love with. How could she pretend something she didn't know anything about? Other than... other than how Betty looked at Henry and Patsy looked at Lane. She'd seen it. Knew they were truly in love. She could do that. It was like posing. She'd done that every time David had taken her picture. Posed like the actresses had in magazine pictures. All those magazines she'd snuck into the house and read cover to cover had shown her how to pose and, hopefully, they'd continue to help her.

"Here we go," David said, and opened his door.

She snapped her head up.

A man had stepped out of a door on the side of the house. "Master David, you're home! Welcome!"

Master David? Jane swallowed twice before she could breathe again.

"Yes, Elwood, I am. Thank you." David closed the door and walked around the car.

The man, older, with gray hair and dressed in a black tuxedo, looked at her through the windshield as David opened her door.

"Have you brought along a guest, Master David?"

Jane slid her hand through the hand-slit opening on the side of her cape and took hold of David's hand. Her insides trembled as she stepped out of the car.

"More than a guest, Elwood," David said, placing an arm around her shoulders. "This is Jane, my wife."

The man's eyes grew wide and the smile on his face quivered as he struggled to hold it in place. "Oh, that is wonderful news, Master David. Wonderful news."

That was a lie if she ever saw one. It was like saying an earthquake was good news. It wasn't. Nor was the news that David was married. Just like she'd known it wouldn't be. However, there appeared to be a lot of things she hadn't known. That David hadn't mentioned.

"See that our luggage is taken to my suite, Elwood," David said, escorting her toward the house.

"Yes, sir." The man nodded at her. "Mistress

Jane." He then held the house door open for them to walk through.

Mistress Jane? This was nothing like what she'd imagined. How could she have? David hadn't told her. "Why didn't you tell me you had servants?" she whispered.

"I didn't think it mattered."

"It did," she muttered under her breath. Everything mattered. "It does."

"I didn't want you to worry," he replied as they walked down a long hallway with windows on one side and a wall covered with felt wallpaper full of colorful red roses on the other. "We'll say hello to my grandfather, and then I'll show you to my—our suite."

"Suite?"

"Yes. My—our bedroom."

"I think we should go to your bedroom first."

He stopped and turned, faced her, flipped her hood back and fluffed her hair around her shoulders and arms. Touching her cheek, he said, "You look lovely. As beautiful as ever."

Her looks had nothing to do with it. She had brushed her hair and applied lipstick as they'd arrived in Chicago, in preparation of meeting his family, seeing his home. That wasn't the problem. It was the things he hadn't told her. The things he thought didn't matter.

"Who is as beautiful as ever?" a booming voice asked. "Davie? Is that you? I thought I saw your car pull in."

"Yes, Grandpa, it's me," David answered.

She didn't have a chance to blink, and David still had his hand on her cheek, when a tall man, with a ring of gray hair that circled the lower portion of an otherwise bald head and went clear down to the sides of his chin, came around the corner of the hallway.

Jane wasn't sure who reacted first. Her or David's grandfather, but he was the one who took a step backward as if startled out of his wits.

He recovered quickly and stepped forward again, gave David a hug and then asked, "Who is this, Davie?"

"Perhaps we should go into your study," David said.

His grandfather looked at him and then back at her.

Despite the fact she was trembling so hard beneath her burgundy cape that her knees were nearly knocking together, Jane couldn't stop the corners of her mouth from tugging upward at the glimmer, the almost mischievous look that formed in his grandfather's eyes. She'd seen that look too many times. From David. It was one thing that never failed to make her smile.

She took a deep breath. Then, lifting her chin, she looked at David out of the corner of her eye and, hoping to mimic her sisters, she let her eyes soften, as if she was dreaming. Then she turned her smile to his grandfather and slipped a hand out through the slit of her cape. "Hello, Mr. Albright. I'm Jane, and I'm very happy to meet you."

He took her hand, but rather than shaking it, he lifted it and kissed the back of it. "Jane," he said, wrapping his other hand around hers. "You must call me Gus, or…" He let the word hang in the air as he looked at David. "Is my thinking correct and she should call me Grandpa?"

It took David a moment to recover. The way Jane had looked up at him a moment ago had nearly knocked his socks off. Her eyes had been smoldering, and for a moment all he'd been able to think about was kissing her.

He swallowed and focused on his grandfather, who, he knew, was going to be the hardest to convince that he and Jane were in love. Grandpa was also the hardest one for him to lie to. He squared his shoulders. "That's up to you, if you want my wife to call you Grandpa, or Gus."

Grandpa didn't look as shocked as David expected.

With little more than a nod at him, Grandpa, still holding Jane's hand, said to her, "Come, dear, your hands are as cold as ice. Let's get you warmed up by the fire."

David followed as Grandpa led Jane around the corner and into his study. A large room that had windows overlooking the driveway, which was why he'd suggested coming in here first, knowing his grandfather had watched him arrive.

Them arrive.

He was going to have to pretend to be in love with Jane, and there was real danger in that because it could be way too easy. The repercussions of this scheme had hit him hard the night they'd shared a hotel bed. Since that night, he'd been fighting a plethora of raging desires.

Grandpa already had Jane near the brick fireplace, where a fire blazed, filling the room with as much heat as the California sun that she was used to.

David removed his wool coat and laid it on a chair near the door. He hadn't told her about having servants because he hadn't wanted her to be intimated because she herself was a maid, but that had probably been a mistake. His ability to think had been hampered lately.

"Close the door, Davie," Grandpa said.

The massive sliding door that separated this room from the rest of the house was rarely pulled closed, and if it was, the house could be on fire and no one would dare to knock on it, let alone open it unless instructed to do so.

He pulled the door closed, and the click of it latching reverberated through him.

Jane was sitting on the high-backed sofa near the large fireplace of ornately carved wood and framed in red tile, and Grandpa was lowering himself into his favorite chair near the other corner of the red-tiled hearth.

"I will see about a cup of hot cocoa or tea for Jane." David moved toward the wall where the servant call button was located.

"Pour her a snifter of brandy instead," Grandpa said. "She looks like she could use it."

He was probably right. No, he *was* right, Jane had been shivering since they'd walked into the house. He should have stopped and made her put on her warm coat, but he'd just wanted to get here.

"Pour me one, too, and yourself of course," Grandpa added.

David bypassed the servant button and went to the bar along that wall, where he poured shots of brandy into two glasses and a half of a shot into a third.

Hooking the short stems of the glasses between his fingers, he carried them across the room, his feet not making a sound as he crossed the thick red-and-black Persian rug. He served Jane first, holding out the hand that held two glasses, including the one containing the half shot.

She looked at him squarely, then took the fuller of the two glasses. He tried not to smile as he held his other hand out to his grandfather, offering him the other glass that contained a full shot.

Grandpa took the glass and laughed upon espying the glass holding the half a shot was the one left. "Sit down, Davie."

He sat next to Jane and took her hand, which was still chilly.

Grandpa held up his glass toward them, but didn't say anything, before he drank the brandy in one swallow.

Both David and Jane had held up their glasses, and then each just took a sip.

Grandpa set his glass on the nearby table that

also held his reading glasses, pipe stand, ashtray and various other things he used while sitting in his chair and smoking his pipe. "Did you open any of the telegrams your brother sent?"

"Not recently." David leaned forward and set his glass on the short wooden table in front of the sofa. "He knew when I was returning."

"My birthday." Grandpa nodded. "Day after tomorrow."

David had planned on the drive being one day longer, but Jane had become too tempting. Far too tempting. He'd driven through most of Illinois before taking rooms late last night, in order to arrive home today and thereby avoid one more night of searching for a hotel that had two rooms available. He'd barely slept last night after the way the clerk had admired her while they'd been walking into the hotel.

David took another sip of his brandy and leaned back, holding the glass. "I knew if it was important, you'd get ahold of me."

Grandpa nodded, then offering her a gracious smile, he asked Jane, "Tell me, dear, when did you meet this handsome grandson of mine?"

It was subtle, the way his arm was stretched out along the wooden arm of his chair, but the way Grandpa held up one finger, David knew he couldn't answer for her and wished he'd taken such questions into consideration, so they could have discussed what they should tell people.

She looked at him and smiled another one of those smoldering eye smiles that made his pulse hammer. Her smiles had done that to him for a large portion of the trip, but he'd never quite seen her eyes smolder like they were now.

"Two months ago," she answered.

David locked his back teeth together, knowing that she referred to the first time she'd seen him play at the speakeasy, not the first time they'd actually spoken.

"Where?" Grandpa asked.

"Los Angeles."

Grandpa nodded, but his finger remained upright.

David was fighting a couple of battles. One of not being able to answer for her, the other of trying to keep his eyes off her. He was totally failing at that. His gaze was stuck on her like the snow outside sticking to the ground and everything else it touched.

"How long have you lived in Los Angeles?" Grandpa asked.

"My entire life," she answered, tilting her head like she did.

"What do you think of Chicago so far?" Grandpa asked.

"That it's cold."

Grandpa laughed. "It is. I hope that Davie warned you that it will become colder."

"He did," she answered.

Grandpa crossed his legs at the knees. "I'm curious to know how and where, specifically, did you two meet?"

She took a sip of brandy and then leaned forward to set her glass on the table.

David clamped his teeth together so hard his jaw throbbed. If Joshua found out they'd met in a speakeasy, that she was a maid, things could turn very ugly. David opened his mouth, about to answer, but just then Jane began to whisper.

"I'll tell you, but you can't tell anyone else," she told Grandpa, still leaning over the table and with a voice so soft it was barely audible.

David bit his lips together at how cute she looked. She did have the most charming whisper. It sucked him in every time she used it.

Grandpa ran a hand over his lips before uncrossing his legs and leaning forward to whisper, "Why?"

In twenty-six years, David couldn't remember a time when his grandfather had whispered anything, to anyone. He couldn't see Jane's eyes but imagined, by the way his grandfather was looking at her, that they were twinkling. They always did while she was whispering.

"Because I wasn't supposed to be there," she whispered.

Grandpa gave a half nod, and then with a grin he couldn't hide, he asked, "Oh? Is that so?"

"Yes, sir, it is." While still leaning forward, she unbuttoned her cape and pushed it off her shoulders, let it fall onto the sofa behind her and expose the simple, yet on her stylish navy-blue-and-white dress. She was also wearing a short strand of white pearls around her neck and a matching bracelet on her arm. He'd thought she looked beautiful, stunning, this morning, and hours later she still looked stunning.

"Where exactly were you not supposed to be," Grandpa whispered, "when you met Davie?"

Her profile revealed how she shrugged and wrinkled her nose. She did that a lot, and it was as cute and charming as her secretive whispers.

"It was an *establishment*, and Davie was play-ing the piano there."

"I see," Grandpa said.

David couldn't help but smile. It was like

watching a movie the way she and Grandpa were whispering back and forth.

"David always says that," she told Grandpa with a little laugh. "I see." She shrugged. "And I ask him, what do you see?"

Once again, Grandpa started to nod and stopped mid-nod. "Well, now, that is a good question, isn't it?"

She sat back and looked at Grandpa expectantly. "I think so."

He chuckled and sat back in his chair, crossed his legs at the knees again. "Well, my dear, in this instance, it means your secret is safe with me."

"Thank you, Grandpa Gus," she said. "That is a relief."

David could have sworn the skin above his grandfather's muttonchops turned pink, and not from the heat of the fireplace. The warmth of the fire had done its job for Jane, though, along with the brandy. Her hand was warm and her cheeks rosy.

"So, Davie, when did you marry this adorable young lady?"

"Earlier this month," he answered. "I have our marriage certificate in my suitcase."

"I'm sure you do." Grandpa scratched the skin

in front of one ear. "It looks like we have a little bit of a situation here. I'm sure Davie mentioned he was expected to marry someone else."

"He did," Jane answered. "I believe her name is Rebecca. As soon as I heard that, I told him that I would come to the wedding and object."

Grandpa lifted a brow. "You did, did you?"

"Yes, I did, and I still would." She glanced his way, then turned back to Grandpa. "I would march right up the aisle of the church, and object, make sure that everyone heard me."

Grandpa couldn't wipe the smile off his face. Neither could David. He was imagining her doing just that, and was certain Grandpa was, too.

David squeezed her hand. She was handling this far better than he'd have imagined. Gramps looked to be nearly smitten with her. Which was an easy feat. She was charming, to say the least.

"Well, the issue we now face is what to do about things." Grandpa shrugged as if he was at a loss as to what could be done. "When you never responded to one of his telegrams, Joshua told Rebecca to mail out the wedding invitations."

David rubbed his temple with his free hand. Whether he'd responded or not, Joshua was going to do what Joshua wanted to do. His brother was dead set on him marrying Rebecca. David was mad, though, that Joshua had taken it that far. "For what date?"

"December eighth."

"Two weeks from now?" David hadn't expected it to be that soon.

Jane looked at him and then at Grandpa. She let out a little huff. "It seems to me that Joshua shouldn't have done that. He didn't have any right to do that."

Chapter Seven

If Jane could ever have a grandfather, she would want it to be Gus Albright. He acted gruff, and on the outside, his frown lines and muttonchop sideburns made him look gruff, but that twinkle in his eyes was too much like David's to fool her. Gus was an older version of David, who was not gruff on the inside. Within minutes of meeting Gus, of talking with him, she'd liked him. Just like she had David.

She had no idea if the way she'd looked at David had convinced Gus that she was in love with him, but it was all she had, so she'd keep using it, keep trying. At dinner. As long as David showed her how to get back down to the dining room.

Right now, he was leading her along yet another hallway of this gigantic house. They were on the third floor, at least she thought it was the third floor. The house was maze of rooms and hallways and staircases that would take her a while to get used to.

David stopped at the end of the hall, grasped the handles and opened a massive set of double wooden doors.

"This is your bedroom?" she asked, peering into a room as large as the living room at her parents' house. There was a couch, chairs, bookshelves, a large credenza like the one downstairs in Gus's study, complete with bottles and glasses sitting atop it.

"Yes," he said. "This is my suite."

"Suite. That's right." She stepped into the room. The entire house was castle-like, with all the dark carved wood, wainscoting, wallpaper, tall decorative tiled ceilings, plush carpets and lush furnishings.

He closed the doors behind her and walked through the room to a single door. "This is my bedroom."

She crossed the room, running her hand over the plush fabric of the brown sofa as she walked past it. David had already entered the room by the time she arrived in the doorway. It was huge. The bed, with four tall thick wooden posts carved into spindles at each corner, was huge, too. There was even a fireplace in this room. In his bedroom.

"This is the bathroom," he said.

She walked into the room, and past the brick fireplace to glance through the door he'd opened. It too was large, with black-and-white-tiled flooring and all the necessary facilities.

"And this will be— What the—?"

"What's wrong?" She hurried to the far side of the room to yet another door he'd opened.

He brushed past her, walked over near his big poster bed and pulled a long cord. Nothing happened, so she wasn't sure why he'd done that.

"What's wrong?" she asked again, stepping through the door he'd left open. The room was like a reading room, or maybe a sewing room, if there were books or a sewing machine. There weren't any of those types of things, but there was a large round upholstered white bench in the center of the room, four full-length mirrors, and two elaborate dressing tables with mirrors. There was also what appeared to be a wardrobe closet that lined the entire length of one wall. She opened the center doors and stared, stunned to see her clothes hanging there, taking up only a minute portion of the massive space.

David entered the room.

"Who hung my clothes in this closet?" she asked.

"One of the maids." He sounded angry.

She closed the closet door. "Why?"

"Because that's what maids do," he snapped. "You know that."

No, she didn't know that. That wasn't the kind of maid she was for her parents. She was the washing-clothes, scrubbing-floors and doing-dishes kind.

He huffed out a breath. "This was supposed to be your bedroom." He waved a hand in no real direction, just around the room in general. "My entire life, there has been a bed in this room. When I was young, my nanny slept in here, and that was supposed to be where you would sleep. In your own bed. Now, it's gone, and it's been turned into—" he spun around "—a huge closet."

"That is what it appears to be," she said, far more worried about having someone unpack her suitcase and put away her belongings without her knowledge than what this room might be or had been.

A knock sounded.

David left the room, walked through his bedroom and into the living room area. "Come in!"

"You rang, Master David?" Elwood, the man

she'd met outside, stepped into the room and closed the door behind him.

"Yes, Elwood." David gestured toward the bedroom. "Why do I have a room that is nothing but a closet?"

Stiff backed, shoulders straight and holding his hands behind his back, Elwood gave a slight head nod. "It's called a dressing room, sir."

"I don't care what it's called," David said. "Who changed it?"

Elwood gave another slight nod. "Miss Stuart, sir. Master Joshua gave her permission to remodel the room."

Jane had never seen David so angry, and couldn't believe he was that mad over a room.

"Where is the bed that was in that room?" he asked.

"It was donated to charity, sir," Elwood replied.

Not exactly sure why David was so mad, but knowing it wasn't Elwood's fault, Jane stepped up and wrapped both of her hands around one of David's arms. "Thank you, Mr. Elwood."

"Just Elwood, Mistress Jane," he said with a nod.

She didn't want to be anyone's mistress any more than she'd wanted to be someone's maid or wife. She just wanted to be Jane. "Just Jane,

Elwood. No Mistress. Just Jane." She waved a hand then toward the door. "Thank you."

"Master David?" Elwood asked. "Is there anything else you need?"

David shook his head. "No. Thank you, Elwood."

He nodded, opened the door without turning around, walked backward out of the room and shut the door.

"Why are you so mad over a room, a bed?" she asked.

He shook his head and let out a sigh. "So that you would have your own bed, your own room."

She wanted that, too. Sleeping with him that one night had left a longing inside her that made her heart race. Just thinking about it still caused that to happen. "Surely a house this size has another bedroom. One that I can use."

"Not when we are supposed to be married." He pulled his arm out of her hold and walked toward the credenza. "Are married. Damn it. She had no right to do that. To remodel my suite."

He was right. On both points. Yet, she was inclined to point out, "No, she didn't, but she was planning on marrying you. Is planning on marrying you." She crossed the room, stood next to him as he poured a glass full of amber liquid.

The brandy she'd had downstairs had warmed her considerably. It had relaxed her enough to tell Gus the truth. She wasn't going to do any more lying. She would withhold certain things that no one needed to know about, but she wouldn't lie.

She picked up a glass and held it out for David to pour whatever he'd poured into his glass, in hers.

He looked at her. "Are you sure?"

She nodded.

He poured a small amount into the glass.

She gave him a look that said that wasn't nearly enough.

He poured more in the glass. "You know, sometimes I wonder if it wasn't the wine that night. The reason we thought this was such a great idea."

"I've wondered that, too," she said, "but neither of us were ossified."

"No, we weren't." He set the bottle down and put the cap back on it.

They had consumed almost an entire bottle of wine that night. "It may have given us a push in that direction." She shrugged. "A touch of courage."

He picked up his glass. "Could be."

She held her glass up to his. "And now we need a bit more courage to pull it off."

They clinked glasses and drank. It was brandy again, and she felt the warmth rising up in her as she swallowed. Right now she needed a solution as much as she needed courage. Glancing over his shoulder, she said, "I can sleep on the sofa."

"No, you aren't going to sleep on the sofa." He drank the rest of his brandy and set his glass down at the same time she did. "You were amazing downstairs. You charmed the hair right off my grandfather's head."

He still looked so mad, which wasn't like him. She reached up and touched the very top of his head, where his dark brown hair was thick and soft. "The hair right here?"

He nodded.

She leaned closer and whispered, "He was already bald there."

He stared at her for a long moment, then shook his head. "That is exactly how you did it, too."

She shrugged. "I was just pretending to be your loving wife." She had to step away from him then, because his nearness was making her heart and other parts of her body do funny things. "So, what did you mean about getting dressed for dinner? We are dressed."

"Dinner is a formal affair, so everyone usually changes their clothes into more formal wear." Reaching up, he unbuttoned the top button of his shirt and then turned, walked toward his bedroom. "But don't worry, you already look beautiful."

She'd never dressed for dinner in her life, but she wasn't about to let others know that.

The dresses she'd worn to Patsy's and Betty's weddings could be considered formal wear. One was green, the other peach. Her only shoes were black, but she did have black pearls, earbobs and a black headband that would tie the outfit together. Oh, and a black silk scarf she could drape over her shoulders.

Not sure how much time she had, she hurried through his bedroom and into the huge closet room.

Used to changing fast due to her nightly excursions, it didn't take her long to be ready to go back downstairs. She'd even brushed her hair so it all fell over one shoulder and then pinned it near the nape of her neck so it would stay that way before she'd put the thin headband around her forehead and positioned it so the tiny cluster of feathers was above her one ear that was showing.

Checking herself in one of the full-length mirrors, she tugged a few small strands of hair to hang in front of her ear and twisted it until it fell in a ringlet.

As she crossed the room, she stopped and put one foot on the round bench to adjust her nylon stocking, and realized that from right where she stood, the mirrors were positioned so she could see herself in each one of them. Her front, her back, and both sides. She wasn't quite sure if that was ingenious or ostentatious.

She settled for ostentatious. One mirror was understandable, but no one needed four mirrors all at the same time.

David was putting on a suit jacket when she opened the door. A gray one that looked extraordinarily spiffy over his black shirt and black bow tie. His pants were gray, matching the coat, and his shined black shoes sparkled in the overhead light.

She glanced up when he let out a whistle, and giggled at the smile on his face. Holding out her arms, she pivoted all the way around. "Is this formal enough?"

"Yes, it is. You look wonderful." He shook his head. "I don't think I've seen you wear the same clothes twice." He walked toward her. "I know I haven't since we left California."

"Of course not. They're all dirty. They're covered with dust from Arizona, New Mexico, Texas, Oklahoma, a touch of Kansas, Missouri—"

"I'll instruct a maid to wash them tonight."

He stopped in front of her, and her breath caught at how badly she wanted him to touch her. Which was strange because she'd never liked to participate in dances where she had to touch her partner and they had to touch her. Then again, it was different with him. They'd been traveling together for days.

They hadn't kissed again, not since the Grand Canyon, and a part of her wished that she hadn't said they shouldn't kiss again. Because she wanted to. Wanted to very badly. And had to tell herself this was all pretend. She was pretending to be his wife.

"When are we going to turn in the camera film rolls?" She really wanted to see the picture of them kissing.

"We can do that tomorrow," he said.

"I can't wait to see the pictures."

"All two hundred?"

She cocked her head, not sure if he was teasing or not. "We didn't take two hundred pictures."

"At least." His smile faded as he held out an elbow. "Time to meet the rest of the family."

She shivered. He'd never said anything mean or nasty about his brother, but from some of the things he'd mentioned and from what she'd heard since arriving here, she had a feeling she wasn't going to like Joshua.

No, it wasn't a feeling. She knew.

He led her downstairs to a room he called the main drawing room, which was like another living room, with more couches, chairs, a fireplace and a credenza topped with various crystal decanters and glasses ready to be filled with the liquids in those decanters.

Gus was already in the room, still wearing the green brocade smoking jacket with black lapels he'd had on earlier.

As if David was reading her mind, he whispered, "It's Joshua's idea that everyone dresses for dinner. Not Grandpa's."

Had she known that, she may not have changed her clothes. No, she still would have because… well, just because. David would have changed, so she would have, too.

"It can't be true, can it?"

Frowning, she glanced at Gus, wondering what he was talking about.

He held both of his hands out toward her.

David put a small amount of pressure on her back.

She stepped forward and laid both of her hands in Gus's.

"It is possible." He released one of her hands and used the other to spin her in a pirouette. "You are even more lovely, more charming, than when I first saw you wearing your Little Red Riding Hood cape."

She giggled, then asked, "Did you read David all of Grimms' fairy tales while he was growing up? Because he knows just as many as you do."

Gus leaned forward and whispered near her ear, "I'll tell you, but you can't tell anyone else."

They both laughed.

David did, too, before saying, "If you two will excuse me for a moment, I need to speak with Elwood."

"Go ahead," Gus said. "I'll get this lovely young woman a drink."

David walked out of the room while Gus led her over to the credenza, as fully stocked as the back room of the Rooster's Nest had been.

"Wine, or something stronger?" Gus asked.

"Wine is fine," she said. "A small glass." She

hadn't been ossified that night with David, and wasn't going to be tonight, either.

Gus handed her a glass, and she was about to take a sip when someone cleared their throat, loudly.

She spun around and her insides quivered at the sight of a tall man with the same shade of dark brown hair and green eyes as David, but that's where the similarities ended. This man, with wide nostrils and narrow eyes, not only looked older, he looked harsher. Meaner.

Joshua. No doubt.

"So, it's true," he snapped, with his nose so high it was like he was sniffing the air. "Where's David?"

"He'll be right back," Gus said. "In the interim, let me introduce you to Jane, David's wife."

"That's not possible," Joshua snarled.

Her spine stiffened so straight Jane wondered if she'd just gained an inch of height. Which was fine by her because she would never cower from someone ever again.

"I assure you, it is," she said.

Joshua's face fell for a moment, then turned red, while the woman at his side gasped and covered her mouth with three fingers.

The woman was petite with brown hair cut in

an angled bob that stopped at her chin, and big brown eyes. She was pretty, but the dull beige dress she wore made her look pale, washed-out.

"No, it's not!" Joshua bellowed.

He was so much like her father, but Jane hadn't even flinched at his shout and, for that, was proud of herself. That was the reason she was here, because she refused to live the rest of her life being barked at, being told what to do, when to do, and how to do it. David had offered a way for her to free herself from that, and that alone was enough to increase her determination to free him of any obligations toward Rebecca, despite his brother, who was glaring at her while Charlene looked as if she was in an ossified stupor.

Jane closed her eyes for a fraction of a second, just to solidify the determination rising inside her.

"Jane, dear, let's sit down while Joshua gets Charlene and himself something to drink," Gus said.

Joshua spun around as if he was leaving the room.

"Josh," Gus said sternly. "I built this house, and I said we are going to have a drink."

Joshua's hands were at his sides, balled into

fists and trembling. She could see them shaking, his knuckles white.

"You and David can speak after dinner," Gus said.

She was here to help David; therefore, she glanced up at Gus, smiled and then turned to Joshua, who was still glaring at her. "I'm sure you're curious as to why David married me."

Joshua's eyes grew narrow. It was like a stand-off between a gangster and an FBI agent, with guns drawn and others watching, afraid to move, not knowing where the bullets would fly. She'd been there, saw it happen with her brother-in-law and the mole, a man Henry had been chasing. It had scared her, but it had also enthralled her. The waiting, the watching.

"Jane, where did you and David meet?" Charlene asked, glancing at her husband and making a failed attempt at smiling.

"Los Angeles." That was the most she was going to say, because anything she said would be held against her. Joshua thought he was going to win in this imaginary guns-drawn standoff between him and her.

He was wrong. She'd waited her entire life to stand up and voice her opinions, and now was her chance. A spiral of a thrill floated up inside her, like the curling smoke of a fire.

"Where?" Joshua snapped.

"Josh," Gus said.

Jane flashed a grin at Gus. She didn't want him to intervene. For twenty-one years she'd lived under the harsh, domineering hand of her father and wasn't going to give this younger version an iota of control over her. Not now. Not ever. She let her eyes harden, as she'd seen her father do for years, and narrowed her gaze in on Joshua.

"In some tavern?" Joshua sneered.

Recalling how Henry had handled the situation with the mole, she slowly took a sip of her glass, lowered it again, but never took her eyes off Joshua. "Where did you meet Charlene?" That's what Henry had done. Questioned the mole rather than answer. Stayed in charge.

Joshua's chin stiffened. "That's none of your business."

She lifted an eyebrow. It may not be any of her business, and she wasn't any of his business. "Tit for tat."

Charlene's eyes widened, and Joshua puffed out his chest like he was about to explode.

Jane held her stance. Didn't move a muscle. Other than to blink, slowly. She wasn't afraid of him. He was nothing but a big goon, a big meanie. She could sit here all night, glaring at him, not backing down, because he represented everything she'd hated about her life.

Joshua squirmed, shifted his shoulders. "Mine and Charlene's family have known each other for years," he said. "It was a given that our families would be united in marriage."

"I see," she said, with a smile that no one but her could see because it was inside her. She teased David about saying that all the time, but she wasn't teasing. She believed no one would marry Joshua because they wanted to, not even the pale woman at his side.

Joshua frowned and glanced around, as if not sure what to say next.

No one would ever know how good she felt inside right now, but it was empowering. Empowering to know she truly could take control of a situation, not by force or bullets or fighting, but by simply being strong inside. She really could be the person she'd always wanted to be. Because of David. He was the reason she had this opportunity.

He entered the room and, with concern on his face, walked directly to her and laid an arm around her shoulders. Flashing an angry look at his brother, he asked, "What's going on here?"

She smiled up at him. "Gus just introduced me to Joshua and Charlene."

He frowned slightly.

Her smile grew brighter and she took a sip of her wine. "Joshua was going to get him and Charlene something to drink. Do you want one?"

That mischievous glint formed in his eyes as he looked down at her again, along with something else. Pride. He was proud of her. She was proud of herself, too, and of him for not giving in and marrying Rebecca. It wasn't over, she knew that. Joshua wouldn't give up that easily. Bullies never did. This was simply the first battle.

"I'll take some Scotch," he told Joshua.

His brother huffed out a breath and, walking past, muttered, "We'll talk later."

"Yes, we will," David answered, looking at her again.

She grinned and then, feeling a sense of sorrow for Charlene, she walked over to the other woman. "How long have you been married?"

Clearly startled, Charlene glanced at her husband before whispering, "Almost four years."

Jane forced herself to smile, all the while reminding herself that she didn't want to get married, perhaps not ever.

David sat in his usual place at the dinner table, with Joshua and Charlene across from him and Grandpa on his right, at the head of the table. What was different was that Jane was beside him, on his left. He wasn't sure what had happened during the five minutes it had taken him to ask Elwood to have extra blankets carried up to his room, but he was proud of the way that Jane had held her own with Joshua. That had to have been what happened. His brother had been nearly squirming in his shoes and speechless when David had walked into the room. Jane had literally knocked the wind out of Joshua's sails.

This wasn't over, not by a long shot, but he found victory in the fact that Joshua now knew that forcing him into marriage to Rebecca wouldn't happen.

David flashed her a smile and hid the chuckle that rumbled in his chest at how she lifted a brow at him.

She leaned closer to his shoulder. "Has your family heard of a little thing called prohibition?"

she whispered as a serving maid began filling the wineglasses near each plate.

Her breath tickled his ear as much as she did his insides. "Yes."

She was about to say something else, but Joshua interrupted.

"If you have something to say, Jane," Joshua said haughtily, "you should say it loud enough for all to hear. It's called being polite."

David's neck muscles tightened, fully understanding how his brother was insinuating she didn't have any manners, therefore not up to the standards of an Albright.

Her giggle sounded as genuine as she was. "Horsefeathers, I forgot my manners." She pointed to her wineglass. "I was curious to know if your family had heard about prohibition. Evidently you have." She held up a finger then, as if she'd just realized something. "Is that why you asked if I met David in a tavern? Because of your involvement in the liquor trade?"

David was taken aback by her comment and angered that Joshua had already insulted her.

"No," Joshua snapped.

"What's this about a tavern?" he asked, glaring at his brother.

"Nothing," Jane said. "I'm sure Joshua just assumed that because he's been worried about the transportation of alcohol. Which is nothing to worry about," she said to Joshua. "After traveling Highway 66 all the way here, you don't need to worry about automobiles transporting more than your trains. Some of those roads were so rough, the bottles would be breaking left and right."

David chuckled at how she'd just insinuated Joshua was doing something far more unjustifiable than being bad mannered or meeting in a tavern.

Grandpa chuckled, too, before he asked, "How was your trip here, Jane?"

Her face lit up as she smiled. "Wonderful. Beyond wonderful! It was copacetic! We saw the Grand Canyon. Didn't we, David?"

The sparkles in her eyes made his heart pick up speed. "Yes, we did."

"We spent the night there," she told Grandpa. "Saw the sunset and the sunrise. It was the most beautiful thing I've ever seen."

"Not for me," David said, still looking at her.

Her cheeks blushed and she touched his arm. "Oh, you."

"There's not a hotel at the Grand Canyon," Joshua said.

"No, there's not," David answered. "But Jane

wanted to spend the night there, under the stars. So we did."

The way she smiled up at him and sighed was enough to make even him believe she was in love with him, and that their night at the Grand Canyon had been very special. He knew differently, and he gave her a wink to let her know she was doing a fabulous job of acting.

"What else did you see on your trip?" Grandpa asked.

Jane started with the attractions in Arizona, and the entire meal was consumed with her accounts of every place they had stopped all the way to Chicago. It was as if she was reading the notions she'd written on the maps. Every once in a while, she'd look at him, ask about something she couldn't quite remember, or just need his assurance in how she was recalling an event.

David gave his assurance and added little things that he knew would make her laugh.

It did, and she promised to show everyone the pictures as soon as they were developed. Joshua tried, but he couldn't quell her enthusiasm and gave up. A surprising occurrence.

David couldn't help but feel sorry for Charlene. He'd been doing it for so long it was just natural. She looked pale and had barely touched her food during the entire time Jane had been making it sound like their road trip had been the most fabulous time imaginable.

She'd even made it sound as if changing numerous tires had been grand adventures. She wasn't making anything up, not even elaborating. It was just her—the way her eyes sparkled and her giggle hung in the air. Everything she said sounded adventurous and enjoyable.

The trip home with her had been enjoyable. David couldn't discount that. He couldn't discount anything about her.

As soon as the meal ended, Charlene excused herself.

David stood, as did Grandpa and Joshua when Charlene stood, bade everyone good-night and left the room.

He then smiled down at Jane, who was looking up at him expectantly, not knowing what she should do. He knew what he had to do, and that she couldn't be a part of it.

"If you will excuse us," David said as he pulled out her chair and took hold of her elbow. "I will show Jane up to our room and then meet you, Joshua, in the office."

Jane frowned slightly, and he gave her elbow a reassuring squeeze.

"In ten minutes," Joshua stated, obviously needing to control something.

"I would prefer that Jane joins me in my study for a cup of tea," Grandpa said. "That way you two boys can have your discussion and I can have some very delightful company." He nodded at Jane. "You, dear, can tell me more about your trip."

She gave Grandpa one of her endearing smiles. "I don't believe I have anything more to share about the trip, but I would enjoy hearing about your adventures. David told me about some, and I'm anxious to know more."

Grandpa tossed his head back in laughter. "I'd be delighted, but you'll be sorry you asked once I bore you half asleep."

"I don't bore easily." She looked up at him. "Do I, David?"

"No, you don't." He kissed her then, a small peck on the cheek, not just for show, but because he wanted to. "I'll see you in a little bit."

She left the room on Grandpa's arm, and David waved a hand, giving his brother the go-ahead to lead the way to his office. Even if he'd left the room first, Joshua would have shouldered past him, needing to be the leader. It had always been like that. Whereas, in reality, it didn't matter who entered the room first or last.

David rubbed the back of his neck and noted how tight the muscles were. He'd grown tired of Joshua's competitions years ago and had stopped participating, but Joshua had continued on as if they were still happening, boasting about being first in practically everything.

They arrived in his office, which was near the front of the house, on the other side of the main foyer from Grandpa's study. David cracked a smile as he glanced over his shoulder, looking at the wall of the study, knowing Jane was on the other side of it. She didn't bore easily and would enjoy hearing Grandpa's stories. The old man was sure to be in his glory.

David pulled the solid wood door shut behind him and crossed the room to the side cupboard. Prohibition hadn't hindered the flow of alcohol into their home, it just increased the cost of it.

"What the hell were you thinking?" Joshua slapped the top of his desk. "You knew what was expected of you! You can't be married to that girl!"

Chapter Eight

David held his temper as he poured himself a cup of steaming coffee from the silver urn that Elwood would have made sure was placed in the office. *Expected of him.* More like demanded of him. That's what it came down to. Joshua always demanded and David hated it. They were brothers, but they were opposite in many ways, and that alone was enough to hinder things. They simply didn't work well together. That's why he focused on expansion, traveled, stayed away from home as much as possible. It was what was best for the railroad.

He had to thank Jane for helping him come up with a plan that would do more than just make him not have to marry Rebecca. Because of her, he could continue to travel, continue to focus on expansion. Marriage to anyone else would have hampered his ability to be gone for six months at a time.

"I am married." He turned around, faced his brother. "To Jane." Leaning a hip against the cupboard as he drank the coffee, he watched Joshua's nostrils flare. "I have the marriage certificate." That piece of paper was already locked in the safe in his suite.

"I'm sure you do," Joshua sneered. "How much are you paying her?"

David refused to bring anything more about Jane into the conversation, but he would offer one warning. He set his coffee cup down. "Don't bring her into this, Joshua."

His brother frowned slightly. "You're the one who brought her into this."

"And you're the one who told Rebecca to mail out invitations to a wedding you knew I wasn't willing to be a part of."

Joshua folded his arms. "She asked me what she should do. I told her you'd be back and to mail them out."

"And you approved for her to remodel my suite." That still angered him. Not because of Rebecca or Joshua, but because sleeping with Jane every night would be tortuous. She was so attractive, so desirable, and not acting on that had already grown extremely painful. Their marriage was in name only, and he'd fulfill his end of the bargain by ending it with her virtue intact, although it might kill him.

"It was to be her suite, too," Joshua snapped. "Until you hauled home some little gold digger."

A ball of fire lit in David's stomach. Jane was innocent in all of this and he wouldn't let her be pulled into it any deeper. "Watch it, Joshua. You can say what you want about me—you always have—but you leave Jane out of this. This is your doing, not hers."

"She's the reason you can't fulfill a promise made by an Albright," Joshua growled. "That's never happened before."

If there was an Albright to be blamed for breaking promises, Joshua merely needed to look in a mirror. There was no sense in pointing out something that would be denied, yet it still had to be said. "No, you are the reason." David shook his head. "And I told you before that I won't be a part of this game."

"Game!" Joshua shouted. "This little wedding sham of yours is going to ruin our reputation."

David had yet to raise his voice even though that's what Joshua was inciting. A shouting match. They'd done that plenty in their younger years, until David had realized it would never do any good. It was too bad, because if they could work together instead of butting heads they could do some amazing things. Joshua was good with the shareholders, making them see what needed to be done, but only when those things were his ideas.

David walked over, sat down in one of the big leather chairs in front of the desk Joshua stood beside. The very desk Grandpa had used to build Albright Railroad into a conglomerate that could provide well for generations to come, if either he or Joshua ever had any offspring. "Me not marrying Rebecca won't ruin our reputation. Marrying her might have." He shook his head. "I told you I wouldn't marry her before I left."

"You said you'd think about it when you left on your research trip."

"Not *my* research—*ours*. It was for the A and R."

Joshua pointed a finger at him. "The shareholders expect a report on Monday."

"They'll get their report. On Monday." He had the report ready, just needed to drop it off so copies for each of the shareholders could be made. A report that included more than automobile traffic interfering with rail lines. Transportation, all varieties, was the future of America. He couldn't understand why Joshua wouldn't get on board with that. "Why did you suddenly decide that I had to fulfill a promise that wasn't even a promise?"

"It wasn't sudden!" Joshua spun around, ran a hand through his hair and scratched the back of his head. Then he spun back around and pointed toward the door. "Our grandfather promised Rebecca's grandfather, on the day she was born, that she would marry an Albright."

David propped an ankle on his opposite knee. "A toast isn't the same as a promise." He'd argued that point before he'd gone to California. More than once.

Joshua's chin quivered before he once again slapped the desk. "Damn it, David! Why are you doing this?"

"Why are you? Why are you so damned set on me getting married?"

Joshua leaned both hands on his desk, stared at the wall where there was a large map of the United States, with a massive web of red lines that indicated all the tracks that A and R trains traveled. "Because it's time you stopped running around the country and settled down. Took your role in this company serious!"

Disgust filled David. "Serious? I've always been serious about my role in the company, and I'm not running around the country—I'm working. Expanding the railroad. Furthermore, if marriage is all you wanted, you should be glad that I married Jane. It's done. I'm married."

"What about Rebecca?"

David didn't like to sound callous, but it was simple. "I'll tell her the truth—that I married someone else."

"She was expecting to become an Albright."

"No, she was expecting money. That's what she wants. That's why she came back here nine months ago, demanding that a comment Gus had made to Orville on the day of her birth—that she'd marry one of his grandsons—was a binding promise. One that I needed to fulfill."

"Gus had promised her grandfather."

David shook his head. "Grandpa said he may have said something along that line to Orville as they'd celebrated Rebecca's birth, and he asked me if I'd consider fulfilling it, when it all started nine months ago. I told him no. He asked me again six months ago. And I told him no again."

Joshua spun around. "So you haul home some little tramp."

David's back teeth clamped together. He'd

never felt the need to protect someone like he did Jane. "I told you not to go there, Joshua." Anger boiled inside him and he shot to his feet. "I'll break more than your nose this time."

It wasn't a fond memory, but a year or so after their parents had died, he and Joshua had had a fistfight. Joshua had lost, but he hadn't learned a lesson. Within no time he'd been back to demanding, back to coercing.

Joshua's nostrils flared, but he didn't say a word.

David shook his head. He wasn't going to go down that road again, battling it out like kids. He turned, walked for the door.

"Walking away again, like you always do," Joshua said.

David's hands balled into fists, but he forced himself to keep walking toward the door.

"We aren't through here!" Joshua shouted.

"I am." David grasped the door handle and turned, faced his brother. The A and R meant as much to him as it did Joshua, as did their reputation, but he was done with this conversation. "Give it up, Joshua."

Joshua let out a harsh laugh. "Like you did when you gave up Charlene?"

A whole new ball of disgust rolled inside

David. For a long time, he'd hurt at how his older brother had had to win at even that. The woman he'd loved since childhood. That Joshua had asked her to marry him on the very day he'd known that David was going to ask her had goaded him, angered him, but right now, none of those old feelings surfaced. "Charlene is your wife, Joshua. I have my own wife." He opened the door. "Whom I am going to go rescue from Gus's tales of yesteryear and take up to bed."

Jane rolled over, not exactly sure what had awoken her other than being chilled. The room had been warm when she'd gone to bed, but it wasn't now. She pulled the blankets up and curled into a ball, but even the sheets and pillow were cold, making her shiver. She scooted across the bed and lifted the clock off the table beside the other side of the bed in order to make out the numbers in the darkness.

Four in the morning.

Setting the clock back on the table, she flipped back the covers, left the bed and rubbed her arms as she hurried into the bathroom.

So cold upon leaving the bathroom that she was shaking, she crossed the room and pulled open the door to the outer room. The rooms were all very dark with all the heavy drapes pulled shut for the night. The servants had done that. When she and David had come up to bed last night, the drapes in all the rooms had been pulled closed, the covers on the bed had been folded back on the bed, and fires had burned in the fireplaces. The one in the bedroom had gone out, and she was hoping the one out here was still going.

"What's the matter?"

She nearly jolted out of her skin and had to slap a hand over her mouth to keep the scream in her throat from sounding. "David, you nearly scared the daylights out of me," she said, holding her other hand over her pounding heart. It was as dark as the tunnel used to be, but her eyes had adjusted enough that she could make out the outline of his head.

"I'm sorry," he said, looking at her over the back of the sofa. "I heard the door open."

"I didn't mean to wake you." She felt guilty about him sleeping out here on the sofa, even though he had insisted.

"You didn't."

She rounded the sofa and sat on the arm. Although she had a good idea, she still asked, "Why weren't you sleeping?" He hadn't been himself when they'd come up to bed last night, after he'd talked with his brother. He'd been thoughtful and quiet. Solemn. It concerned her that brothers could be so different and so distant from each other.

His sigh seemed to fill the room. "Several reasons. Why are you awake?"

"I'm cold." She rubbed her arms. "I was hoping the fire was still going out here, but I see it's not." Like in the bedroom, there weren't even any coals glowing in the fireplace.

He pulled her onto the sofa and covered her with a blanket. "Tomorrow, we are going to buy you a nightgown that goes clear to the floor, with long sleeves and buttons up all the way to your chin."

She pulled the blanket beneath her chin. The short-sleeved yellow silk dress that she was wearing to sleep in didn't offer any warmth. "That sounds warm," she admitted. "But I'm cold right now."

He wrapped an arm around her and pulled her close to his side. His warm side. She snuggled against him.

"You are cold." He rubbed her upper arm and shoulder.

She tried to keep her teeth from chattering as she said, "I know." The yellow silk dress had been one of the few things hanging in the closet when she'd gone into the dressing room to change for bed. At her alarm of her clothes being gone, David had assured her that he'd instructed Elwood to see that her garments were laundered and returned to the closet in the morning. She had nothing else to put on, other than the blue coat or burgundy cape. Both would be uncomfortable to sleep in, but they'd at least be warm.

He pulled her off the sofa as he stood. "Come on."

"Where are we going?"

Wrapping the blanket around her, he said, "Back to bed, so you can warm up before you catch pneumonia."

Still cold and tired, she was more than happy to comply, and stayed at his side as they walked into the bedroom.

The sheets were chilly as they climbed back into the bed, and she snuggled so close to David she was almost on top of him. The familiarity of his warmth and scent was so comforting it made her feel gooey and tingly inside. It also made her want to kiss him and have him kiss her.

Those feelings kept getting stronger and stronger, and fighting them was getting harder and harder.

"Go back to sleep," he whispered.

She wanted to, but couldn't. Her mind was suddenly busy, full of all sorts of thoughts. Mainly about kissing him, how amazing that had been, and when she tried to push them aside other things formed, danced in her head.

"David?" she whispered.

"Hmm?"

She smiled at how his chest rumbled beneath her ear. "Why are you so nice and your brother so mean?" She and her sisters weren't all that different from one another. Not like David and Joshua. She and her sisters were nice to each other, too. They loved each other.

"You think I'm nice?"

"I know you are."

She wasn't sure why he found that funny or why his short chuckle sounded strained. It was true. He was not only nice, he was likable and fun and handsome, opposite in every way from his brother. "And I know your brother is mean." She also added, "Gus isn't mean. It's just Joshua. Why?"

He sighed. "I can tell you what I think is the reason."

"What?"

"For eight years Joshua had everyone's attention, and then I was born, and he had to share that attention, and he didn't like it."

"That's silly. He can't blame you for being born. Furthermore, he's a grown adult and should have gotten over any childish jealousy." She'd never been jealous of Patsy for being born, and Betty certainly had never been jealous. They'd had tiffs over the years, but they'd gotten over them quickly. They'd had to. They were all they had—each other. She missed Patsy and Betty and had so much to tell them.

"Well, he hasn't, and adult jealousy can be far more dangerous than childhood jealousy."

A shiver tickled her spine. "Dangerous?"

He rubbed her arm, pressed his cheek against the top of her head. "I mean stronger, harsher. You aren't in any danger."

That wasn't her full concern. "Are you?"

His chuckle sounded false. "No. No, I'm not in any danger from Joshua."

She couldn't think of any other danger he might be in, yet the way he said that made it sound like he was. "Then from who?"

He chuckled again and then sighed. "No one. Let's go to sleep now."

She nodded, and closed her eyes, but her mind was too full of thoughts about him, his brother and all sorts of other things. Before long, she once again whispered, "David?"

"Yes?"

"Why did Joshua want you to marry Rebecca so badly?"

"He's says it's time I settle down, stop traveling so much."

The exact reason he didn't want to get married. He'd told her that while they'd been traveling. "Did Joshua stop traveling when he had to marry Charlene?"

"Joshua never traveled. He took over the chairmanship of the railroad when our father died. And he didn't have to marry Charlene. They wanted to get married."

"But I thought they had to get married because of the railroad. Your family and her family each owned half of it, and it was agreed the two families would get married. That's what Gus said." Not in those exact words, but Gus had said something along those lines while they'd been visiting.

"It was always assumed our families would unite in marriage," David said.

The same bout of sorrow for Charlene formed as it had when she'd first met her. Charlene had looked so pale and unhappy. "I feel sorry for Charlene, having been forced to marry him."

"Charlene wasn't forced to marry him. She wanted to. She said she loved him."

"They don't act like they are in love."

"They don't?"

"No. They barely even look at each other. Is that what happens after a few years? People forget they love each other?"

"I don't know," he said. "Maybe it does for some."

She would have to think about that later. Right now, her wandering mind had a different question, a far more important one. "What about Rebecca? Does she want to marry you because she loves you?" The idea of that made her stomach queasy.

"No. Rebecca does not love me. She loves herself, and the idea of being an Albright. Wants the prestige, the lifestyle, the money."

All the times she and her sisters had talked about their father's ploy to marry them off to rich men, she'd never looked at it from the other side. The man's side. Of knowing someone only wanted to marry them for their money. It was all just so wrong, and so sad.

Her stomach did an odd little flip, and she

knew why. She'd married David for money. Not all his money, as in forever and ever. Just enough so she could start a life outside of her parents' house. However, theirs had been an agreement, one that would help both of them. That had to be different.

Maybe, but she still felt unsettled.

"You need to go to sleep now, you have a big day tomorrow," David said.

"I do?"

"Yes. We are going shopping for a nightgown, and we will turn in the films to be developed, and then…"

She couldn't wait to see the pictures, but his teasing tone was what intrigued her more right now. "And then what?"

"Have a snowball fight."

She'd forgotten about that and shot upright. "There's enough snow?"

His laugh was genuine. "Haven't you looked out a window?"

"No." She tossed back the covers while scooting across the bed and jumped to her feet. Her breath caught as she tugged apart the drapes. There was a streetlight at the end of the driveway, and everywhere the light shone, there was a pristine, sparkling blanket of white. She practically had to tell herself to breathe because she'd never seen anything like it. "Oh, David, it's so pretty."

David's arms encircled her from behind and he rested his chin on the top of her head. "And so cold."

She giggled, happy because his arms around her kept her from shivering, and tomorrow she'd have a snowball fight. Then she grew sad, because no matter how she tried to justify it in her mind, she was no better than Rebecca Stuart. The only thing that made her feel a tiny bit better was that she and David would get a divorce. Then, someday, he could marry someone he loved.

That should, but didn't, make her feel any better.

David did, though. The following morning. She couldn't help but feel happy, excited, when shortly after breakfast, which included a caramel roll that was still warm, fresh out of the oven, he escorted her outside. The first thing she did was grab a handful of the white snow and pack it into a ball shape.

"Wipe that little impish grin off your face," he said as he opened the door of his car. "I told you, we have to buy you some trousers and boots before we can have a snowball fight."

A gust of wind that had to have been on his side whipped around her legs, beneath the hem of her blue coat, icy and cold, making her shiver. "I know. I know!" She threw the snowball on the driveway and laughed at how it splattered as she climbed in the car and he closed the door.

The car was already running, sending warm air from the engine down on her feet. She waited until David climbed in and shifted the car into gear to ask, "Why isn't there any snow on the driveway? There was last night."

"The servants shoveled it this morning," he answered. "That's why it's piled up along the edge."

"But why?"

"So we don't get stuck. Cars get stuck in the snow very easily."

"Oh." That made sense, and so did so many other things he told her while they were out and about.

Things about how the films would be developed, why she needed at least two pairs of trousers and two nightgowns, and a long-sleeved dress, and why it was so cold and windy in Chicago. That one he proved to her by driving her along the shore of Lake Michigan. Even with the bright sun shining down, she had never seen water look so cold. The lake water was dark, almost black, the waves white tipped, and there were long, frosty white icicles hanging off the docks and on everything else the rolling water splashed up against.

"Why are all those people lined up on the street?" she asked as they drove along the road after leaving a restaurant where they'd eaten lunch near the lake.

"It's a soup kitchen."

"Soup kitchen?" She stared harder at the long line, which included children. "Do you mean a breadline?"

"Yes."

The church her family attended often had a special offering to support the breadlines for the poor. Father always gave them extra money to put in the offering on those days.

"Soup kitchens were one of the charities my mother used to raise money for," he said.

They turned the corner, and she had to spin around to look out the rear window until the line was no longer visible. She couldn't imagine standing in line to get something to eat. Turning back around, she asked, "Who raises money for them now?"

"The ladies' aid group that she belonged to still does, and we donate money to them, both the railroad and our family. Grandpa encourages people to give money to the soup kitchens instead of buying him gifts."

"That's nice," she said, but couldn't get the image of the children she'd seen out of her mind. Someday, she would find a way to help people like that. Like his mother had. That would be a wonderful thing.

Upon arriving at the house, David asked Elwood to assist in carrying the packages and boxes they'd purchased while in town.

"Shall I send a maid to put these items in their proper places, Master David?" Elwood asked after all the packages had been delivered to the dressing room.

"In a few minutes, Elwood," David replied. "We are going to change our clothes first to play in the snow."

Jane bit back a giggle as Elwood nodded and frowned at the same time.

David lifted her blue coat off her shoulders. "My wife has never seen snow before, and she wants to have a snowball fight."

Elwood's somewhat elongated face softened

and his eyes emitted a hint of twinkle as he nodded at her. "In that case, I shall have the kitchen prepare a kettle of hot chocolate for when you are finished."

"Hot chocolate!" She'd read about it but had never tasted it. "That sounds delicious!"

"Thank you, Elwood," David said.

"My pleasure, sir."

Elwood backed out of the room and she began opening boxes and packages, searching for the trousers and boots David had purchased for her, as well as the thick cardigan sweaters and heavy socks he'd also insisted upon buying.

"Find everything?" David asked.

"Yes!"

"All right." He walked to the doorway. "I'll meet you in the other room once you're dressed."

"Aren't you going to change clothes?"

"Yes, but it won't take me nearly as long as it will take you."

She planted her hands on her hips. "I'll have you know I was the fastest dresser of me and my si—friends." She wished she'd told him about her sisters, but it felt as if it was too late now. That should have been something she'd told him before, but hadn't been able to then because she'd been afraid that he'd take her back to Los Angeles if he knew about her family, knew she'd run away.

"Shall we have a race?"

"Yes!" She kicked off her shoes and was nearly out of her dress before he had the door closed.

Within minutes, she was pulling the door back open and found him tugging down a thick, navy blue sweater he'd just pulled over his head.

"I win!" She walked into the bedroom and spun around, proving she was completely dressed. Including a knitted scarf, hat and mittens.

He sat down on the bed to pull on a pair of boots. "What's under that coat?"

It wasn't fastened, and she pulled the front opening wide, exposing the dark purple cardigan. The top three buttons weren't buttoned because this was how it had come out of the shopping bag, and she'd merely pulled it over her head.

He stood, walked over and buttoned the sweater, then pulled her coat closed and fastened that button. All of which she couldn't do with mittens on.

"Thank you," she said. "But I still won."

Laughing, he shrugged into his black wool coat. "Yes, you did." He reached up and tucked some stray hairs around her face beneath the folded cuff of her hat. "You are unlike any woman I have ever known."

The urge to kiss him struck so hard and fast her muscles tightened. Even those in the very lowest point of her body. The tingles were everywhere, too, especially in her breasts. She'd noticed that before, during their trip to Chicago, but it was getting stronger and stronger each time he was near.

Especially when he looked at her as he was doing right now. She couldn't look away—it was like their eyes were locked together, staring at each other.

Her heart skipped several beats when he leaned forward, and her breath caught, certain he was going to kiss her.

He looked away quickly and backed away from her. "Ready?"

"Y-yes," she said, swallowing against the disappointment flooding her. She walked toward the door, hoping the distance would make the strange sensations inside her go away faster.

Gus was walking across the foyer when she and David stepped off the last stair of the massive curved stairway that led to the front door.

"Where are you two off to now?" he asked.

"A snowball fight," she answered. "You're

welcome to join us. There will be hot chocolate when we are done."

David had the best laugh she'd ever heard, but Gus's came in a close second.

"I may join you for the hot chocolate." He shook his head. "But not the snowball fight."

"You don't know what you're missing!" she said as David pulled her toward the door.

She hadn't known what she was missing, either! The most fun of her life. Better than dancing even. The wind was cold, and nipped at her cheeks, but the sunshine and the joy inside her, along with layers of clothing, kept her warm as she and David threw balls of snow at each other and ran across the yard to keep from getting hit by one.

She had never laughed so hard or run so much just for fun. It was even more enjoyable than the magazine picture had made it look.

When a snowball hit the side of her stocking cap, David raced over and caught her around the waist. "I'm sorry. Are you all right? I didn't mean to hit you."

She slapped her hands together to get rid of the mini balls of snow stuck to her mittens. "You are supposed to hit me, we are having a snowball fight."

He brushed the side of her hat, knocking snow off. "Not in the head."

"I didn't know that," she said honestly. "I was trying to hit you anywhere I could."

"And you did," he said, laughing.

His cheeks and nose were red, and it made him so handsome that her toes curled inside her boots.

He grasped one of her wrists and held that arm over her head. "I proclaim Jane Albright the winner of her first ever snowball fight!"

She cheered for herself, for him, for the fun they were having.

As he lowered her hand, he grasped her waist again and picked her up, so she was looking down at him, and then spun them around and around as if they were in the middle of a dance floor.

They both laughed, until he stopped spinning and slowly lowered her. Jane had no idea if she kissed him or if he kissed her, but their lips were suddenly pressed together, and it was wonderful.

She tightened her hold on his neck and held on as her entire body came to life. Tingling, tightening, curling, it was all there inside her. She pressed her body up against his and kissed him, kissed him exactly how he was kissing her.

When their mouths separated, she was gasping for air and wondering…wondering what all the commotion inside her was about.

He stared at her for a moment, and she stared back, not sure what to do. Then, fully realizing what had happened, she stepped back. They'd kissed and they shouldn't have. "You…uh…we…uh—"

"I know," he said. "Joshua was watching out the window."

"Oh." Once again, disappointment washed over her. She'd wanted David to kiss her because he wanted to, not because someone was watching.

Chapter Nine

"I'll show you something else we can do in the snow," David said, taking her hand. "We have to go to the side of the house, where the snow hasn't been disturbed."

Even though he'd only done it because Joshua had been watching, David's kiss had left her so dizzy she could barely see straight. Her heart was still pounding. Everything inside her was still swirling and throbbing. The tip of his nose had been cold against her cheek, his lips warm against hers, but when his tongue had slipped inside her mouth…

Just thinking about that made her feel as if she might swoon. It had been so wonderful. So…she couldn't even describe how amazing that had been. Or how disappointed she was because it left her wanting to experience that all over again, and more.

"Here we are. This will work." He grasped both of her hands. "Lay down on your back."

"What?" Jane asked, having been completely lost in thought.

"I have a hold of you and will lower you slowly. Just lean back, all the way to the ground."

She glanced over her shoulder at the ground. "Why?"

"So you can make a snow angel."

"What's a snow angel?"

"I'm going to show you."

Trusting him fully, she nodded. "All right." She leaned back, and he lowered her all the way to the ground, before he let go of her hands and told her to stretch her arms out at her sides and then drag them through the snow, all the way to above her head until they met, and then repeat that several times.

"Now give me your hands," he said, holding his out to her.

She grasped hold of his hands and let him pull her back up on her feet.

He held her until she was steady, and then twisted her around. "Look."

She laughed at the image she'd left in the snow. "It does look like an angel." She knelt down. "Even the buttons on the back of my coat are imprinted in the snow." Jumping around to face him, she held out her hands. "Give me your hands so you can make one. I'll lower you to the ground."

"You are going to lower me to the ground?" he asked, sounding amused.

"Yes!" She reached for his hands, but he held them out to his sides and then fell backwards. Snow puffed into the air and got caught on the wind, swirling as it blew away. He then dragged his arms up and down and jumped upright.

She laughed at how he'd done that, and at his angel. Then she ran to a fresh spot of undisturbed snow, spun around and fell backward, laughing as she hit the ground and made another snow angel. "Bee's knees," she said, staring up at the bright blue sky. "I've never had so much fun."

His face appeared before hers. He was on his hands and knees, and kissed the tip of her nose. "I'm glad."

She threw snow in his face, just for fun. Well, partially in fun, because it had been that or kiss him again, and she couldn't do that. She leaped to her feet and squealed as he chased her and as they threw snowballs at each other again.

She was getting better at making snowballs, and dodging them, and throwing them.

Jumping up and down, and clapping her snow-covered mittens at how the snowball she'd thrown had hit him square in the chest, she squealed and started to run when a mischievous grin formed on his face and he started running toward her.

Twisting fast in order to avoid his outstretched arm, she wasn't sure how it happened, but she lost a boot. It just went flying off her foot.

She tried to hop away, but he caught her instantly and pulled her down on top of him as he fell into the snow.

"That wasn't fair!" She rolled off him, into the snow. Lying on her back, she held up one foot. "I lost a boot."

"I'll get it," he said, jumping to his feet. A moment later he picked her boot out of the snow. "We need to buy you boots that come up to your knees instead of your ankles."

She reached for the boot, but he shook his head and grasped her hand. He pulled her to her feet, so she stood on one foot, and then he turned around so his back was toward her.

"Jump on."

"On your back?" She and her sisters used to give each other piggyback rides when they were little.

"Yes, I'll give you a piggyback ride to the house. This boot is packed full of snow."

She grasped hold of his shoulders and jumped, swinging her legs around his hips as her body landed on his back.

He caught her under both knees. "Hold on."

"I am," she said, while looping both arms around his neck as he walked toward the house. "This is much easier than walking."

He dipped down as if he was going to drop her and laughed when she squealed again.

They were both laughing as he carried her around the corner.

He instantly stopped laughing, and she saw why. A long black car was rolling to a stop next to the house.

"Who is that?" she asked.

He didn't answer for a moment, but then said, "That is Rebecca Stuart."

Jane's heart sank. "Put me down, David."

"No, you only have one boot."

As he trudged through the snow of the front yard, Jane got her first look of Rebecca Stuart as the woman climbed out of her car. She was tall, slender, with short black hair that was pressed flat against her head in perfect finger waves. Her coat was fur, black fur, and she held a long cigarette holder high in the air with one hand as she walked toward the house.

The closer David carried her toward the woman, the faster dread rose up in Jane. Rebecca was classy, sophisticated, beautiful, glamorous.

Everything Jane was not.

David had known Rebecca would show up at some point, and it wasn't as if any time would be a good time. He was just thoroughly disappointed she'd arrived now, spoiling the fun he and Jane had been having. Almost too much fun.

Joshua had been watching them out of the window, so he'd kissed her, but he'd taken that kiss too far. Way too far. He'd known that the instant his tongue had parted her lips and would have stopped, but the way she'd been kissing him in return, he hadn't been able to stop. Tongue swirl for tongue swirl, he'd let it continue until he'd been breathless.

Afterward, well, it was safe to say, he'd never had a kiss affect him so deeply.

Huffing out a breath, he silently admitted his heart had never turned so cold as it had a moment ago, either. Upon seeing Rebecca's car. At one time she'd signified everything he didn't want. He still didn't want her, but the whole marriage idea—of sharing his days and nights with someone—didn't seem as distasteful.

"Hello, Rebecca," he greeted distantly as they met her on the sidewalk that led to the steps beneath the pillared archway over the front door.

"David," she said, with her chin tilted up, nose in the air as if something smelled.

Elwood had already opened the front door, and held it open for them to enter the house.

David let Rebecca go first, and once he'd traversed the steps, with Jane on his back, he said to Elwood, "My wife is in need of dry socks."

"I have a pair at hand, sir, and her house slippers."

"Thank you," David replied, glad he'd also purchased her a pair of slippers this morning, despite her insisting she wouldn't need them.

"Thank you, Elwood," Jane whispered as he carried her into the house.

"My pleasure, Jane," Elwood replied quietly.

David grinned at how even stiff old Elwood had been charmed by her.

They entered the foyer with an audience in waiting. Grandpa near the door to his study, Joshua in the doorway of his office, Charlene on the staircase and, of course, Rebecca. Front and center, with the smoke of her smoldering cigarette making a curlicue before her face.

Jane was trembling, and David considered putting her down, but then she would have to walk, cockeyed with only one boot. He kept walking, carrying her. "Rebecca." He extended the invitation only to her. "You may join my wife and I in the front living room."

Rebecca blew a puff of smoke into the air. "Why don't you let...her get dried off while we speak, David?"

"Because there is nothing that you and I have to say to one another that my wife cannot hear," he replied, already close to losing his temper.

Elwood was standing near the open French doors that led into the front living room, and David carried Jane through them and across the room to the cluster of furniture near the blazing fireplace.

She slid off his back as soon as he released her knees, and the trepidation in her eyes when he turned around touched him deeply. He set her boot on the floor, and while removing his gloves he kissed her forehead—for show, he told himself.

After dropping his gloves on the coffee table, he removed her hat, and while smoothing the hair away from her face, whispered, "Just be yourself, Jane, that's all you have to do."

Her smile was tentative, but enough to let him know she would try.

Once they'd both removed their outer clothing and she had on dry socks and her house slippers, David helped Elwood load his arms with their coats and other items.

As the butler dipped as usual before making a departure, he bowed farther and whispered to Jane, "I shall keep your hot chocolate warm."

Thank you, she mouthed more than said.

Rebecca was still standing near the door and cleared her throat as Elwood approached.

"Would you care for me to take your coat, Miss Stuart?"

"Yes!" she snapped while waving a hand at his armload. "But get rid of those first. I don't want snow on my fur."

"Yes, Miss Stuart."

"Then she shouldn't wear it," Jane said, standing up from the chair. "There's snow everywhere."

David winked at her and touched her chin, very happy she was indeed herself.

Elwood returned within moments, removed

Rebecca's coat and left the room, closing the doors behind him.

Rebecca sashayed her way across the room. "Imagine my surprise, to learn you brought—" she paused, scathing Jane with a narrow glare as she took a long draw on her cigarette and waving her other hand dismissively to indicate Jane "—home with you."

Jane, with her purple cardigan, tan trousers and snowflakes still melting on the corkscrews of her long honey-gold hair, was far more beautiful than Rebecca could ever hope to be. And Rebecca knew it. He saw that on her puckered face.

Jane looked up at him with wide eyes and whispered, "What a high hat!"

Rebecca was a snob. More than a snob, and David wondered if he'd ever been as happy as he was right now. Happy he'd met, and married, Jane. "Rebecca," he said. "This is my wife, Jane Albright."

Rebecca's entire torso rose and fell with her heavy sigh as she stood, shoulders back and chest purposefully protruding out to emphasis the low-cut neckline of her gold blouse. Neither her stance nor her outfit made her any more appealing.

"Jane, is it?" She took a long draw on her cigarette holder and blew the smoke out between her pursed red-coated lips. "What a common, plain little name."

"No, it's not all that common, people just think it is. Sort of like how Rebecca isn't all that pretty—" Jane paused while hooking her arm through his "—of a name."

Once again, pride filled David. Jane was being herself all right and had just leveled the playing field. He gestured toward the furniture. "Would you care to sit down?" That was the most he'd offer Rebecca.

She lowered herself onto the chair at the end of the furniture grouping, legs crossed at the ankles. "We had an arrangement, David."

He assisted Jane onto the one of the sofas flanking the table and then sat down beside her. "No, *we* did not, Rebecca. As I've stated prior, there was never a solid contract between your grandfather and mine, and I'd deemed I had no obligation in fulfilling any contrived promise stemming from a toast two men made over twenty-five years ago." David paused only long enough for that to settle. "As far as the invitations you mailed, provide me a list of addresses and I'll arrange for a letter to be sent, apologizing for any inconveniences that may have occurred, and relaying that there will not be a wedding between the two of us."

Her face was turning redder by the minute. "There is more to it than just the invitations. There's the church and caterer and—"

"Give me a list," he said. "I'll pay any expenses caused by the cancellation."

"It's not that simple, David," she snapped. "You can't cancel mere weeks before a wedding!"

"It's actually simpler than that." He draped an arm around Jane. "I'm already married. Therefore, a marriage between you and I is impossible. It will never happen. Ever."

Her chin quivered as she took a breath. "Your family has a reputation to uphold. I never imagined you would shame it, destroy it, by canceling a wedding everyone expects to happen—" She slapped the arm of the chair. "That's not like you, David. The announcement has been in all the newspapers. Gifts have already arrived. It will create a scandal. Is that what you want?"

"Scandals come and go." That was true, they did. The Albright name had never been associated with one, and he wasn't pleased it would be now, but in truth, marrying her would have been scandalous. He'd have disgraced himself.

He stood. "Please have the lists of every invitation, announcement, vendor and individuals couriered over to me. I'll take care of it."

Her cigarette had burned down to the stub and gone out, but she still took a long draw on the holder before realizing. With a scowl at the cigarette and then at him, she stood up. "You'll be sorry you did this, David."

"No, Rebecca, I'm not, and I won't be. Ever."

Elwood opened the door from the outside before Rebecca reached it and held up her coat for her to slip on.

"I'll be right back," David told Jane. He crossed the room in time to catch the exchange of looks that Joshua and Rebecca shared until he was noticed. Rebecca stormed for the door, her heels clicking loudly on the tiles.

He stood there staring at Joshua until Rebecca had gone. Without a word, Joshua entered his office and shut the door. David couldn't help but think about what Jane had asked him last night, if Joshua had had to stop traveling when he'd married Charlene. He'd never thought about that before. Joshua hadn't traveled, but he'd never been given the opportunity to. He'd had to step into the chairmanship role when their father had died. David had assumed that's what his brother had wanted, just like he'd wanted Charlene. David now wondered if that was true. Or if Joshua had wanted something different but had never been given the choice.

A maid arrived with a tray of hot chocolate and cups, closely followed by Grandpa and Charlene.

"We are going to join you for hot chocolate," Grandpa said, walking past him and into the room.

David nodded, but was still staring at Joshua's office door.

"I saw you and Jane out the window," Charlene said, her voice a soft whisper. "You appeared to be having fun."

He glanced into the living room, where Grandpa and Jane were already in conversation, before he looked at Charlene. Her skin was pale and he was certain she'd lost even more weight during his absence. "It was fun," David admitted.

"I haven't had a snowball fight since we were young and you and I used to have them," Charlene said. "Remember?"

"I remember." What he remembered was a lively, outgoing girl, not the solemn, demure woman she'd become the past four years.

"Sometimes I think I made a mistake, David," she said. "That I didn't know what I was thinking or feeling, or—" she shrugged her delicate shoulders "—hoping for."

David had to wonder what he would have felt if she'd have told him that a year ago, or two, or three. Even a month ago. He had no idea, but knew all he felt right now was sorrow. Sorrow for her, perhaps a small amount for him and for what may have been. And, if truth be told, he even felt a sense of sorrow for Joshua, and that surprised him. "None of us know what the future holds, and we've all questioned decisions that we've made." His gaze had gone past her to Jane, who was sipping hot chocolate and smiling as Grandpa spoke. What she'd asked him last night, about people forgetting that they'd loved someone, made sense. It hadn't last night, but it did now. His heart had forgotten that it had once loved Charlene. It was only his mind that hadn't figured that out. Until now.

David gently took Charlene's elbow and escorted her into the room. "I hope you've left some for me," he said to Jane as he waited for Charlene to sit on the sofa next to Grandpa.

Jane flashed him one of her impish grins. "I may have." She shrugged. "Or I may not have."

He sat down next to her and grasped the handle of the china cup sitting atop the saucer she held. "Then I'll just have to steal some of yours."

"You wouldn't."

"I would." He lifted the cup and, watching her, rather than taking a sip he guzzled the warm chocolate, emptied the cup.

"David! You bum!" Laughing, she pulled the cup from him and tipped it up to her lips, drinking the one final drop he'd missed.

"There is plenty more, David," Charlene said. "Would you like me to pour you a cup?"

"No." He took Jane's cup out of her hand. "Please refill this one, though."

He held the cup as Charlene filled it, thanked Charlene, and took a sip before he handed the cup back to Jane.

She took a sip and licked her lips as she shook her head at him.

"Jane tells me she won the snowball fight," Grandpa said.

David leaned back and rested an ankle on his other knee. "Yes, she did." Her hair hung over her shoulder and down her arm. He stuck his finger in one of the twisting curls. "The first one. I would have won the second one if she hadn't kicked off one of her boots."

"Kicked off!" She shot him a pretend scowl.

"It fell off and you know it. And I would have won that fight, too."

"Perhaps we need a rematch?" He was thinking about the kiss they'd shared more than he was about the snowball fight. Even though he knew he shouldn't be.

"Perhaps we do." She took a sip from her cup.

Oddly enough, he felt more comfortable, more at ease than he had in years. Twirling her long hair around his finger, he turned his gaze on Charlene. She was staring into her cup of hot chocolate. "Who is on the guest list for tomorrow?" he asked.

Charlene's cup clattered against its saucer. "Surely you wouldn't be considering having a snowball fight with guests present?"

He knew that wouldn't bother Jane, but he shook his head. "I'm just curious as to who will be here."

The light pink tinge in Charlene's cheeks was the most color she'd had in a long time. She set her cup down and glanced at Grandpa.

"I'm not having a birthday party," Grandpa said.

David frowned. "You're turning seventy. I'd assumed it would be a large party." That had been the reason he'd had to return in time for tomorrow, because his grandfather always had a birthday party, with a large guest list.

"I changed my mind," Grandpa said.

"Why?"

Charlene softly cleared her throat. "With a wedding so close, and Thanksgiving, Joshua felt that was too much for me to handle by myself."

That explained it. Joshua. David looked at Jane. "There won't be a wedding now."

"No, there won't be." Jane set her cup on the table. "And I'll help you, Charlene. Whatever you need." She then leveled one of her doe-eyed gazes on Grandpa. "You have to have a birthday party. Anyone who reaches seventy deserves one."

Grandpa laughed. "Are you calling me old?"

Jane's cheeks turned red, yet in her cute, charming way, she grinned and shrugged.

Grandpa laughed. "What do you think, David?"

"I think you're old, too," he said teasingly, "and I think you should have a party, if you want one."

"There's not enough time now," Grandpa said.

"Yes, there is," Jane answered. "Furthermore, if you don't have a party, people might go hungry."

Grandpa frowned. "They will?"

Her eyes were full of compassion as she looked

at David, then back at Grandpa. "Yes, David told me you give to the soup kitchen for your birthday, and the line I saw today was really long. There were children in it." She leaned forward. "Please have a birthday party. I'll help. I'll do whatever needs to be done."

David looked at his grandfather, challenging him to defy her plea.

"Well, all right then," Grandpa said. "Let's have a birthday party."

David had known that would be the answer, and he laughed at how Jane jumped up and gave Grandpa a hug.

"David!" Jane stared at the closet before her, at the array of dresses hanging there. Beautiful dresses made of velvet and velour, corduroy and other heavy fabrics, that she would never have chosen because they would be much too warm for California weather.

"Yes?"

Twisting, she saw him leaning in the doorway to the changing room, wearing only an undershirt and black pants. "Where did all these clothes come from?"

"The stores we visited this morning."

"Why? How?" He had bought her one dress this morning, not a dozen.

"Why? Because the short-sleeved dresses you brought with you are much too cold for winter. How? I had the stores deliver the ones I saw you eyeing." He winked at her and stepped back into his bedroom. "Make your choice. We are expected at dinner in twenty minutes."

She loved clothes, always had, but his generosity was making her feel guilty.

"How is the party planning coming?"

Her thoughts instantly moved past the clothes hanging in the closet. "Wonderful!"

"Get dressed and then you can tell me all about it," David said.

"I will! Just give me a minute!" She closed the door, quickly changed and then, as they made their way down to dinner, told him all about the planning and preparations that had kept her and Charlene, who was very nice, busy all afternoon.

The discussion over the party, and tales of past parties that David's mother used to host, continued through dinner and afterward.

By the time she crawled into bed that night, a different sense of guilt filled her. She may have been isolated while growing up, due to her father's rules, but her ignorance of the needs of others was her own problem. Selfish was what she'd been. Her entire life she'd thought about what she wanted and what she didn't want. The plight of others, and if she could do anything to help them, had never crossed her mind other than putting money in the collection plate at church.

In fact, it wasn't until David told her about marrying Rebecca that she'd ever thought of helping someone outside of her family. Hearing about how much his mother had done to help others was also inspiring. Made her want to do more things like that. More ways to help the less fortunate. Because she was fortunate. She'd never gone hungry. Never not had clothes to wear or a home to live in. She'd never stood in a food line, hungry and cold like those people she'd seen today.

She wasn't cold right now, either. The new nightgown she had on had long sleeves, and a fire was burning in the fireplace. In fact, she was toasty warm beneath the covers of the big bed.

Alone.

Because David was once again sleeping on the couch in the other room.

That saddened her and made her feel lonely. She hadn't felt lonely since leaving California.

She rolled over onto her side, near the edge of

the bed, and stared for a moment at the wedding band on her finger. Six more days. She'd consulted the calendar. Tomorrow was Thursday. David had to give his report to the shareholders on Monday and had said they'd leave after that. Tuesday. Six days from now.

Pretending to be in love with him was not hard at all; in fact, it was easy, and she didn't even need to think about it.

"Is the new nightgown warm?"

Her heart fluttered and she flipped around, looked toward the doorway where he stood. "Yes."

He walked in. "I thought I'd throw another log on the fire so it won't go out as fast as it did last night."

She sat up and laid her arms over the edge of the blankets. The nightgowns he'd purchased were as pretty as the dresses. This one was made of thick flannel in a pale pink with darker pink roses and delicate white eyelets around the neckline, cuffs and hem. "Thank you, but it's not necessary. I'm sure I'll be fine tonight."

He walked over and put a log on the fire, causing sparks to fly up the chimney. "You say that now, but it'll get cold again when the fire goes out. I'll come stoke it again."

"When will you sleep if you're up all night putting wood on the fire?"

He grinned and walked to the bed. "In between trips."

She smiled in return and sighed. "I wish I could have met your mother. I bet she was as nice as you are."

"I wish you could have met her, too," he said, sitting down on the edge of the bed.

Her thoughts instantly went to their kiss outside today. How the tip of his nose had been cold against her cheek, but how that kiss had set her insides on fire. The heat was still there, churning up desires she'd never experienced. Womanly desires and thoughts that she'd only read about in magazines.

He took a hold of one of her hands. "Thank you, Jane."

"For what?"

"Stepping in and helping Charlene with Grandpa's party."

She'd never planned or attended a house party. Her family never had large numbers of people over for a meal or any other reason. There had been a lot of people at her sisters' weddings, but that had been different. The receptions had been at the church, and there hadn't been anything more than coffee, punch, and cake served. "It's been fun, and it hasn't been that much work at all."

"You say that now—tomorrow you might think differently."

The receptions following Patsy's and Betty's weddings had each only been an hour long, but Gus's party would start at five and go until people left. The planning had greatly helped her with one thing—all the different rooms in this house and the layout made more sense. The buffet evening meal would be served in the billiard room because it was the largest. "No, I won't. I'm looking forward to it."

"I truly never expected you to assume any duties of your role."

Chapter Ten

The shiver that crept up Jane's spine wasn't a chill. It was more of a creepy sensation. The kind she'd get if she saw a big hairy spider or slithering snake. It didn't scare her, it just disturbed her. "My role?"

"Yes, as my wife, you would eventually be expected to take over certain household responsibilities, including being the hostess for parties, but I never expected you to do that. You won't be here that long."

She was aware of that, yet, the way he said it hurt in an odd way, and it left her with an odd emptiness.

He kissed the back of her hand before releasing it. "I'll let you get some sleep now."

Not trusting her ability to speak, she nodded and lay back down as he walked across the room and out the door. She closed her eyes against the way they stung. Everything seemed to be far more confusing than she'd anticipated when she'd agreed to come to Chicago with him. And complicated. Far too complicated. In part because she'd never expected to feel the things she was feeling. Things she'd never felt before, including this odd emptiness at the idea of leaving David.

She rolled onto her side again and wiped aside the tears slipping out of her eyes.

Sleep had eventually overtaken her, but it hadn't taken away the emptiness that had formed last night. Out of sorts because of it, she told David she would prefer to take a bath the next morning instead of joining him for breakfast.

He agreed cordially, including placing a small kiss on her forehead, which made her eyes sting again. And again, after she'd completed her bath and discovered a caramel roll and other breakfast foods on a tray covered with a silver dome lid.

She ate a small amount, mainly because she didn't want to be rude to those who'd cooked the meal and carried it up, and because David had gone to the effort of seeing that it was brought up for her.

Her time alone gave her time to think and she concluded that her best plan would be to distance herself from David because he was becoming too dear to her. That way he wouldn't become even more dear, and when the time came for them to return to California, to get their divorce, it would be easier to say goodbye.

The issue with that, was that she couldn't. Especially today, with a house full of people who must believe she and David were in love. That their marriage wasn't a sham. Which it was, in more ways than one. She hadn't even used her real name on the marriage license. One more issue that weighed her down.

Furthermore, even if she avoided him now, they would still spend six days together traveling back to California, and then more time in Nevada, waiting for their divorce.

The only thing she could do was to make sure she controlled her own inner senses, inner workings that were getting out of hand when it came to David. She was beginning to wonder if she was falling in love with him. If that's what was causing all the commotion inside her. She sincerely wished she could talk to her sisters about it, about everything. They would know. They were both in love with their husbands and could help her make sense of all that was happening.

She couldn't talk to them, though, because David didn't know she had any sisters. Any family.

Her own deceitfulness in all of this was burning a hole inside her. The only way to change that would be to tell David the truth, but if she did that, and Joshua learned that they weren't truly married, he might find a way to make David marry Rebecca in two weeks and everything would be for naught.

She didn't understand why, but it certainly appeared to her that Joshua wanted David and Rebecca married. She'd felt him glaring at her last night across the table more than once.

Which was the precise reason she would remain here and make everyone believe that she and David were in love, until Tuesday.

Mind made up, deciding what to wear became her focus. David had purchased several lovely dresses for her, and choosing which one to wear was difficult. She finally decided on a shin-length layered dress made of olive-green velvet with an overlying frock of sheer black silk enhanced with sparkling gold embroidered flowers and swirls above and below the empire waist and down the three-quarter-length sleeves. The square neckline was the perfect opportunity to wear her black velvet choker necklace that had a single gold bead dangling off the very center.

She took extra care in winding her hair as it dried so the ringlets fell evenly down her back, and she pinned both sides up behind her ears. She then placed a headdress made of various lengths of black chain over her crown and tucked a single black feather into a chain above her right temple.

She applied mascara, a light dusting of rouge, and lipstick, before stepping into her black shoes.

Drawing a deep breath, she eyed herself critically in one of the full-length mirrors, checking that the hems of each layer of the olive dress and black frock hung smoothly and that the empire waist was situated evenly beneath her breasts.

Satisfied, she spun around and pressed a hand to her heart, startled at seeing David standing in the doorway. "Horsefeathers! You scared me!"

There was a small smile on his face, but he didn't move, just kept staring.

She glanced down at her dress and then back up at him. "Is this dress not—?"

"Beautiful?" He walked toward her, shaking his head. "You make everything look beautiful."

Her heart was thudding, because if a man could be beautiful, it would be him. Because he was beyond handsome. His thick brown hair was parted on the side, smoothed back slick, and his green eyes were shimmering. He wore black pants, a white-and-green-striped shirt, and while the front of his vest was black, the back of it was gold. Simple attire that he made look very elegant.

He grasped her hand and leaned forward, kissed her cheek.

She drew in a deep breath, inhaling how wonderful he smelled, even while telling herself that she shouldn't have let him kiss her cheek since no one was watching them here.

Looking at her, with a smile that produced his dimple, he said, "People have started to arrive, but I'm not sure that I want them to see you."

She nodded, knowing some of Gus's friends were arriving in time for lunch, but then anxiety formed. "You don't want them to see me? Why?"

He twisted a finger around a curl of her hair. "Because every man at the party is going to try and steal you away from me."

She sighed with relief, even as her cheeks felt flushed. "Baloney. I'm the one who needs to worry."

He frowned. "About what?"

Shrugging, she said, "Everything."

Looping her hand around his elbow, he said, "I'll be at your side all day. All you have to do is be yourself."

He had no idea how impossible that was for her. An imposter, a liar, couldn't be themselves.

They left the suite side by side and traversed the hallways and stairways until they were in the front living room, where a fire blazed and a half a dozen people were being entertained by Gus.

"Jane, dear, come here, let me introduce you to a few close friends." Gus waved them into the room. "This is Wilbur and Grace Coulter, Donald and Ann Wainwright, and Gerald and Ruth Johnson." Smiling down at her, he then said, "This is the newest member of our family. Jane, David's wife."

If she'd expected surprise, she'd been wrong. All three of the couples greeted her courteously and offered both David and her congratulations on their marriage. She greeted each of the couples, two older and one middle-aged, in return, thanking them. At Gus's invitation, she and David sat, and she shared details of the trip from California to Chicago with them. Reliving that trip always filled her with delight, and it did so again.

A few other people arrived before the noon

meal was served, a substantial feast that was served in the large dining room. After that, the front door was nearly flooded with the flow of people that were soon filling the rooms on the first floor of the house.

"There are certainly a lot of people here, and it's not even time for the party to start yet," Jane told David as they wandered from room to room for him to make introductions to people that she was certain to never remember. The names were all swirling together in her mind, and the swirl kept getting larger and larger.

"I figured this would happen as word spread," he said.

"Word of the party?"

"No. You."

"Me?" She then grasped he meant word of his and Rebecca's wedding being canceled because of her. "Would all of these people have been at your wedding to Rebecca?"

"Most of them. A few would have boycotted it, knowing I'd been railroaded." He winked at his pun.

She smiled at him, even as the weight of just how deep this deception went grew.

David introduced her as his wife to more people, and she didn't even have to think about making her eyes look dreamy when she looked up at him. They did that all on their own now. Somewhere in the back of her mind, she knew this was pretend, but with so many people congratulating her, and with David boasting about being very lucky to have found her while he'd been in California, she was caught up in it, forgetting that it wasn't real.

She joined David and his friends in a game of billiards, laughing at her own mistakes and hugging him when she'd managed to make one of the balls roll in the net pockets in the corners and center edges. They played cards later, games she'd never heard of but caught on quickly. His friends were jovial, both the men and women, and she was truly enjoying herself. His friend named Jeff was married to Cora, a friendly and pretty woman with short, curly, brown hair and the cutest little mole right next to her nose.

"David," Cora said as the card game ended. "Play some music so we can dance!"

Jane set her cards down and looked at David, astonished, because she hadn't seen a piano in the house.

"What do you say?" he asked her.

"I say yes!"

"All right then!" He took her hand and a group

of friends followed as they hurried down the hall past Joshua's office, where he had spent most of the day standing in the doorway, and into a large room with a piano.

"Why didn't you tell me you had a piano?" She hadn't yet explored the rooms down the hall past Joshua's office, for obvious reasons.

David shrugged. "Never thought of it. You can help me play."

They sat as they had at the Rooster's Nest, side by side, and he told her which key to hit and when, as others danced in the center of the room, having pushed the furniture out of the way.

Jane didn't think she could be happier, until one of his friends took over playing the piano and David led her to the center of the room. They danced the Charleston and the tango, and when the notes of the shimmy struck, Jane tossed her head back with glee. Shooting David a teasing grin, she held her arms out at her sides and twisted her shoulders, making her torso shimmy. He tossed his head back with laughter. She bent her knees, and keeping her back straight while twisting her shoulders, she shimmied down to the floor and back up.

David, still laughing, clapped his hands.

She spun around, so her backside was to him,

and shimmied her way down to the floor and back up again.

David grasped her waist and spun her around, planted a kiss on her lips and then joined her in dancing the shimmy. Arms out, their bodies almost touching as they shimmied down to the floor and up again. She'd never laughed so hard. Her heart was pounding from the fun as much as it was from dancing.

When the song ended, David caught her around her waist and lifted her up like he had after their snowball fight, and then slowly lowered her until their faces were even. That's when he kissed her, just like he had outside in the snow. She clung to him, pressed her body against his and returned his kiss, her tongue dancing as wildly with his as their bodies had during the shimmy earlier.

It wasn't until their mouths parted and David lowered her to the floor that she heard the clapping and laughter. She laughed and whispered, "I think we won."

"I know I did."

Her heart was so full it nearly floated right out of her chest.

"Let's get something to drink." With his hand on her back, David steered her toward a table with a punch bowl and glass cups, as well as an assortment of other beverages.

"I need to use the powder room first," she said. "I'll be right back."

Jane crossed the room and met Cora at the doorway.

"Powder room?" Cora asked.

"Yes," Jane answered.

"There's a line," Cora said. "I've had to go for twenty minutes, but the line is getting longer instead of shorter."

"We can use the one in our suite," Jane said.

"Oh, you are a doll!" Cora said, and hooked her arm as they entered the hallway. "I am so glad that David met you. You could have knocked me over with a feather when we got that wedding invitation in the mail."

"For his wedding to Rebecca?" Jane asked as they started up the curved staircase that made sweeping loops to the second, third and fourth floors of the house.

"Yes. Jeff and I knew David was still in California, so we were so flabbergasted. Truly flabbergasted. We didn't think he'd ever get married. Not after Charlene married Joshua. Everyone had assumed it would be her and David, he'd been in love with her for years. We are so glad he got over that. You and he are..."

Jane had stopped listening.

David had been in love with Charlene?

She could barely breathe, and it was as if the walls around her were spinning.

"Jane? Jane?"

She shook her head. Focused in on Cora.

"I said which way? I've never been up here before."

Jane tried to smile and looked around, tried to get her bearings. "This way."

"Are you sure?"

No, she was hoping. Hoping she wouldn't faint. Wouldn't cry. Wouldn't... Oh, how had she been so stupid? So blind? "Yes, I'm sure."

"Oh, dear." Cora held onto her arm tighter. "You knew, didn't you? About Charlene? David—"

"Yes, of course I knew," Jane lied.

Cora looked relieved. "I figured David had told you. He's as honest as the day is long and he so deserves you." Cora grinned brightly. "Someone fun and beautiful. I am just so happy for both of you!"

Jane was glad someone was happy, because she'd never felt this rotten in her entire life.

* * *

David kept one eye on the doorway, waiting for Jane to return, while listening to friends and a few foes joke and laugh and carry on, mainly about him finding gold in California. Jane.

He had to agree. The way she'd danced that song, shaking her torso, teasing him so openly, yet so secretively with her eyes, had nearly been his undoing. He'd been half-ready to carry her upstairs and make their marriage real. Yet, at the same time, he knew he'd never do that. It wasn't part of their bargain.

He just hadn't expected this to happen—how she'd changed things inside him. Whatever he'd felt for Charlene was long gone. He couldn't even remember, or imagine, that what he'd ever felt for Charlene was close to what he felt for Jane.

She was so beautiful, sassy, smart and charming. So charming. There was no one more lovable than her.

Charming, though, wasn't what he needed. Knowing she was here at home would be enough to make him stop traveling for work, and that wasn't what he wanted. Nothing else had changed, certainly not with Joshua. His brother had been angry that Jane had offered to help

Charlene. He'd pulled David into his office this morning and laid into him about it.

Even though his friends were still talking, David walked away to the door where Jane had exited, wondering what was taking her so long.

In all actuality, it may not have been that long. He'd just grown so used to her being at his side that it felt as if something was missing when she wasn't.

As he stepped into the hallway, his spine quivered. A crowd was forming at the end of the hall, near the front foyer. He started walking that way, and quickly picked up his pace when he realized silence filled the air.

He knew why when he saw who was walking through the front door.

Rebecca.

Of course, she'd have to show. She didn't have the decorum not to.

The silence echoed in his ears as he made his way through the crowd. Charlene had been at the door, greeting guests earlier, but wasn't now.

No one said a word as the door closed and Rebecca stood there, in the center of the foyer like she was a queen. He clenched his back teeth, knowing, in the absence of Joshua and Charlene, it was his duty to greet a guest, no matter how unwanted that guest may be. Before he had a chance to speak, someone else did.

"Hello, Rebecca, it's nice that you could join us."

David looked up the stairway, saw Jane walking down the last few steps with Cora at her side.

"Well, if it isn't plain Jane," Rebecca said, with a sneer. "You can address me as Miss Stuart."

David pushed his way through to the front of the crowd and started across the foyer.

"And you can address me as Mrs. Albright," Jane said.

David laughed in order to break the silence as he arrived at the staircase, took Jane's hand as she stepped off the bottom step.

There had been a few chuckles in the crowd, but silence ensued again.

"Do you find humor in her absurdity, David?" Rebecca asked drily.

Anger roiled inside him. "I find your audaciousness pitiful, Rebecca, as always, and yes, I found joy in my wife's response to you because she *is* Mrs. Albright." He leveled a serious glare on her that came from the pit of his soul. "Let me inform you this once, because I won't repeat it, so take heed. If, in your simplemindedness, you believe you've been wronged by me, then take your wrath out on me. Don't ever attempt to take it out on her. Ever."

He let the silence remain for a few moments so his oath could take roots for all who had heard, and then he smiled down at Jane. "I believe the buffet is ready to be served. Shall we?"

Her smile was gracious, though it looked strained, and he lifted her hand, kissed the back of it, hoping that might help before he escorted her through the main room and into the billiard room, where long tables were heaped with various foods.

It didn't take long for the crowd to return joyous, and Jane was soon laughing and responding to the teasing she'd already become accustomed to by some of his friends, but she didn't have the same amount of sparkle as she had prior to Rebecca's arrival. Others probably didn't notice, but he did.

Rebecca didn't leave, either, which irritated him, but he chose to ignore her and the few cronies that huddled around her as if they were a congress of crows in session.

After Grandpa had blown out the candles on his cake, which Jane insisted upon, as well as everyone singing happy birthday, Jane excused herself, and David watched as she met Charlene near the doorway, where they talked, laughed and then spent time overseeing the household staff clear away the buffet.

"Why don't you just go ahead and haul her upstairs?" Jeff Rogers asked while slapping his shoulder.

He and Jeff had been friends since childhood and had attended college together. There was little they didn't know about each other. "Is it that obvious?" David asked, laughing because he already knew. He'd been undressing Jane with his eyes for half the day. No, for the entire day. From the moment he'd seen her looking at herself in the mirror upstairs, tugging at the waistband of her dress that came up to right beneath her breasts.

Tall, with black hair and dark eyes encircled with laugh lines, Jeff threw back his head in laughter. "I'm not even going to answer that, old boy. You're in enough pain."

David grinned because that was true. "She is something, isn't she?"

"She has *it*!"

David laughed and nodded. The *it* Jeff was referring to was sex appeal, and Jane had a load and a half of that.

"All I can say is that you should have gone to

California a year ago—it would have saved us all a lot of grief. Mainly you, but also for me and Cora because we're your friends." Jeff handed him a cue stick and nodded toward the pool table where a rack of balls was set up.

David bent over and shot the cue ball into the triangle of other balls, wondering if he would have met Jane a year ago.

Jeff slapped his back. "You'd have been married when Rebecca arrived back home from Europe last year, nearly broke and looking for a sugar daddy."

David stepped back from the table so Jeff could take his turn shooting. Most everyone knew that was exactly why Rebecca had set her sights on him.

"So where did you meet Jane?" Jeff asked when he'd missed pocketing a ball.

"You wouldn't believe it, if I told you." David took his turn, pocketed two balls and walked around the table to hit the white ball again. "Which I'm not going to do."

Jeff laughed. "I'm your friend, so you will sooner or later."

Remorse washed over David. Sooner or later Jeff and everyone else in the house would be shocked to hear he and Jane were divorced. He missed pocketing a ball.

"Also, as your friend," Jeff said, leaning down for his turn to shoot. "I need to tell you that Rebecca has amassed significant debt since she arrived home."

"I can believe that."

Jeff looked up. "Would you also believe it's mostly in your name?"

"My name?"

"Yes, she used the upcoming nuptials as collateral."

"How do you know that?" David shook his head as soon as he'd asked, knowing full well that Jeff's firm would know everything about Rebecca. His father and hers had been friends. "What are you doing tomorrow morning?"

"Working," Jeff answered.

"Got time for one more meeting?" David asked. He would need some legal advice to make sure everything Rebecca had done in his name was completely settled.

"Yes, in the morning," Jeff said. "I'm booked all afternoon because I transferred appointments from this afternoon to tomorrow so I could take the afternoon off, as did half the city from the attendance here today."

"Nine o'clock?" David asked. He had to drop off his report at the railroad office in the morning to have copies made for Monday and Jeff's office was only a block away from there.

"That works for me." Jeff took a shot and pocketed the eight ball. "My game."

Chapter Eleven

It was several hours later when David finally escorted Jane up the staircase. Nearly everyone at the party had stood in line to say goodbye to her. There was a plethora of invitations for her to join others for tea, shopping and various lady activities, and for both of them to attend dinner parties and other events.

The only one he fully committed her and him to was an evening out with Jeff and Cora on Saturday. He wasn't looking forward to Tuesday, to taking her back to California, or returning home and telling everyone they'd divorced.

They were all going to think he was crazy.

He'd have to agree. It had been foolish to think a plan he'd conjured up over a bottle of wine would actually pan out. He did know one thing for certain—if he'd shared a bottle of wine with any other woman, he'd never have put such a plan in place.

He'd had second thoughts from the start, but it had been because of her that he'd gone ahead with it. He wasn't blaming her, just admitting the truth. The other truth was that he'd been attracted to her from the first night he'd played at the Rooster's Nest.

He'd played there that first night because the other player hadn't shown up. After watching her dance that same night, he'd agreed to play again, as often as his schedule would allow, because he had been working while there. The playing had given him an escape, and she'd kept him coming back.

That hadn't been something he'd admitted to, not even to himself until tonight. Not that it did any good. It didn't change anything, other than give him insight that he'd refused to admit a lot of things over the past few years.

He'd gone to the Rooster's Nest that last night to see her one last time, and when he learned she wanted out of her previous employment, he'd been ready to do whatever he could to help her. He did wonder what type of maid she had been in Los Angeles. Every household was run differently, but she didn't seem to understand the duties of the maids in his house. She made the bed every morning, and cleaned their bathroom, and did other little things that were the duties of the maids.

That was probably why. Because she had been a maid.

She'd done an amazing job with the party. Everything had gone very smoothly. "Did you have fun today?" he asked as they exited the stairway to walk down the hallway that led to their suite.

He already thought of it that way. Their suite. Though he'd been angry, and still was that Rebecca had been allowed to remodel his suite without his permission, he no longer was upset about the absence of the second bed. He didn't mind the couch.

"Cora is very nice," she replied. "And pretty. I really like her."

"Everyone really liked you." He rubbed her upper arm as they walked. "Gus was in his glory."

"He did seem to have a good time," she said as they arrived at the door.

Opening the door, he stepped aside so she could enter first. Although she'd continued to play the part of his loving wife all evening, her sparkle hadn't returned after Rebecca's arrival, even now. "I'm sorry about Rebecca," he said while closing the door. "I should have known she'd have gotten word of the party."

She shrugged. "She didn't cause any trouble."

"No, thankfully, she didn't." He followed her into the bedroom, unbuttoning his vest as he walked. "You handled her arrival perfectly."

She walked directly toward the bathroom. "That's what I'm here for."

The door closed behind her, and something in her tone had him moving to the door. "Are you all right?"

"I'm fine," she answered through the wood. "Why wouldn't I be?"

She didn't sound all right. He questioned opening the door but went to the bed, instead, to wait. Tossing his vest on the chair in the corner, he sat on the bed and removed his shoes and socks.

The door opened and she left the bathroom, going into the dressing room and closing that door. That wasn't unusual. It was her quietness that was unusual, very unusual.

He took off his shirt and suspenders and emptied his pockets, leaving on his pants as he had every night since returning home. In part because he didn't trust himself, and in part because he didn't want to tempt fate, either.

Plucking a pillow from the bed with one hand, he picked up the blanket draped over the foot with his other and carried them out to the sofa.

He returned to the bedroom when he heard the dressing room door open, and she was in bed, snuggled beneath the covers, when he exited the bathroom a short time later.

"Good night," he said, pausing near the foot of the bed.

Her response was barely audible. He could understand why she was so tired. She'd been the spotlight of the party and handled it all with grace and the jubilance of no other, besides all the hostess duties she'd performed.

It was impossible not to wonder about the future, wonder if being married, to her, wouldn't be as awful as he'd led himself to believe. He had some very good employees who could do a lot of his traveling for him, but he truly did love that part of his job.

Furthermore, thinking of making their fake marriage real was selfish. She'd told him right from the beginning that she didn't want to get married. To anyone.

That thought was still on his mind the next morning when he returned home from his appointment with Jeff. It would be weeks before he knew the full cost of this debacle with Rebecca.

He parked the car in the driveway and entered the house as Elwood opened the door.

"Thank you, Elwood, do you know where my wife is?" His heart rate increased every time he called her that. All on its own, and he had no control over it.

"She was with your grandfather earlier, Master David," Elwood answered. "They were recording the gifts he received yesterday."

"Thank you." He walked down the hallway, toward Grandpa's study, but found it empty. Deciding to check their suite, he took the stairs two at a time, growing anxious to see her. It had only been a few hours, but it seemed longer.

As he arrived on the second-floor landing, he nodded at Charlene, fully prepared to continue to the stairs that would take him to the third floor, but she stepped forward and grasped his arm.

"I've been waiting for you, David," Charlene said.

"Why?"

"I need to talk to you."

"We can talk later, right—"

"You need to see something, David, right now."

She glanced around as if not wanting anyone to hear.

He huffed out a breath. Seeing Jane was what he needed right now, yet, Charlene did look concerned. "What is it?"

"We can talk in my sitting room," she said, grasping his arm.

The rooms on the second floor were all assigned to Joshua and his family, other than the suite that Grandpa still occupied, just as the rooms on the third floor were assigned to him. The fourth floor was reserved for guests and the basement was where all the servants had their rooms.

Charlene remained silent as they walked down the hall and into a room that was decorated with pink-and-white furniture and window treatments.

"What did you want to show me?"

She crossed the room, lifted a newspaper off the table beside the floral sofa and unfolded it. Looking up at him, she sighed and then began to read.

"It appears as if the wedding of the year will not happen—that of David Albright and Rebecca Stuart. This reporter has learned on good authority that Mr. Albright is already married. The nuptials appear to have happened while David Albright was in California on business. He arrived home on Tuesday along with his new wife. The new Mrs. Albright, whose first name is Jane, has been described as a beautiful and very modern woman, which was displayed during Augustus Albright's birthday gathering held last night at the Albright residence. Mrs. David Albright demonstrated dances that might be popular in California establishments, but seem rather immodest and perhaps inappropriate for private home parties. That did not appear to dissuade Mr. David Albright, as the two were seen displaying deep affection for one another—which was, again, perhaps inappropriate during a social event. The guest list at the Albrights' gathering included none other than Miss Rebecca Stuart, along with…"

Charlene set the paper aside. "It lists many of the people who were here yesterday."

David was rubbing a hand over his lips, had been for some time to keep from laughing aloud while she'd been reading. Now that she was done, he let the laugh out.

"You can't find that funny!" Charlene stated with more emotion than he'd seen in a long time. "Joshua certainly doesn't. He was quite angry upon reading it."

"Yes, I do find it funny," he admitted. He could also believe that Joshua was quite angry upon reading it, namely because there wasn't anything about him in the article.

"You can't be serious," Charlene said. "This could create a scandal."

He shook his head. "The only people who might find anything scandalous are the jealous old prudes who weren't here to see it themselves. Jane did nothing wrong yesterday, and neither did I."

"I'm not saying she did anything wrong. I like her. It's impossible not to, but…"

"But Joshua doesn't," he finished for her.

Charlene shook her head. "He doesn't believe she is up to the standards of this family."

A bout of anger instantly roiled inside him. "Standards of this family?"

"Yes." She sighed, and it looked like true concern in her eyes. "I wanted you to see the article before Joshua shows it to you. I'm sure he will."

He was still controlling his temper, but it was gaining steam. "I'm sure he will, too."

She shook her head. "I'm sorry, David. I never wanted to come between you and Joshua. I truly never thought that my marrying him would cause such problems. I'd loved him for so long, and when he said he loved me in return, I thought all of my dreams had come true."

David's mind was still on Jane, but a piece of it did focus on Charlene, on what she was saying. "And now?"

She wiped at a tear trickling down her cheek. "I still love him, but he doesn't think he's worthy of it. He just keeps getting angrier and angrier at everyone and everything."

"Why?"

"Yes, yes, I'm fine," Jane said into the phone, in answer to Betty's questions. "I'm having the most wonderful time. I just missed you and wanted to hear your voice."

"Where are you?" Betty asked.

"I can't tell you that, in case you decide to send Reuben to drag me back home." Jane was trying her best to sound happy and carefree, and hoped to demonstrate that by using the nickname she'd given to her brother-in-law Henry, but hearing Betty's voice was increasing the sadness inside her.

"I'd only do that if I thought you were being mistreated," Betty insisted. "Please, Jane, I've been so worried about you. So has Patsy. And Father, oh, Jane, he is so worried. He told Henry that all he'd wanted to do was protect us, keep us safe, but that all his rules had done just the opposite."

A shiver rippled over Jane's arms. "He did?"

"Yes, and Mother is beside herself. I've told them that I'm sure you're fine, but it's been so hard, because I didn't know that for sure. None of us did. Just please…tell me where you are."

Jane twisted the cord of the speaker with her opposite hand as her stomach roiled. She couldn't lie to Betty. Had to let them know something. "I'm in Chicago, and I'm fine. I truly am."

"Chicago! Dear heavens! That far away? How did you get to Chicago?"

"We drove, and it was so amazing. I can't wait to show you the pictures." She glanced at the door of the library that Elwood had led her into when she'd asked him if there was a telephone she could use, privately. David could be home any moment, and Elwood had promised to let her know when he arrived. "I have to ask you a question, Betty."

"What?"

"How did you know you were in love with Henry?"

"I just knew. My heart felt it. He made me feel alive and I—I— Why? Were you not in love when you eloped? Who is this piano player? What's his name?"

She couldn't answer all those questions. "Yes, yes, I was in love with him," she lied. "I just wanted to make sure that's what I was feeling."

"Was? Do you not feel that way any longer? Does he love you in return?" Betty sounded worried again. "Do you need money for a train ticket home?"

A knock sounded on the door, and a second later, Elwood stuck his head in the room. *Master David*, he mouthed.

Thank you, Jane mouthed in return, and then said into the speaker, "No, I don't need any money. I have to go now. I miss you and will see you before Thanksgiving. Give Patsy my love. And tell Mother and Father I'm fine. I really am." She hung up then, knowing Betty would keep talking if she didn't.

She made sure the phone was sitting exactly

on the corner of the desk as it had been when she'd entered the room, and then rushed to the door. The library was huge, with shelves that went from the floor to the ceiling, and there was a rolling ladder in order to reach them all. It also had dark leather furniture and, like most every other room in the big house, had a large fireplace on the one wall.

The room was on the same floor as David's suite, just on the opposite end of the long hallway. Elwood had said David used the library a lot while he'd been in college. She pulled open the door and, seeing the hallway empty, stepped out and closed the door quietly behind her.

She then hurried along the hallway and into their suite. Once the door was shut, she went into the bedroom, and then the bathroom, where she shut the door and took a moment to let her racing pulse slow. She owed Elwood a huge thank-you for showing her the telephone, and for watching out for David.

Ever since he'd left that morning, she'd thought about calling Betty, but hadn't dared ask just anyone about using a phone. Through a process of elimination, in which most everyone was quickly eliminated, she'd ended up with Gus and Elwood on her list. She felt she could trust them, Gus was David's grandfather, so Elwood was who she'd asked.

Once she'd built up the courage.

He'd assured her he wouldn't tell anyone, and that he'd inform her of David's arrival. Which he had.

Thank goodness.

The trouble was, she wasn't sure the phone call had done any good. Actually, it may have done more harm than good. She now missed her family more than ever, and her heart definitely felt something for David, but it couldn't be love. She didn't want to love anyone. Neither did David. That's why they'd agreed to this plan. Because neither of them wanted to get married. To be married.

If he had, he'd have married Charlene.

But Joshua had married her first.

She'd pretended she'd known all about it, even as she'd asked Cora a few subtle questions, and that, along with not telling David about her family and writing the wrong name on the marriage license, increased the guilt inside her.

Cora's answers had included that David had been in love with Charlene since he was little and had asked her to marry him, but Joshua had already asked her, just hours before. That also increased the sadness inside her. No wonder he hadn't wanted to marry Rebecca, or anyone else.

This plan that she'd agreed to, back at the Rooster's Nest that night, was anything but foolproof.

She wanted to cry, and she never cried.

Never ever.

That had been the only thing she'd had control over whenever she'd become frustrated with her life.

She sucked in several deep breaths until the feeling eased and her eyes no longer stung. Letting out a long breath, she looked at herself in the mirror. It was only a few more days. She could do it.

What choice did she have?

None.

When she got home, she was going to tell her sisters to never, ever, let her come up with a plan again. Especially one she thought was foolproof.

"Jane?"

Her heart began to pound, even as it dropped into her stomach. Staring at herself in the mirror, she pulled up a smile. Which looked as fake as she felt, but it was all she had at the moment.

Turning, she pulled open the bathroom door.

"There you are." David crossed the bedroom

and a frown formed as he looked at her. "Are you feeling all right? You look a little pale."

"I'm fine." She stepped around him. "How was your meeting with Jeff?"

"Fine."

He'd told her it was about debts that Rebecca had acquired in his name. "Was it a lot?"

"I won't know that for several weeks."

"Oh." She walked out into the living area.

He indicated the sofa. "Let's sit down."

Her nerves started jumping around beneath her skin, but she nodded. "Why?"

"Because I need to talk to you."

"About what?"

He waited for her to sit and then sat down beside her. "I just spoke with Charlene."

Her skin shivered, especially around her neck. Her throat, which was trying to lock up.

"Don't look so worried," he said, patting her knee. "It's not that bad."

Her heart was also constricting. "Charlene?"

"Yes, she just told me she believes that she and Joshua haven't had any children because he's unable to due to having the mumps when he was a child." He stood up and walked a few steps. "I never knew that, or that it has caused strain in their marriage."

"That's why he's so angry all the time?"

He shrugged. "They were happy when they first got married. I started traveling more then, and have been gone so much the past few years that I never questioned…"

Her heart constricted again, now for a different reason. He was truly concerned. Despite all the anger between him and Joshua, he cared. Still loved his brother. She took his hand. "Why would you?" she asked. "You were gone, and when you came home, Joshua was angry."

"And I thought it was at me." He cursed under his breath. "Why didn't he say something? Things would never have gone this far."

She thought of Betty, and what she'd said about their father. All his rules to protect them had done the opposite. She'd run away because of them. Right or wrong, her father should have talked to them, told them why he had so many rules. An urgency rose up inside her. "Go talk to him, David. Before it's too late. Before it gets worse."

"I might already be too late."

"No. It's never too late. It can't be."

"We'll find that out after I talk to Joshua at lunch."

"It'll be fine," she said, wanting to assure him.

"You say that without knowing what I'm going to talk to him about."

She frowned. "You just told me."

He shook his head. "There's something else." Bending down, he picked up a newspaper lying on the table in front of the sofa. "You made the news."

"I what?"

He handed her the paper. She began to read and her heart fell a bit more with each line she read. Especially about her being immodest and inappropriate. Ashamed, she whispered, "Oh, David, I am so sorry." She'd never cared what others had thought while dancing at the speakeasies, but they hadn't known who she was, here they did. His wife. Mrs. David Albright.

"Sorry?" He lifted her chin with one finger so she had to look at him. "You have nothing to be sorry about. You made the society page."

The mischievous twinkle was in his eye, and for the first time, it didn't make her smile. "David, this is serious. They think I'm—"

"A beautiful, modern woman," he interrupted. "And you are."

"It also says I'm immodest and inappropriate. It's says your wife, Mrs. David Albright, is immodest and inappropriate." She pressed a hand to her churning stomach. "I've brought shame to your entire family."

"No, you haven't. You are not immodest or inappropriate, and everyone who was here last night would agree with me." He took the paper and dropped it on the table. "I also know where that came from. My brother. Joshua. He's the one who needs to be ashamed. And he owes you an apology, one I'll make sure you get."

"No, David. No. I don't want—"

"I do."

Chapter Twelve

Jane had never been so nervous in her life. David had been angry when Rebecca had been allowed to remodel his suite, but that didn't compare to how mad he was right now, as they walked down the stairs to the first floor. She was trembling so hard she could barely walk. If she had the choice, she'd be on her way back to California.

As that thought crossed her mind, she looked up at David, and an odd sense of power rose up in her as she recalled that first night, when Joshua had tried to intimidate her. He hadn't intimidated her then, and he wouldn't now, either.

These two brothers needed to figure this out. Learn to get along again because they should love each other as much as she and her sisters loved one another.

She tightened her hold on David's arm as they entered the dining room. He glanced down at her and she smiled. Nothing about this plan had been as simple as objecting to a church full of people, but she sure had learned a lot. Not just about the things she'd read about in magazines, either. She'd learned about real life things. About people, all kinds of people, and how to help them. She liked that. It was difficult but, in the end, worth it.

Head up, she kept the smile on her face as David pulled out her chair and she sat. Her first glance was to Gus, who smiled at her in return, but she noticed it was strained. He must have read the article, as well. That made her feel bad, but she held her smile and offered it to Joshua and Charlene.

"Dexter Rogers said hello," David said to Gus once the meal had been served.

"How is he doing?" Gus asked. "I missed him at the party yesterday."

"He sends his regards for that as well," David answered. "He's fine, but Stella is just getting over pneumonia."

"I hadn't heard that," Gus said. "I'll have to give him a call."

"Dexter Rogers?" Joshua asked. "Where did you see him?"

"At his office," David answered. "I had a meeting with Jeff this morning."

"For what?" Joshua asked.

"It appears that Rebecca Stuart has acquired a rather large debt, in the Albright name."

"What did you expect?" Joshua asked. "You had promised."

"No, I had not," David replied. "And what I expect is respect from my family. For me and my wife. Since that didn't happen, let me assure you, brother dear, if it's a scandal you want, that what's you'll get."

The room grew so quiet Jane could hear both David and Joshua breathe as they stared at each other. She glanced at Gus, who was eating his meal as if nothing was wrong. That confused her considerably.

Joshua pushed away from the table. "We'll take this into my office."

"There's nothing to take," David said. "I told you what would happen if you dragged Jane into this. You chose not to believe me."

Joshua jumped to his feet. "I said—"

"Shouting won't change anything. I heard what you said." David remained seated, but lifted his napkin off his lap and laid it over his plate. "And only because you are my brother, I'll give you one last chance."

Not hungry at all, Jane laid her napkin on her plate, too.

David pushed away from the table and stood.

A hint of satisfaction crossed Joshua's face, until David pulled out her chair.

Jane was confused, but stood up as David took her elbow.

"A retraction," David said to Joshua. Then he looked at Gus. "Jane and I will not be home for dinner this evening. We have some errands to complete and will then be dining downtown."

Gus nodded. "I'll let Elwood know."

She waited until they were well out of earshot before saying, "I thought you were going to talk to Joshua."

"I did."

"No, you didn't. That wasn't talking."

"That's how Joshua talks. He yells and makes demands."

"Maybe you could explain—"

"I've tried. Believe me, I've tried."

Her insides shivered. She did believe him, but also wondered if he hadn't tried hard enough. Both he and Joshua were stubborn when it came to each other.

"Excuse me, Master David, Jane," Elwood said as they rounded the corner into the foyer. "Where would you like me to put the gifts that are starting to arrive?"

She looked up at David. "Gifts?"

He shrugged and looked at Elwood. "Wedding gifts, I'm assuming."

"Yes, sir." Elwood bowed and then waved an arm toward the front foyer, where a table had been set up near the French doors of the main living room.

Gaily wrapped packages and envelopes covered the white lacy tablecloth, and several larger packages sat beneath the table.

"Would you like me to have them transferred to your suite, or do you anticipate a gift-opening reception?" Elwood asked.

"I would guess a reception is expected," David said.

Jane's insides quivered all over again.

"I believe you are correct, sir," Elwood said.

"Set one up for Sunday afternoon," David said.

"Very well, sir." Elwood nodded, but then looked at her, "Perhaps Jane would have a few moments to meet with Mrs. Kennedy to provide the details?"

David was looking at her, too. Smiling, she nodded. "Of course."

"Meet us in our suite in a few minutes, please," David said. "We will then be going out for the rest of the day and evening."

"Very well, sir. We'll be there momentarily." Elwood bowed before walking away.

Mrs. Kennedy was Elwood's wife and in charge of the kitchen. Jane had met with her and Charlene about Gus's birthday party. She was also the person in charge of the caramel rolls that continued to be served each and every morning. She was short, squat and adorable. Her face was as round as Elwood's was long, and Jane thought the woman was a marvel. Everything that had come out of the kitchen since her arrival had been delicious.

"Who are all these gifts from?" she asked as they walked past the table and up the staircase.

"People who were here for Gus's birthday, and those who read about our marriage in the newspaper. I hadn't thought about it, but a gift reception would be expected."

Expected. More like unexpected to her. Just like everything else that had happened since that night at the Rooster's Nest. "What will you do with the gifts?"

"We'll open them during the reception."

"No, I mean afterward. After Monday, when we leave for California?"

He put his arm around her and gave her a hug as they walked up the steps. "Don't worry about that. I'll take care of it."

She couldn't help but worry about it, and so many other things. Many more things than she'd ever imagined, and far more than she'd had to worry about back home.

True to his word, Elwood and his wife arrived at their suite practically the same time she and David did, having walked up the back set of stairs that came out on the other end of the hallway, near the library where she'd used the telephone. One more thing she would have to tell David about. Eventually. While on their way back to California.

Mrs. Kennedy proved to be a marvel all over again. As soon as the four of them sat down in the living room of their suite, Ora, as she told Jane she could call her, started making suggestions. Jane was drawn into the party planning as quickly as she had been for Gus's birthday. Other than the small amounts she'd helped with for Patsy's and Betty's weddings, she didn't have any experience in planning parties, but it was fun. A lot of fun.

It would be an open house, on Sunday in the billiard room, from two to five in the afternoon, with hors d'oeuvres, various drinks and cake. Ora assured that the invitations would be hand-written that afternoon and delivered to everyone who had already sent a gift, as well as several others that David suggested.

Jane insisted that she would help decorate the room the following day, and with anything else that she could do in advance of the party, despite Ora's insistence that the staff could manage it all.

The planning couldn't have taken more than half an hour, but Jane had felt as if she was in her glory during that time. She hadn't known planning such an event had so many facets, but having experienced that with Gus's birthday party, she nearly felt like an old hand organizing this one. As the meeting ended, she asked Ora to please let Charlene know about everything they'd discussed, since she and David would be leaving soon.

"You enjoyed that," David said after Elwood and Ora had left.

"I did," she agreed.

"It was nice of you to ask Mrs. Kennedy to include Charlene."

She shrugged. "Charlene's planned far more parties than I have, and I like her."

"She said the same thing about you."

"She did?"

"Yes."

That made her feel good. David may have loved her at one time, but that was no reason for her to not like Charlene.

"Time to get your coat," he said.

"Where are we going?"

"To pick up your pictures."

Her heart leaped into her throat. With everything else going on, she'd forgotten about the pictures. "They're done?"

Laughing, he nodded. "Yes."

Despite all he'd come to discover during his short discussion with Charlene, his anger over the newspaper article, and the caution he told himself he had to maintain when it came to how he was feeling about Jane, David couldn't help but get caught up in her excitement over the pictures. Unable to wait until they were in the car, she'd pulled them out of the packages in the photography shop. Proclaiming every picture was her favorite, she showed them to him, the clerk and other customers. She also knew exactly where each one had been taken and explained all about it. No one seemed to mind; in fact, there was a cluster of people around them, vying for their turn to see the pictures.

He'd also bought a leather-bound album, with large black pages that she'd be able to paste the pictures onto, which she clutched so hard he didn't think she'd ever let go of it.

There were several pictures that had truly taken his breath away, she'd looked so beautiful, so happy. He had, too. He had been happy. Happier since he'd met her than he'd ever been. Her exuberance did that. It was contagious and followed her everywhere she went.

"You know, David," she said as he drove away from the shop. "We haven't taken a single picture since we arrived at your house."

"No, we haven't. The camera's in our suite. In the credenza, along with the rolls of films we bought when we dropped these ones off to be developed. You can use it whenever you want."

She nodded. "I will." Biting her bottom lip, she giggled.

"What's so funny?"

"I was just thinking about our snowball fight. I wish I'd gotten a picture of that."

"We can have another one."

She nodded and leaned her head back against the seat. "And Gus. I need to take a picture of Gus."

"I'm sure he'll let you." He'd never seen his grandfather's eyes light up the way they did when he looked at her. David knew that feeling. What he was going to do about that was his main problem right now.

"Do you know that he received over a thousand dollars in gifts yesterday?"

"No, I did not know that."

"He did. I helped him count it, and he wrote a check for that same amount, matching it."

David grinned. He was proud of his grandfather's generosity. If there was a man he'd like to follow in the footsteps of, it was his grandfather.

"I saw the card you gave him, with both of our names on it, and a hundred dollars."

He nodded. There was nothing he needed to say. He believed in supporting the soup kitchen and other charities, and did so regularly.

"That was very nice of you." She let out a long sigh. "I wish I could see it."

"See what?" he asked.

"The soup kitchen when they get the money.

Gus said he'd have it sent over to them," she answered. "I'm sure they'll be surprised and happy."

He was sure, too, but was thinking more about her comment. "You want to see it?"

She nodded.

"We could go home and get the envelope and deliver it."

"We could?" Her eyes were sparkling.

"Yes, we could."

"Oh, David, let's! I'd much rather do that than go to a restaurant."

"All right then, that's what we will do."

She never failed to surprise him, but what happened once they arrived home nearly shocked him. She not only invited Gus to go along with them, she invited Charlene and Joshua.

A plethora of mixed emotions rolled around inside him. He was still angry at his brother for the article. It had been malicious and hurtful and he wouldn't forget it, but he was also proud of Jane, the way she was insisting that the entire Albright family had helped in raising the money, so they all should see where it went. It was a blatant display of her true character, how authentic she was in caring about others, even people who had wronged her.

"That's all right," Charlene said. "Joshua doesn't like those types of things."

"But you'd like to go, wouldn't you?" Jane asked.

Charlene lowered her gaze to the floor, but Jane raised hers, to stare at Joshua.

David watched them both, his brother and wife. It was a showdown of sorts, and he didn't feel right stepping in to voice an opinion either way.

"If you really want to go, Charlene," Joshua said.

Charlene shook her head. "Not without you. I'd feel out of place."

Jane was still staring at Joshua. David pinched his lips together to hide the smile that was pressing hard to show, because he knew his brother was not going to win this.

"All right," Joshua said. "Let's go."

Within a short while, they were all piled in David's car, with Joshua and Charlene in the back seat and Gus and Jane in the front with him.

"Bee's knees, but this is fun!" she said, scrunched up next to him.

"I wouldn't consider visiting a soup kitchen fun," Joshua said drily.

"Have you done it before?" Jane asked.

"No."

"Then how do you know?"

David glanced over and met his grandfather's gaze, which was full of delight, as he steered the car around the corner to head toward the lake. The soup kitchen she'd seen the other day was near there.

"Grandpa," she said. "You should be the one to give them the envelope—it was your birthday."

"But it was your idea to deliver it," Grandpa answered. "So you should be the one."

"It wasn't my idea," she said. "It was David's."

"As I recall you said you wanted to see it," he corrected.

"I did, but you're the one who said we could deliver it," she argued.

David had to laugh at the groan that came from the back seat. Jane had been good for him and his family, but he'd never expected her to be good for Joshua, too. She was, though. This was the first time they'd gone anywhere together in years. Once again, he thought about when she'd asked if people forgot that they loved each other. They did. He was sure of that. He also knew there was a lot about Jane to love.

He found a parking spot near the soup kitchen and they all climbed out.

"Are they open?" Jane asked. "There is no line."

"They don't start serving until later," Charlene said. "The workers will be inside, cooking."

"How do you know that?" Joshua asked.

"From one of the ladies who has asked me to be on her committee," she answered. "They serve meals twice a day."

"How nice of you," Jane said.

"I haven't joined," Charlene said, eyes downward.

"You can, if you want to." Joshua put his arm around her. "I won't mind."

David put an arm around Jane and walked toward the kitchen, with Gus on her other side, giving Joshua and Charlene a moment alone.

"You are like a star in the night," Gus said to Jane. "A bright, shining star."

Her giggle floated on the air, and as David looked down at her, saw her shining face, his heart once again reacted. It was moments like this, when he was looking at her, that he had a hard time remembering his reasons for never wanting to get married, to never want to have someone to share his life with. The big moments and the little ones. Actually, she made the little moments big with her enthusiasm and charm.

She was adorable in so many ways, too, and lovely. The brilliant blue of her coat matched her eyes, which were sparkling brightly right now. The moment he'd seen that coat, he'd known he had to buy it for her. Her blond hair flowed over the fur collar, her shoulders and down her back, in those soft corkscrews, and her cheeks were rosy, making her smile brighter.

The desires that were alive and growing inside him for days now were once again so strong he couldn't stop looking at her, couldn't stop thinking about kissing her.

"David, the door."

As his grandfather's words entered his mind, he heard someone else shout his name. He twisted, glanced up the sidewalk and instantly recognized the reporter. "Hello, Wesley. How are you doing?"

"From what I hear, not as good as you." Still walking toward them, Wesley Clinton gave a slight nod toward Jane. "It's true, I see."

David laughed and squeezed Jane's shoulder. "It is."

Wesley smiled as he reached them. "Looks like the entire Albright family is here."

"We are," Grandpa answered. "Good to see you, Wesley."

After a round of handshakes, David asked,

"What are you doing here, Wesley? I don't see any police cars."

Known as a news-breaking reporter, Wesley laughed. "Slow news day. I'm walking the streets trying to find something. What are you doing here?"

David glanced at Jane. This was her project, and he'd let her answer.

She flashed one of her charming grins at Wesley. "We are delivering a donation to the soup kitchen."

Both of Wesley's dark brows rose. "You are?"

Glancing up at Grandpa, she nodded. "Yes, Gus is making a donation in honor of his birthday."

"Well, it looks like I found a story." Glancing at Grandpa, Wesley then asked, "Do you mind, Gus? If I write about this. Take a picture or two?"

"Not at all," Grandpa answered. "While the economy may be good for some of us, there are always those who are down on their luck. Maybe an article in the paper will encourage more people to make a donation."

Jane gasped and, full of exuberance, said, "Wouldn't that be wonderful!"

The next half hour included an interview with

Wesley, where Jane gave her thoughts in her vibrant way, emphasizing how the entire family was a part of delivering the donation. David was sure not even Joshua would be able to find anything wrong with the article.

Her compassion and sincerity as she described seeing the line outside the soup kitchen the other day was spellbinding. The way she talked about the people—how they must not have families to help them, and the children, with their scarfs whipping around in the chilling wind, holding on to each other's hands… He could see them in his mind. Others must have, too, because by the time she was done, not only had Wesley pulled out his wallet and handed several bills to the volunteers, so had Joshua.

Wesley took several pictures of all of them inside the small soup kitchen facility with the volunteers, who were overjoyed and assured them all that they'd be able to feed many, many people with the generous donations they'd just received.

The festive feeling that Jane brought to the simple occasion stayed with them as they exited the building.

"Thank you, all of you," Wesley said. "This is going to be a great article." Then, as he tucked his little notebook in his pocket, he leaned closer and whispered, "Take me with you to California next time you go, will you?"

David laughed as Wesley walked away. Then, when he turned back to his family, he was surprised to see the way Joshua was looking at him. His brother was smiling and gave a slight nod before climbing into the back seat of the car.

They drove home then and remained there, ate with the family, and for the first time in a very long time there was no tense, heavy air hanging around the table. Instead, there was laughter and lively conversation.

Afterward, they spent a couple of hours in the main living room, with Jane showing everyone the pictures of their trip. She also showed them the leather photo album he'd purchased, which led to him asking Elwood to provide her with a jar of paste to put the pictures in the album.

Later, in their suite, she said, "Oh, David, this was such a wonderful night!"

She was in the dressing room, sitting on the large, round stool, removing her shoes. He leaned against the door frame and determined the dressing room wasn't a bad thing at all.

She was the best thing, though. It had been years since he'd felt the unity with his family that he'd experienced this evening, and she was the reason.

"Yes, it was." He pushed off the door frame and walked toward her. The way she smiled up at him, with the corner of her lips tilted upward, ignited his already heightened desires to yet another level. Stopping in front of her, he held out his hands.

She glanced at them hesitantly, then laid hers in them and stood as his fingers folded around hers.

His pulse quickened as her lids fluttered shut and opened again as she looked up at him.

She swallowed, licked her lips and then dipped her chin slightly, breaking eye contact.

"I can't even begin to describe you," he said, quietly, sincerely. He couldn't. "There are no words that do enough justice."

"David," she whispered, shaking her head.

"There aren't. You bring brilliance to life in a way I've never seen. Never knew existed. You are like everything that's pure and true, and amazing and wonderful, all rolled into one."

"No, I'm not."

Yes, she was. He wasn't doing his thoughts justice. "You are something that needs to be cherished." He wanted to do that. Cherish her.

Forever. Damn the consequences, the reasons he'd previously told himself. They no longer held true. Couldn't, because he hadn't known her when he'd adopted any of those previous thoughts or ideas.

He traced the side of her face before cupping her cheek and burying his fingers in the mass of her hair. Slowly he leaned forward and kissed her. Softly. Tenderly.

She let out a tiny whimper and pulled out of the kiss, leaned back, looked at him.

He didn't release her, not her face or how their gazes were locked. He couldn't. The brief kiss hadn't been enough. He waited, though, for her reaction. It was her call.

She shook her head, then gasped and, wrapping her arms around his neck, pressed her lips against his feverishly.

Exhilarated, he grasped her waist, pulled her closer and kissed her with all the passion flowing through his veins. The heat of her mouth, the sweetness of her tongue twirling with his, the curves of her body pressed against his was thrilling, tantalizing, but it wasn't enough. His body begged for more.

She broke the kiss and, breathing heavily, buried her face against his chest.

He held on to her, laid his cheek atop her head.

"We can't do this," she whispered. "No one's watching us."

He grinned at her reasoning. "No, they aren't, but we are married."

"But it's not real." She sniffled slightly. "It can't be."

He wanted to say it could be, but the way she stiffened, he chose not to. Furthermore, she was right. Something that started out as a lie was always a lie. It can't become the truth just because someone wanted it to.

He held her a while longer, then kissed the top of her head and released her. "Good night, Jane."

She kept her gaze averted. "Good night, David."

Sleep evaded him for a large portion of the night. Convincing himself that although he may have changed, nothing else had. As in their bargain. He'd created this plan and would see it through to the end. The end they had both agreed to.

The following morning, he forced himself to pretend nothing had happened last night and was relieved to see that Jane did, too. She was better at it than him, just like she was better at so many other things.

As soon as breakfast was over, she disappeared into the kitchen, which he visited several times throughout the morning to find her laughing and working alongside the others, preparing things for the gift reception the following day. After the noon meal, she spent hours in the billiard room, helping with decorations, rearranging furniture and determining how everything would be set up the following day.

The room did look spectacular, with vases full of flowers and white tablecloths covering an array of tables that had been set to serve the food and drinks. As usual, it once again was Jane that made the room sparkle.

"It's time for us to get ready," he said.

"Already?" she asked, straightening the hem of the white cloth draped over the top of the billiard table, which was covered with gifts.

"Already?" He grasped her waist and forced her to turn about. "You've been working since the moment you woke up this morning."

She laughed. "This hasn't been work. It's been fun!" She took his hand. "Come, look where I put the photo album. I thought people might enjoy looking through it." She led him toward a table.

The album was in the center of a small table. He flipped open the first page and noticed how she'd written where they were under each picture. "When did you find time to do this? Write in it?" Her penmanship was perfect, so was her memory.

"Here and there."

"Here and there? We just picked up the pictures and album yesterday."

She laughed. "It didn't take that long. Where are we going with Cora and Jeff?"

He'd been going to let it be a surprise, but chose to tell her instead. "To dinner and a performance."

"What kind of performance?"

"The theatre."

Her adorable eyes widened. "A play? A real play? With actors and everything?"

"Yes."

She pressed both hands over her heart. "I've always wanted to see a play."

"David, I would like a word with you."

Joshua stood in the doorway. David nodded. He hadn't seen Joshua all day. "I'll be there shortly."

Withholding his desire to kiss her, he tapped the tip of Jane's nose, told her he'd meet her in their suite and then walked to Joshua's office.

"This was in the social page today," Joshua said, handing him a newspaper.

David had already read it, but did so again. It was a short paragraph, near the bottom of the page and written by the same reporter as the article yesterday.

It has come to this reporter's attention that yesterday's article may have been misconstrued by some.

Mrs. Jane Albright is not an immodest person, and nor was her behavior inappropriate while she and her husband, David Albright, entertained their guests with some of the new dances from California.

Indeed, everyone at Gus Albright's birthday gathering enjoyed the music and dancing.

The article wasn't much, but it was more than he'd expected and had surprised him when he'd seen it this morning because, from Joshua, it was a big step. He handed the paper back to his brother.

Joshua laid it on his desk. "You may not believe this, but I didn't have anything to do with the first article."

David sat down in the chair. Yesterday he wouldn't have believed that, but today maybe his mind was more open. "Rebecca?"

Joshua nodded. "I paid her a visit today and informed her of exactly what a charge of slander toward an Albright could mean to her, presently and in the future."

Surprised, David asked, "You did?"

"Yes." Joshua shook his head. "I'm sorry, David."

An olive branch from his brother was the last thing he'd expected, since their difficulties were as much his fault as Joshua's. "I am, too," he replied. "About a lot of things." Shaking his head, he added, "I don't even know how things got to the level they did between us."

"Me." Joshua sighed and shrugged. "My wife pointed that out to me last night. She told me you know."

Accepting it as a delicate subject, David nodded. "How long have you known?"

Joshua let out a bitter laugh. "That I'm sterile? Years. Before Mother and Father died. Mother always said there was a chance it wasn't true, but four years of marriage is a pretty solid confirmation she was wrong."

Not sure how to respond, David asked, "Have you seen a doctor?"

"Several." Joshua leaned forward, planted his elbows on his desk. "I was jealous when you were born. Everyone knows that, and then, as a kid, I blamed you for getting sick. You had the mumps first, but you were young. I was older, at the age where it can cause more issues, and it did." He sighed. "And then I fell in love with Charlene. I knew you liked her, too, and for years, ignored my feelings for her, but when I knew you were going to ask her to marry you, I— Well, I knew I'd hate you if I let you marry her. I loved her then, and I love her now."

"I'm glad," David said, meaning it. "I never loved Charlene the way a man should love his wife. I thought I did because I knew it was expected that our families marry." He could say that honestly now, because Jane had proven it to him. The way he felt about her didn't compare to how he'd ever felt about anyone.

"I never told her," Joshua said solemnly. "That I was sterile, and I should have. Before we were married."

"It wouldn't have changed her mind," David replied, as certain of that as he was everything else. "She was in love with you, and still is."

"I still should have told her, and I should have told you that it was the reason I insisted upon you marrying Rebecca. After Charlene and I were married, you became dead set against marriage.

I thought it didn't matter at first, but then, realizing you are the only chance for our family to have future generations, I decided to force that to happen."

"That's what it was all about? A new generation of Albrights?" As he was asking the question, he knew the answer. It made sense. Everything Joshua said made sense. It also felt good, to have this all out in the open between them.

Joshua nodded. "Yes. The entire time you've been out there, focusing on expanding the A and R, I've been here, brooding about it because I can't have a child to pass it down to. I still was, up until last night when, because of your wife, I realized that even my choice for a wife for you was wrong. I was afraid you might marry someone who wasn't upstanding enough to bring into our family. Rebecca's family connection seemed to meet that qualification, but I now realize that doesn't mean she does." He leaned back in his chair. "But Jane does. She's quality, and I'm happy that you found her."

David felt pride. For his brother to have admitted all that he had. For Jane, because she was quality and someone to be proud of. But he felt no pride for himself. For the false marriage he'd used to get his way, and for the way the desolation of it would affect his family. All of them.

Knowing he needed to acknowledge Joshua, David nodded. "Thank you." He nodded toward the newspaper. "For that and everything else."

"You're welcome." Joshua grinned as he stood up. "I have a feeling our family is finally going to be a family again. Thanks to you."

David stood, took ahold of his brother's extended hand and shook it, while internally full of regret.

Chapter Thirteen

Jane was tired. Not in the sleepy, worn-out way, but in the I-can't-keep-doing-this way. Pretending that all was wonderful in the world was growing harder and harder.

David… Everything about him was wonderful. Too wonderful. Not falling in love with him, not loving him, was exhausting.

The play he'd escorted her to this evening was amazing. The meal was outstanding, and the performance was thoroughly gripping, but she had no doubt that it was David at her side that made it truly extraordinary. Just as he had everything else.

"You two are so in love," Cora said while they were using the powder room during the intermission. "It's like Cinderella and Prince Charming."

Jane finished applying a new coat of lipstick and dropped the tube in the pocket of her gold brocade dress. Keeping up her facade, she replied, "I can't deny that David is truly charming."

"And handsome, and lovable," Cora said teasingly.

Jane nodded. "Yes, he is all of those things."

"He thinks the same about you," Cora said. "He makes love to you with his eyes every time he looks at you."

Jane shook her head. "No, he doesn't."

"Yes, he does." Cora laughed and patted her cheeks. "There's no need to blush. You're married."

No, they weren't married. Not in any true sense of the word. There were times where she wished she'd used the right name, so she could just let her heart have its way and fall in love with him. The womanly desires she'd only read about in magazines were alive and running hard and fast inside her. She'd been unable to sleep last night after the way he'd kissed her. The way she'd returned his kiss.

Now, just looking at him brought her insides to the point they nearly exploded. She'd been counting the days since she'd arrived in Chicago, and now she was counting the hours, too, forcing herself to believe she could get through just one more. Then another, and another.

"Come on," Cora said. "Our princes are waiting for us."

"You will be at the reception tomorrow, won't you?" Jane asked as they left the powder room. It was helpful to have others around, because she needed the escape from being at David's side all the time. Her restraint was waning.

"Of course," Cora said, looping her arm through hers. "So will my parents and my in-laws. It's going to be the party of the year. Everyone wants to meet you. The woman who stole David Albright's heart so deeply he made his brother post a retraction in the newspaper. That's the talk of the town!"

An entirely new fear rose up inside her. She didn't want David to be the talk of the town, not because of her. Once again she thought she might cry, but wouldn't. Couldn't. She couldn't give up that control, either.

She made it through the rest of the play, and through another night of David sleeping on the sofa on the other side of the bedroom door. Somehow.

Dressed in a lovely blue corduroy dress with wide white lace cuffs and a draping collar, she stared at herself in the mirror, wishing she had a pair of white shoes rather than her black ones. All she'd have to do was say so and David would buy her a pair, she had no doubt about that, but she wouldn't say anything. He'd already bought her far too many things. She wouldn't take any money from him, either, once they were divorced. Nor would she live in his apartment.

She would return home, explain to her parents why she had left, why their rules drove her away. A home should be a safe place, but also a happy place, a place where people work together, and if her parents couldn't understand that, she'd find somewhere else to live. With one of her sisters for a short time if needed. She'd learned so much in the time since she'd left home that she didn't even feel like the same person.

She wasn't. Now, she realized that there had been options other than running away. She could have stood up to her father. She could have gotten a job. She could have done a dozen other things rather than run away.

With David.

There was a knock on the door of their suite. She stepped into her black shoes and walked through the bedroom and into the living room. "Come in."

"As always, you look lovely," Gus said as he walked into the room and closed the door.

"You look very dapper yourself," she replied. Instead of a green smoking jacket, he was wearing a red one. She truly adored him.

Laughing, he waved toward the sofa. "You do an old man's heart good. Come, sit for a minute."

She sat on the sofa while he sat in an armchair next to it. "Are people arriving already?"

"No," he said, smiling.

"Good, I want to help with the finishing touches. I just thought I should get dressed first in case I don't have time later."

"That's what David told me, and I wanted to give you something to wear." He reached inside his jacket and pulled out a sizable golden tin box. "My wife, Mary, died many years ago, and this is the first piece of jewelry that I bought her after I'd made enough money to buy her quality jewels." He winked. "Before then they'd been baubles, not real jewels, but she never complained. You remind me of her." He held the box toward her. "And I would like you to have it."

Her heart swelled so fast she pressed a hand to her breast at his words, yet also knew she couldn't accept whatever was in the box. "I couldn't take—"

"Oh, yes, you can. I want you to have it, as my wedding gift to you." He leaned forward. "You, Jane, are the best thing that has ever happened to David. I always knew his time to shine would come, he just had to find something important enough to fight for. He'd never had that so he'd been satisfied standing in the back, letting Joshua run the business, run the family. You changed that in him, and I am very grateful for that."

"I didn't do that."

"Oh, yes, my dear, you did." He opened the box. "You've touched our entire family."

Jane gasped. She'd seen the diamond-and-sapphire necklace before, in a painting of Mary in Gus's study. The necklace was undoubtedly more gorgeous in person.

"My Mary's eyes were as blue as yours, and I'd be honored to see you wear this today."

She shook her head. "Gus, I couldn't—"

"Yes, dear, you can. It will make me extremely happy to see you do so."

With her hand still over her heart, which was starting to hurt, she said, "I'd love to make you happy, but that's a family heirloom."

He took it out of the box. "And you, my dear, are family." His smile softened. "I've given Charlene things of Mary's, if that's what you're worried about."

It wasn't. Charlene deserved those things, she didn't. "Gus, I—"

"No more arguing." He held the necklace toward her. "If you feel that strongly about not keeping it, just borrow it for today. It will make me proud to see you wear it."

Accepting his compromise, she nodded. "Just for today."

After she put the necklace on, Gus escorted her downstairs. The weight of the necklace made her feel like even more of an imposter. The party increased that feeling inside her because everyone noticed the necklace and it lifted more than one brow. It also had people whispering. She managed to play her role of being David's loving wife throughout the afternoon, opening an array of elaborate and beautiful gifts including crystal vases, gilded picture frames and engraved silver platters.

Thanking people for items she'd never see again was awful, and accepting the soft kisses David placed on her cheek was so bittersweet her eyes stung. Looking around the room, at all the people, all the happy people, made her throat sting, too. Even Joshua was happy, and nice to her.

He had been all day. So had Charlene. Very happy, and insisted it was because of Jane and how she'd made them all go to the soup kitchen. Charlene said that Joshua had told her that night that he needed to repair things between him and David. That their family needed to heal their differences and become a family again.

That made Jane think even more about *her* family and their differences. How she'd run away rather than try to heal them.

Most of the guests left by the end of the open house, but a few remained and joined the family for dinner that evening before making their departures. By then, Jane's worries had given her a headache.

David turned to her as they entered their suite and kissed her forehead. "Once again, your beauty and charm had everyone in awe. I'm very proud of you, Jane. Very proud."

She wasn't, and moved away. This lie she was living had gotten out of control, and the truth was that she wasn't going to be able to escape it. Not on Tuesday when they left, because she'd still be with David. All day. Every day. He had become dear to her. So very, very dear.

So had his family, and leaving here, divorcing him… The thought made her headache worse. Removing the necklace, she placed it in the box on the table in front of the sofa.

"Are you all right?" he asked.

She shook her head.

He grasped her arms, turned her around. "What is it?"

"I just have a headache," she said honestly.

He kissed her forehead again and then placed a hand behind her knees and picked her up, carried her toward the bedroom.

She should protest, but her head really hurt. Her heart really hurt.

In the bedroom, he laid her on the bed, removed her shoes and silk stockings, and then whispered, "I'll be right back."

He was back momentarily, with a glass of water and two aspirins.

She sat up and took the pills, using a sip of water to wash them down. "Thank you."

"Lay back down," he said, taking the glass from her hand.

"I need to take my dress off. I don't want to ruin the lace." The matching blue silk slip wouldn't be warm, but she didn't care about warmth right now.

"All right, I'll help you."

He did and, as he lifted the blue dress over her head, offered to get her a nightgown.

"No, I just need to lie down." Her head was pounding so badly she hoped sleep would help. It had to.

He covered her with the blankets. She closed her eyes, willing the aspirins to quickly take effect.

Even with her lids closed, she could tell he turned out the lights, and a moment later he laid a cool, damp cloth on her forehead.

It may have been one thing or a combination of things, but when she opened her eyes, she knew she'd been dreaming. She had no idea how long she'd been sleeping, nor could she recall what she'd been dreaming about, but her head no longer hurt. Lifting a hand, she touched a temple, gingerly, just to make sure.

"Do you need another aspirin?"

David was lying on the bed beside her. She shook her head. "No. Thank you."

He slid an arm beneath her neck and wrapped the other one around her waist. "Then go back to sleep," he whispered.

Her headache might be gone, but the reasons

for it were still there. "They are going to hate me, David," she whispered.

He kissed her temple. "No one hates you."

"They will. Your family, your friends, when they find out we aren't really married, they'll all hate me. So will you."

"I'll never hate you."

Her eyes burned and so did the tears they released, hot as they trickled out of her eyes. "Yes, you will." She'd lied to him the most.

"Go back to sleep, sweetheart," he whispered. "You'll feel better in the morning."

No, she wouldn't. She might never feel better. "I need to go home, David. I can't do all this any longer."

"All right, I'll take you home. Now, just go to sleep."

The tears were falling faster. "I wanted to see the world. See all the things I'd only dreamed about, but I've hurt people in doing that."

"Shh," he whispered. "No one's been hurt."

"Yes, they have, and it's my fault."

He tightened his hold around her waist, rubbed her stomach. "I'm the one who asked you to run away, so it's my fault, and I'm sorry, but we'll make it right. I promise. I never meant for you to get hurt in all this."

They had agreed together to run away, but that didn't make her feel any better. Pain constricted her heart, as if it was breaking in two. "I lied to you, David. I wasn't a maid. I just felt like I was because of my father. He's the reason my sisters and I snuck out at night. To visit speakeasies."

His hand on her stomach went still. "Oh?"

"My father is very strict." She swallowed against the burning in her throat. "He didn't allow us to go out. To do anything. I hated it. He should never have treated us like that, I don't care if he thought he was protecting us, keeping us from making bad decisions. It was wrong."

"He doesn't know, does he? Where you are at right now?"

She squeezed her eyes shut, holding back more tears. "No." Swallowing a sob, she continued, "I couldn't tell you because I was afraid that you'd take me back to Los Angeles, and then I couldn't tell you because, because…" Unable to come up with a solid reason, she merely said, "It was too late."

His hand slid off her waist and he rolled onto his back.

The pain in her heart increased. "I'm sorry, David. I truly am."

"Your family has to be worried about you,"

he said. "I want you to call them tomorrow. Let them know that you are fine, safe, and will soon be on your way home."

She pinched her lips together to keep from saying that she'd already called her sister.

He rubbed her shoulder and then patted it. "I'm glad you told me now, Jane. Go to sleep, we'll get it all worked out."

No, they wouldn't. It wasn't his problem. It was hers.

She eventually fell asleep, and woke to David pulling on a gray suit coat.

"How's your headache this morning?" he asked.

"It's gone," she answered, not looking directly at him.

"I have the shareholders meeting this morning. Would you like me to have a caramel roll sent up here?"

"No. I'm not hungry."

He walked around the foot of the bed and touched her beneath the chin, forcing her to look up. "Are you sure?"

She nodded.

"All right, I'll be home after the meeting. We'll contact your family then." He leaned down and kissed her forehead. "Don't worry. We'll work it out."

She nodded again, because he expected it, but as soon as he shut the door, she heaved out a sigh and willed the tears to not start flowing again. He was so nice, so likable, right from the first night she'd met him. Even back then, before running away, when she'd tried to not talk to him because she'd thought he was a piano player, it had been impossible for her not to talk to him, not to like him.

She crawled out of bed and walked into the changing room. After hanging up the blue dress from yesterday that was lying over the top of the footstool, she put on a long-sleeved brown dress with a black belt, pinned back the sides of her hair, and then sat down to put her shoes on.

Her life had changed so much since meeting David. Not just in seeing new places and things, but on the inside. Up until a week ago, her life, all her wants and needs, had been all about her. She'd thought about her sisters and parents, but even all those thoughts had been about her. It hadn't been until David, that she started thinking about others and about how she could help them. That had felt good, too. Helping others. It was something she wanted to continue to do.

Hearing the outer door to their suite open, she stood. David appeared in the bedroom door as she was walking around the bed.

"There is someone downstairs who would like to see you," he said coldly.

A shiver rippled through her. "Who?"

"Your brother-in-law. Henry Randall."

Her heart sank as her entire being went cold. She shouldn't have called Betty. Shouldn't have said she was in Chicago. Henry was the best FBI agent in the bureau. Tracking down criminals was his job. Finding her would have been a simple feat once Betty asked him to do it, which had to have been exactly what had happened.

"An FBI agent," David said.

Bile burned the back of her throat. "Yes, I—"

He held up a hand. "Don't say you're sorry. There are things I didn't tell you, too. So rather than being sorry, we need to focus on what we are going to do about it."

She'd never thought she'd wished to get yelled at, but she did. She was used to that. Would know how to respond. She'd seen him mad at Joshua, so why not now?

He held out a hand. "Come on."

Stepping forward, she asked, "Why aren't you mad at me?"

He took her elbow. "Would it make a difference?"

"No."

"I'm disappointed that you didn't trust me
enough—"

"I do trust you, I just...couldn't tell you."

"We'll talk about it when I return from the
shareholders meeting." He opened the door to the
hallway. "I've already explained to your brother-
in-law that I need to be gone until noon, and
asked Elwood to prepare a room for him."

Jane was glad all her tears had been used up
yesterday; otherwise, she would have had to hold
them back right now. As it was, all she felt was
broken inside, like a plate that couldn't be glued
back together.

Her legs, her feet, grew heavier with each step
she took down the flights of stairs, and even
though she wasn't in a joking mood, she pulled
up a grin as Henry walked across the foyer from
Gus's study to the bottom of the stairs. "Hey,
Reuben." That was a nickname she'd come up
for him when he'd won a dance-off with her sister. He didn't wrinkle his nose; nor did his light
blue eyes twinkle. Instead, he studied her before
pulling her into a hug.

She returned his hug and whispered, "I should have known you'd find me."

He released her. "As soon as Betty heard you were in Chicago, Patsy searched newspapers delivered to Lane, and found an article that made them both so mad they convinced me that I needed to come check on you." He shook his head. "Did you really think a Dryer girl could run away and the other two would sit home waiting for her to return?"

"Dryer?" David asked.

She closed her eyes at how another lie was being revealed.

"Sorry, I know she's an Albright now," Henry said.

"Yes, she is," David said, frowning.

She pulled up a smile for her brother-in-law. "David told you he has a meeting this morning, Henry. I'll walk him to his car and be right back."

David held his hand out to Henry. "As I explained, it's a meeting that I can't miss. I'll be back within a few hours."

Henry, as tall as David, but with black hair, shook David's hand. "I understand. I'm sure Jane will tell me all about everything."

Even though her heart fell to her feet, Jane

looped her arm through David's as they walked to the hallway, hoping that made it look like everything was fine between them.

"Your last name isn't Bauer, either?" he said, once they'd arrived at the door.

"No."

"So we aren't even married?"

Everything about her was trembling. Cold. Nearly as cold as his voice. "No."

He nodded. "You could have just said no right from the beginning."

Blinking fast against the burning, she shook her head. "No, I couldn't."

He nodded, an odd and slow nod, before saying, "Answer me one thing."

She nodded.

"Is there anything else I should know?"

Three things that he might consider important came to mind. "My other brother-in-law owns the largest newspaper in Los Angeles, my father is one of the richest men in Hollywood, and Henry's uncle is the United States Attorney General."

He looked at her as if he couldn't believe what she'd just said, then shook his head and walked out the door.

She wanted to shout she was sorry, but he was right—there was no point saying it. Doing something about it was what she had to do. There was only one thing she could do. She ran down the hall and up the set of stairs at the back of the house, all the way to her suite, where she grabbed her suitcase and started tossing things in it.

Henry was in the living room of the suite when she walked out of the bedroom. He was a blur, due to her tears, but she knew it was him.

"What's going on here, Jane?" he asked. "And don't lie to me."

Her chest burned with pain as she admitted the truth. "I have to go home, Henry. Now."

David was trying hard, very hard, to keep all he was feeling inside. It had taken him several blocks to even be able to think. To breathe. Confusion, hurt, anger—it was all there, vying for space. Shock was there, too. She wasn't a maid or a flapper or poor or without family.

Above all, she wasn't his wife.

He'd been fully prepared to take the blame today. He had practically railroaded her into helping him, to coming to Chicago, and even when questions had arisen in his mind about her he'd chucked them aside—justified them to himself without asking her.

She was right in saying she couldn't tell him about her family because he would never have brought her all the way to Chicago. No matter where they'd been along the road, he'd have turned around and taken her back to Los Angeles.

He'd practically kidnapped her. All because he'd chosen to deceive his family rather than find out the truth, get to the bottom of why Joshua wanted him to marry Rebecca.

Because of her, he had gotten to the bottom of it, and his relationship with Joshua was—he huffed out a breath—better than it had been in years.

All because of Jane.

He turned the corner, saw the A and R building.

Damn it. What the hell was he thinking?

The shareholders could wait.

Jane couldn't.

He whipped into the parking lot, slammed on the brakes, hit the clutch and grabbed the shifter to put the car in Reverse to back out and head home.

The passenger door opened while he was shoving the shifter into gear.

"I have to go home," he told Joshua. "Shut the door."

"I know." Joshua jumped in and shut the door. "That's why I was standing out here, waiting for you. Both Charlene and Gus called."

David froze. "Why? What's happened?"

"I don't know. Charlene was crying. I couldn't understand her, and Grandpa just said to tell you to get home right away." Joshua slapped the dash. "Drive, man! I told my secretary to cancel the shareholders meeting."

Urgency filled him, and the drive back to the house felt a hundred miles long. The car was still rolling to a stop in the driveway when David shut off the engine, opened his door and jumped out.

Joshua was on his heels.

"Jane!" he shouted upon entering the house. "Jane!"

He ran down the hall. "Jane!"

"She's not here."

David slid to a stop as he rounded the corner. "What's happened?" he asked his grandfather. "Where's Jane?"

Charlene ran past him, to Joshua, sobbing.

Shaking his head, Grandpa said, "She's gone, David. I tried to convince her to stay until you got here, but she refused."

His insides froze. "Gone? Gone where?"

"Back to California. To her family."

It was as if a fist grabbed hold of his heart, squeezed it and wouldn't let go. "What are they driving?"

"You aren't going catch them. Henry didn't drive out here. He flew, and had an airplane waiting to fly her home."

David's mind spun. There had to be a way he could catch them. Stop them. "Chicago doesn't have a municipal airport."

"There's a military one. That's where he flew in and out of. They are probably already in the air." Grandpa sighed heavily. "She wouldn't even take her coat."

David cursed under his breath as his throat burned. "It's freezing out there!"

"I made her take a blanket," Elwood said from where he stood near the staircase.

David's heart hurt even more. Jane may not have been forthcoming with him, but she had been genuine. Completely genuine. The entire household had been charmed by that genuineness. The house itself hadn't been so alive in years.

"It was that damned article," Grandpa said. "In the society page. Claiming she was immodest and inappropriate. Her family read that article. I tried to explain, but she stopped me. Said it didn't matter."

Fury like he'd never known struck. David slapped the wall. "Damn it!" That stupid article may have been the reason her family had arrived, but he was the reason she'd left. Him and him alone. He'd handled everything wrong right from the beginning. Justifying everything to meet his wants. The things he thought he wanted and those he thought he didn't, and by doing that he'd robbed himself of the one thing that deep down he had always wanted. Love. He loved Jane more than this family, more than the railroad. Above and beyond all he'd ever known, ever had.

Worse though, than robbing himself, was what he'd done to her. She'd healed his family, opened his heart to love again, while he'd damaged her family, and her.

"You have to go after her, David," Charlene said.

Damn right, he did. He had to repair the damage he'd done. His anger grew stronger. It would take him at least five days to get there.

A hand landed on his shoulder. He spun, saw Joshua. His anger was still there and it needed a release. "She wasn't a gold digger."

His back teeth were clamped so hard his jaw stung. He'd accused her of that himself, thinking she wanted a sugar daddy.

Chapter Fourteen

Joshua shook his head. "I know she wasn't, David. As I told you before, she was—is— quality. Albright quality."

David huffed out a breath. "Albright quality? Her father is one of the richest men in Hollywood. One of her brothers-in-law owns the *Los Angeles Gazette* and the other is an FBI agent, whose uncle is the United States Attorney General."

"At the end of the day, boys, none of that matters," Grandpa said. "Not who her father is, or her brothers-in-law. It's who Jane is. She's what this family needed. A tie to bind us all together. She gave us that. Within a matter of hours."

David's heart warmed at the thought of her, at how she said that people forgot they loved one another.

"And you love her, David," Grandpa said.

"Damn right, I do!"

"We all do," Charlene said.

"We need to get you to California," Joshua said.

David questioned Joshua's sincerity. They'd butted heads for so many years that a complete turnaround couldn't have happened so quickly. Yet, it had. Because of Jane. With one little action, she'd proven that despite years of difficulties, they were a family who loved each other. "I need an airplane."

"Yes, you do, and that's exactly what you are going to have," Joshua said. "You'll be on one today, if we have to buy a whole damn airport!"

Jane lay in the bed she'd slept in for years, but there was no comfort in the familiarity. In fact, she felt rotten. Sick to her stomach.

She'd done it again.

Run away.

Rather than trying to find a solution, she'd run. It was time she stopped doing that.

Her parents had been so happy to see her last night. Father had chided her for worrying them, but he'd also apologized while hugging her, hard, and said he was so relieved that she was safe and sound. She'd told him that she was sorry, too, but that she'd had to leave. That she'd been unable to take being smothered any longer.

It had been very late when Henry had delivered her home. Betty had offered for her to stay with them, but Jane had declined, knowing that putting off the inevitable wouldn't make it any easier.

She had so many wrongs to right.

Those wrongs included David. She had to fix those, just like she had to fix the ones here at home.

Her happiness wasn't dependent upon others. It was dependent upon herself.

She'd spent years sneaking in magazines and reading them, dreaming of living the lives of people in the pictures in those publications. Thought that would make her happy. That she'd discover what she wanted. Who she wanted to be.

The problem had been that she'd been looking outside instead of inside.

A long, cold airplane ride had given her time to realize that. Something David had said kept repeating over and over in her head.

Rather than being sorry, focus on what you are going to do about it.

He'd said *we*, but he hadn't run away. She had.

* * *

She didn't sleep well if at all that night, and the following morning she got dressed, tied her hair back and went downstairs to face her parents.

To right her wrongs.

The pan of caramel rolls on the counter made her eyes sting.

"Your father suggested that I make those for you this morning," Mother said.

"That was kind of him, and of you to make them," Jane replied. "I'm sorry that I worried you both."

"I know you are, dear, and your father knows he was wrong. I know that I was wrong, too," Mother said softly. "I should have put a stop to things, like I did when your father and I eloped."

Jane was so taken aback the plates she was lifting out of the cupboard rattled together. "You and Father eloped?"

Mother's smile was secretive as she nodded. "Yes, we did. We were gone for almost a month before returning to Seattle."

"Where did you go?"

"We came here. Your grandfather, Sylas, was alive then, and he wanted to sell some land, but couldn't because your great-grandfather had put all the property in your father's name. So we eloped, came here, and after he sold some property we used that money to return to Seattle."

Amazed, because she'd never heard any of this, Jane asked, "Then what did you do?"

"We lived there for a few months, with my mother, and then we moved back here and your father sold more property. We've been here ever since." Mother filled a platter with scrambled eggs. "Your father has provided me with a life that I'd never imagined when we eloped. Three amazing and wonderful daughters, a beautiful home." She sighed. "I'd known he'd make me happy, but I'd never dreamed of how happy."

Confusion filled Jane. "But wasn't it wrong? To run away, to elope?"

Mother's smile was soft and serene. So was the gentle kiss she placed on Jane's cheek. "Sometimes we do things without thinking of the consequences. I saw you girls growing into strong-willed women and was proud of that, but I overlooked how unhappy you were in the process. I should have told your father it was time for us to let each of you grow, live but, like him, I was afraid of losing my little girls. Now, it's time to focus on what happens next. How all wrongs can become rights."

Jane thought about that, tried to decipher what

her mother meant as she followed her into the dining room and quickly set the table before returning for additional platters.

Then, during the meal which, in the past had always been silent, she was surprised all over again when her father spoke.

"I'm sorry, Jane," he said quietly but firmly. "I thought my rules, my expectations, for you girls would keep you safe. I saw all three of you growing up, but in my eyes, you were still three little girls that I needed to protect from the world." He glanced at Mother sitting across the table. "When your mother pointed out that you no longer were little girls, I then tried to find ways to make sure you were taken care of. I realize now, that in doing so, I was wrong, that I was too heavy-handed, too controlling, and I hope you can forgive me."

Dumbfounded, Jane was speechless for a moment. Then, realizing how difficult that had to have been for her father, she said, "Yes, you were—but, yes, I forgive you. You always provided everything we needed. More than what we needed."

He nodded at her and smiled.

That wasn't enough for her. She had a greater

need. Standing up, she walked to his chair, leaned down and wrapped her arms around him.

He returned her hug, which brought tears to her eyes.

"I love you, Jane," he whispered.

Her heart tumbled. "I love you, too, Father. I always have."

He patted her back and cleared his throat. "So, this young man you married. I understand he's a piano player."

The thought of David made her grin. She returned to her chair. "Playing the piano is just a hobby of his. He works for a railroad."

"In Chicago," Father said. "Henry said that's where you were."

"Yes, in Chicago." A sigh seeped out of her. "With his family." During the plane ride, after she'd told Henry everything, he'd suggested that she not say much to her parents about her marriage until he knew what needed to happen because of how she'd used the wrong name on the license. That was one more wrong she had to right.

"Will he be returning to California so we can meet him?" Mother asked.

She swallowed, but was done lying. "David

had an important meeting this week with his business."

"What is his business?"

"The Albright and Roberts Railroad. His grandfather Gus, Augustus Albright, founded the railroad."

"The A and R?" Father asked.

"Yes."

"I've heard of them. That's a very large railroad," Father said.

A rich man, just like he'd wanted. So they would be protected. Safe. Money didn't do that. She and David had slept outside, next to the Grand Canyon with nothing except two pillows and two blankets and she'd felt safe. Protected. She then thought of the other couple they'd met there, Sam and Sarah, and how David had left money for them in their car. "Yes, it is a large railroad, but I believe it's not important if a person has money, it's what they do with it that matters."

"Hello!" sounded in the room at the same time the front door closed.

Recognizing Patsy's voice, Jane jumped to her feet and hurried to the hallway, where she met her younger sister.

Hugging each other, Patsy said. "I wanted to

come over last night as soon as Betty called me, but she told me to wait until morning." Patsy released her. "I missed you."

"I missed you, too." Jane stepped back and gasped upon realizing what was different about her younger sister. "You cut your hair!"

"I did!" Patsy patted her short-bobbed hair, which barely touched her shoulders. "I'd been thinking about it, and just finally did it. Do you like it?"

"I do," Jane said. Then she whispered, "What did Father say?" Their father had always opposed them cutting their hair. Mother, too.

Patsy frowned. "Nothing. Why should he?"

He had changed. She just hadn't realized how much. Because she'd been so focused on herself.

"Lane loves it," Patsy said. "But he'd love me if I was bald."

"Patsy, come and have breakfast with us," Mother said.

Patsy hooked Jane's arm and they walked back into the dining room.

As soon as they entered the room, Patsy exclaimed, "Caramel rolls! Yum!"

They'd barely sat down when the kitchen door opened. "Hello!"

"In the dining room!" Patsy replied to Betty's greeting.

Once again, Jane realized how blind she'd been to everyone else before she'd run away. After her sisters had gotten married, they had come over for Sunday dinners and those meals hadn't been silent. She'd just been so focused on the things she didn't have that she'd overlooked the things she did have.

She gave Betty a quick hug as her sister sat down beside her.

"Henry said that David's house is very nice," Betty said, sliding a caramel roll onto her plate.

"Beyond nice," Jane said. "It's like a castle."

"Did you feel like a princess?" Patsy asked.

Jane had to smile at her sister's teasing grin. "Yes, I did." She had, but David had made her feel that way, not the house or even the clothes he'd bought her. He'd made her feel special because he was so special.

"Then your dream came true. You always wanted to be a princess," Patsy said. "Do you have a maid?"

Jane shrugged, then grinned, knowing her sisters would love to hear all about David's house. "Yes. Several of them."

"Maids?" Father asked.

"Yes," Jane answered. That led into a conversation about David's house and the people there, and Jane couldn't stop herself from telling them about all of the wonderful people, places and things she'd experienced since meeting David, especially the money they'd raised and delivered to the soup kitchen.

Patsy said she'd seen the picture of that in the Chicago newspaper that was delivered to Lane's office, which led Jane to talk about all the pictures she'd taken.

Long after Father left for work, Jane's tales of her adventures continued. Once the dining room and kitchen were cleaned, she, her sisters and mother moved into the living room, where she told them more, including the snowball fight.

"You really love him, don't you?" Betty asked.

"Yes," Jane said. Then the world came crashing down around her. Tears came. "I do, but I had to come home."

"Why?"

"Because you were all so worried about me."

Betty wrapped an arm around her shoulder. "You could have just told Henry you were fine. He said the people there didn't want you to leave. That the butler had tears in his eyes when you

344 The Flapper's Scandalous Elopement

left. Henry said he didn't know what to do, but that you insisted on him bringing you home."

"Is that true, dear?" Mother asked.

Jane bit her lips together to smother a sob. "Yes. I'd lied to David. I hadn't told him about any of you. I couldn't. Not in the beginning. I was afraid that he wouldn't take me to Chicago with him. And then it was too late."

"Not take you?" Patsy shook her head. "You eloped. Henry told Lane that you got married in Arizona."

Jane glanced at Betty, and the empathy she saw in Betty's eyes told her that Henry had told her everything. "We did," Jane admitted. "But I used a different last name on the application."

"Why?" Patsy asked.

Jane covered her face with both hands. "I don't know. I truly don't."

"Didn't you want to marry him?" Patsy asked. "Don't you love him?"

Flustered, Jane stood, threw her arms in the air. "All I knew then was that I didn't want to be a maid forever." She took a few steps, turned and faced the others. "I didn't even know what love was. Not the kind I feel for him now."

"Goodness," Mother said. "You girls have certainly never failed to surprise us. I agreed to your father's idea about finding husbands for each of you for two reasons. One, because I was worried about all three of you sneaking out at night, and two, because it was time that you each stood up to him. Showed him who the women were that you had become."

Jane shivered as she looked at her sisters, who were both as wide-eyed as she was.

Mother smiled at all three of them. "Yes, I know you all snuck out at night. I know a lot more than you girls think I do." She lifted her brows. "Do you honestly think I never noticed the hundreds of dollars of material, makeup and jewelry that I paid for and watched snuck into this house?"

Too stunned to speak, Jane once again glanced at her sisters.

Mother chuckled softly. "Someday, you'll all three know how a mother knows everything, and why they don't always tell everyone everything that they know." She waved a hand to the sofa, where Jane had been sitting. "Come, dear, sit back down. I have more to tell you."

Jane sat down between her sisters again, not sure what to expect next.

Mother folded her hands in her lap. "Your father's mother, though I never met her because she died when he was a boy, was a frail, fragile woman who didn't have the stamina to live the life her husband provided. They lived in the hills, searching for gold. Your father thought all women were like that. And he wanted nothing to do with them. With me. I fell in love with him at first sight, and the third time he pushed me away, had an excuse as to why I couldn't love him, I knew I had to do something, so I told him that I was coming to California with him. That we were eloping, that I was going to be his wife, so he'd better just get used to it."

"You did?" Patsy asked.

Mother was so soft-spoken, so dedicated to Father, that it was shocking to think of her standing up to him. For all of them.

"Yes, I did," Mother said. "And he tried backing out of us getting married, even after we'd run away together, but I wouldn't let him." Smiling, she continued, "He eventually realized that not all women were as fragile as he'd thought, but then you three girls came alone. Precious little babies are fragile and need to be protected. That's all he saw when he looked at you, and I knew why. As you grew up and started challenging him, like I had, he was overwhelmed. Four females against one male. There were days that

I felt so sorry for him, because despite every rule he set down, you found a way around them. That's where I found myself torn because, like him, you were the things we loved most about our lives, and yet…"

Jane took ahold of Betty's hand when her sister laid it on her knee, and ahold of Patsy's hand, on her other side.

"I felt sorry for you girls," Mother continued. "You'd grown into beautiful, amazing women who deserved the opportunity to find happiness. Love. But you were all so different. There's you, Betty, the oldest. The one to always follow the rules. You even made up your own rules to follow. And expected others to follow them."

Jane looked at Patsy and shared a look about how right that was.

"I was at my wits' end on your wedding day. I thought I was going to have to stand up and object myself. I say a prayer of thanks for Henry every night."

"Oh, Mother, that's why you kept insisting I needed to wait," Betty said.

"Yes, it was." Mother sighed. "And Patsy, as the youngest, you thought rules were made to be broken." Smiling, she shook her head. "I was so proud of you when you convinced your father to let you go to secretarial school. You knew what you wanted and you'd break every rule to get it."

Patsy laughed. "Lane was worth breaking every rule."

"I say a prayer of thanks for him, too," Mother said. "And then there is you, Jane. You were the reason we needed rules. When you convinced your sisters to start sneaking out, I didn't know what to do. But then I knew Betty would lay down the rules, and that you'd follow them. As long as someone didn't need your help, because that's where you always got stuck between following the rules and breaking them. You'd side with Patsy in breaking one, or side with Betty in enforcing one, depending upon who needed you at the time, because to you it wasn't about the rules, it was about who needed your help."

Mother was right about all three of them, and Jane wondered how they'd all thought they were pulling the wool over her eyes. They hadn't been, yet Mother had never revealed that she knew. Not at all.

"After your sisters were married, I became concerned about you sneaking out alone, so I spoke to your father about not securing a husband for you. I'd hoped that would give you the freedom you'd always craved." Mother chuckled softly. "I didn't expect you to elope two days later."

"I didn't either," Jane admitted. "It just happened. David was leaving for Chicago, and I—" She'd wanted to help him. Just like her mother said. Just like she'd wanted to help those people in the soup kitchen line.

"You wanted him to be happy," Mother said softly. "That's what we all want, for those we love to be happy."

Jane nodded. She still wanted him to be happy.

"Your father went about it wrong, the way he said you didn't need to get married. He assumed you knew that he meant not right away, to someone he chose, and you assumed that he meant you would remain home, forever. We all assume things at times. Betty knows, but I don't think you other girls know that your father is up in the hills, sluicing for gold in the creek," Mother said. "That's where he goes every day."

Jane hadn't heard anything about that. "Why?"

"Because it makes him happy," Mother said. "Shortly after we built this house, we had more money than we'd ever dreamed of having, had you three girls, and a beautiful home. I couldn't believe he wanted more and told him he had to stop searching for gold. That it was a pipe dream and that we didn't need the money. He stopped, for a time, but then he snuck out to do it. I was mad that he'd lied to me, but then I realized it wasn't the gold he was after, it was the searching that he loved."

Mother sat back and sighed. "And now you are all wondering why I just told you all of this."

Jane nodded, although she had just learned more about her family, her parents, than she'd ever known.

"Because no one is perfect. We all make mistakes. We all make assumptions. We all find out there are things we were wrong about. It's called living and there is nothing—no mistake, no assumption, no lie—that is too big to fix when we love someone."

Jane's grief returned tenfold. "But I didn't even use the right name."

"What are you going to do about that?"

Jane shrugged. She didn't know how, but she knew what. "Make it right."

Chapter Fifteen

David drove past the corner near the studio where he'd picked Jane up that night a week and a half ago and couldn't stop an influx of excitement at the idea of seeing her. In less than two weeks, she'd changed his life a hundred and eighty degrees. Changed it for the good in ways he'd never thought could change.

What he'd failed to understand was that he'd made himself believe he didn't want them to change. He'd justified the reasons to himself, and that had been enough, or so he'd thought. In reality, he'd been stuck in a rut, and had grown so accustomed to it that he'd thought he liked it.

It was simple. In the end, it all came down to the fact he didn't know what he wanted until he had it. Until it had landed in his lap.

Actually, it had landed on the piano bench beside him, in the form of an adorable blond-haired flapper who'd made him laugh, live and love.

He hadn't been looking for love, but he'd found it. An all-consuming love that made him realize he'd had things all wrong. He'd thought he could get married and then divorced and be just fine, because of what had happened with Charlene. He'd been mad because, to him, Joshua marrying Charlene had been the last straw for him and Joshua, after butting heads for years. He knew now that he'd confused the childhood friendship between him and Charlene for love, because it didn't compare to the way he loved Jane in any way.

He also knew now that Charlene had never loved him, either, but she did Joshua, and he truly was happy for them.

True to his word, Joshua had found a plane and a pilot. David had been in the air before midnight. He'd never ridden for so many hours in an airplane, but he would have walked all the way to California if that's what it would have taken. Now, after flying here in twelve hours, he was even more convinced that the A and R might need to invest in air travel. Building an airport in Chicago could be a very worthwhile venture.

Before Jane, that was all he'd cared about,

working at the railroad and expanding the family business. He still cared about that, but now he was also thinking about family and future generations of Albrights.

He hoped Jane wanted that, too. He didn't know why she'd used the wrong name on the marriage license, but in all honesty he didn't care.

He glanced at the note on the seat beside him. Joshua had arranged to have a car waiting for him in Los Angeles, and the note said that Henry had called last night to let them know that they'd arrived safely.

It also said to let Jane know that everyone in Chicago was looking forward to seeing her again soon.

If she didn't want to be married to him, he'd give her a divorce, but not without having a chance to let her know how much he loved her, how much he wanted to be married to her.

He found the house, an impressive two-story redbrick home with large white pillars, and pulled into the driveway. David picked up the note and shoved it in his pocket. He was sure there would still be times he and Joshua disagreed, but he was grateful that his brother and family had rallied behind him now.

He also wanted to provide Jane with the same support she'd shown him when it came to her family. Whatever had made her feel as if she were nothing more than a maid, which had made her want to run away, needed to be repaired.

A woman with short blond hair answered the door upon his knock, one who resembled Jane to the point he had to take a second look. There were two other blond-haired women standing behind her. One older, but both of them also resembled Jane in some ways. Just not nearly as beautiful.

"I'm assuming you are Jane's sisters and her mother," he said.

"We are," the older woman said. "Am I assuming right, that you are David?"

"I am," he answered with a nod. "Is Jane here?"

"She is. Do come in, David." Waving a hand, the older woman continued, "I'm Marlys Dryer, and this is Betty, our oldest daughter, and Patsy, our youngest. Jane is the middle one. The most outgoing, but also the most stubborn."

David wasn't sure why she was pointing that out, so he nodded before asking, "May I see her?"

"Of course," Marlys said. "She is up in her room, resting. She didn't sleep well last night."

"I'm sorry," he said, wondering if he should offer to wait until Jane woke, but he didn't want to wait. He wanted to see her now.

"Her room is the last door on the left," Marlys said, pointing toward the staircase behind her. "We'll be in the kitchen."

David hadn't expected her to say that and wasn't waiting for her to change her mind. "Thank you." Wanting to run, he forced his feet to walk up the stairs and down the hallway to the last door on the left.

The idea of knocking crossed his mind, but he chose to just try the knob instead.

It turned.

He pushed the door open. She was lying on the bed, facing away from the door and curled in a ball. His heart constricted at the same time it began to race. Quietly he entered the room and closed the door. Her blond hair was tied in a ponytail, hanging over one shoulder.

It was as if he was walking on ice, hoping it didn't crack beneath him, give way and send him to the bottom of an icy lake, as he crossed the room. It had only been a day, little more than twenty-four hours since he'd seen her, yet it felt like years. Lonely, pain-filled years. He didn't want to be separated from her again. Ever. But it had to be her choice. He wouldn't railroad her this time.

Arriving at her bed, he stood there, fighting the urge to lie down beside her and hold her.

She let out a little moan and rolled over. Her long lashes fluttered, and she smiled. "David."

Her voice was barely a soft whisper, but it rippled through him.

Her eyes snapped open then and she slapped a hand to her throat. "David?" She sat up. "Wh-what are you doing here? How did you get here?"

"The same way you did. An airplane." He sat down on the edge of the bed and, needing to touch her, he brushed the ponytail over her shoulder, and then a few tendrils away from her temple. "You aren't going to get rid of me that easily."

She laid a hand on his arm. "I wasn't trying to get rid of you. I just thought—" She sighed. "Oh, David, I don't know what I was thinking."

He cupped the side of her face. "That's why I'm here, so you can tell me what you were thinking."

"I was thinking about all the lies I'd told you, and how wrong that was," she whispered.

He leaned forward, pressed his forehead to hers. "You withheld some information, and I'm glad you did." Lifting his head, looking into her eyes, he continued, "If I had known about your family I wouldn't have taken you to Chicago, and that would have been tragic, because then I'd never have met the woman I love with all my heart and soul."

She blinked several times and pinched her lips together.

"I withheld information from you, too," he said.

"Not telling me about servants doesn't compare," she said, shaking her head.

"There's more." Guilt churned in his stomach because he should have told her this a long time ago. "I never told you that I'd planned on marrying Charlene, and that I asked her, but she turned me down."

"Because Joshua had already asked her." She cupped his face with both hands. "I'm so sorry about that, David. You had to have been heartbroken."

He wasn't sure if he'd expected her to be mad, or upset, but she wasn't either. Just compassionate. "No, I wasn't heartbroken. I was mad, mainly at Joshua because I thought he was just being vindictive. Now, I know the truth. They were in love, and they truly love each other."

"They do. They truly do, and I hope they think about adoption," she said.

"Adoption? You know about their issues?"

She lowered her hands and sat back. "Yes, Charlene told me while we were working on the gift-opening party."

That made sense since they had spent a lot of time together. Curious, he asked, "Did she tell you about her and me?"

"No. I found out about that the night of Gus's birthday party."

"From who? Why didn't you say something? Ask me?"

She shook her head. "Because it didn't matter. She's in love with Joshua. But she loves you, too, like a brother. And you love her, and Joshua. Just like I love my sisters and brothers-in-law."

Her ability to be so genuine would forever amaze him. "I do," he admitted. "They are my family." He took hold of her hands. "I just met your mother and sisters."

She smiled.

"They seemed very nice."

"They are."

"Why did you feel as if you were just a maid?"

She sighed and closed her eyes. "My father was very strict with us growing up, and, wanting to keep us safe, to protect us, he felt we needed to marry rich men. When I told you about someone objecting at a wedding, that was Henry, at Betty's wedding. She almost married a man Father had chosen. Lane was on the list he'd made, too, but he and Patsy had already fallen in love by the time they were married."

"That explains why you were so quick to offer to object for me." The muscles in his neck tightened at the same time his heart constricted. "Is that why you used the wrong name, and came home? For your wedding?"

Her smile was gentle as she shook her head. "No. I had expected the same thing, to be forced into marriage, but then Father changed his mind. He said I would remain here at home with him and Mother, inherit everything from them." Sighing, she continued, "I felt one was as bad as the other. When I heard your dilemma, I thought it would solve all my problems. But it didn't. It just created more."

He was so relieved she hadn't returned to marry anyone that he wanted to kiss her, hug her, but he always wanted to do that. Concentrating on what she'd said, he asked, "Because you ran away? Your family didn't know where you were?"

"There was that, but there was more."

"What?"

"I didn't want to fall in love with you, David. I think that's why I wrote the wrong name on our marriage application, because I already was falling in love with you. I think that happened the night we played piano together. I didn't admit it, even to myself, but I could see myself doing that again, playing the piano. I could see myself with you, and that scared me."

"Why?"

"Because I'd told myself that was what I didn't want. To marry anyone."

He grinned. "That's exactly what I was doing. Telling myself I didn't want to marry anyone, yet I did. I married you." He kissed the tip of her nose. "My heart knew long before my mind did."

"What are we going to do, David?"

"Is that what you want, to not be married to anyone?"

She shook her head. "I wish I'd used my real name. Jane Marie Dryer."

His heart began to pound. "What do you think of the name Mrs. David Albright?"

Bowing her head, she whispered, "That's not me."

"It's not?" He lifted her chin. "You are the

woman I stood with in that judge's chamber. The woman I vowed to take as my wedded wife, to have to and hold, to love and to cherish."

"I didn't use my real name." A tear slipped from the corner of her eye. "I wish I could change that, but I can't."

He wiped away the tear with his thumb. "I don't care what name you used, what I care about is if you want to be married to me?"

She nodded. "Yes. Yes, I do."

His heart soared, but he needed to control himself, because once he started kissing her he wasn't going to stop. "Then we are."

She smiled, but shook her head. "It's not that easy."

"Yes, it is. You filled out the application as Bauer, but you signed our marriage certificate as Dryer."

"I did?"

"Yes, you did." When he noticed that, he'd been as shocked as she was right now, and while waiting for the flight here last night, he'd called Jeff. "It's a clerical error—they happen all the time—and Jeff said it's a simple matter to correct."

"He did?"

"Yes, he did."

362   *The Flapper's Scandalous Elopement*

She sat up on her knees as her eyes lit up. "We're married? Really married?"

His heart was racing and the smile on his face kept growing. So did hers. "Yes, we are really married."

"Oh, David!" She looped her arms around him, hugged him tight. "I love you. I love you so much."

Unable to wait any longer, he kissed her. She not only returned his kiss, she plastered her perfect, supple body against his and held nothing back.

He released the passion he'd always held back while kissing her, and by the time their lips parted they were both gasping for air, but also wanting, needing more.

It was either stop now or lay her down on the bed and share all his love with her. "Will you come to my apartment with me?" he asked, wanting to have more privacy than they had here.

"Yes! Yes!" She flipped her legs over the edge of the bed and, while sticking her feet into her shoes, said, "My suitcase is by the door."

He grabbed the suitcase as they walked out of the room. "Do you have nightgown in here?" he asked, teasing her.

She batted her eyelashes at him. "No."

They both laughed and hurried down the steps.

Marlys met them at the bottom of the staircase. "Would you two care to join us for lunch?"

"We can't, Mother, we are taking my things to David's apartment," Jane said, glancing up at him with sparkling eyes. "But we'll be back later for dinner. So Father can meet David."

His body was on fire with need, anticipation and excitement. "Yes, we will," he agreed. "What time?"

"Six?"

"We'll see you then," Jane said as she pulled him to the door.

The drive across town couldn't have taken more than half an hour, but it seemed much longer. In their rush to get inside, he didn't notice he'd forgotten both of their suitcases in the car until they were in his apartment, arms locked around each other and kissing.

"Your suitcase is still in the car," he said when their mouths parted.

She giggled. "I don't need it right now."

"Me, either."

"I bet I can get undressed faster than you!" she challenged while running toward the bedroom.

He was right on her heels, and the undressing of both of them was like a snow flurry, with articles of clothing being tossed about instead of snowflakes.

"I won!" Naked, she leaped onto the bed so hard the springs creaked, which made her laugh harder.

The sight took his breath away. Her blond hair was flowing across his pillows, and her bare skin glistened in the sunlight coming in through the windows, but it was her eyes, the shimmer, and the passion, that he couldn't look away from.

She held out her arms.

He kicked off his final article of clothing and climbed over the foot of the bed. On his hands and knees, he crawled toward her, running a hand along the glorious smooth skin of her leg, her hip, her side. This was his wife. His wife. He was awed by that and fully enchanted.

Cupping the side of her face, he whispered, "You are so beautiful and I love you so much."

"I love you, David," she whispered against his lips. "So very, very much."

Her breasts were round, firm, and one nipple hardened as his forearm brushed over the top of it.

That was merely the beginning.

He kissed her, loved her, from top to bottom, as he'd dreamed of doing a hundred times over.

The restraint he'd managed to maintain in the past had completely evaporated, and he knew he'd never find the capacity to ever hold back from her again. He wasn't sure how he'd managed it this long.

Her skin against his, her touch, exploring him as lovingly as he was her, was beyond arousing. It was the epitome of a glory-filled torture.

Her little gasps and pleasure-filled moans of approval as he caressed her and stroked her was pushing him to the limits. He positioned himself over her, keeping his weight off her.

She grasped his hips and bent her knees, giving him full access to what he'd merely teased and gently explored before.

"There's no need to be afraid," he whispered as he touched the tip of his erection against her womanly folds.

Her giggle was soft. "I'm not afraid. I'm excited." She tugged on his hips. "I want you."

"I want you, too." The desire was greater than all he'd known. Carefully, he guided himself into her, just a small amount, giving her time to accept him.

She arched her hips upward.

He eased in further.

There was a catch in her breath and he stopped. "Does it hurt?"

"No." She arched upward again and this time wrapped her legs around his thighs, taking him fully inside her as her hips returned to the bed. "It's amazing."

His pleasure rumbled in his throat as her heat closed around him, soft and tight. He reveled in it a moment, and then he started to move, to glide in and out. The friction was magnificent, but it went beyond that. His heart, his mind, as well as his body, was fully consumed by her.

Their bodies united, her breasts brushing against his chest, was so good, so very, very good, a slow burn of pleasure built at the base of his spine. As it grew more intense, his movements grow faster, quicker.

She was moving faster beneath him, encouraging him to continue, go faster, thrust harder.

"David…" she gasped. "Oh, my, I'm going crazy inside."

"Me, too," he admitted, barely able to speak at the upsurge of pleasure because he could feel hers, too. Her body was gaining speed, too, as if they were rushing toward the same destination, hand in hand, heart in heart.

"David!" she shouted as her entire body shuddered.

His crescendo hit a moment later, shrouded him with satisfaction that was so pure it consumed his entire body even as the aftershocks slowly faded.

He kissed her long and slow as they both sank deeper into the mattress.

As their mouths separated, she cupped the sides of his face. "Tell me one thing," she said between gasps.

Instantly concerned, he asked, "What?"

"Why have we not done this sooner?"

He laughed and kissed her again. "Don't worry, we'll make up for lost time."

Jane had never imagined her body was capable of feeling so utterly glorious. No magazine article had prepared her for that, or for how amazing it was a second time, or for how fun it was a third time in the bathtub at David's apartment. She determined right then and there that she would never take a bath by herself again.

He laughed when she told him that, but he also agreed, as she knew he would.

Hours later, after they were both dressed in clothes out of the suitcases that he'd had to retrieve out of the car, they were ready to leave his apartment and go to her parents' house. She was wearing the blue-and-white dress that she had worn the day they'd arrived at his house in Chicago and he had on black pants, a red-and-white-striped shirt, covered with a black vest with a red silk back, and looked so very handsome. Smiling up at him, she said, "Thank you for coming to California. I regretted leaving you, even before I left."

He grasped her waist and pulled her close. "It was the longest twenty-four hours of my life."

She laid her hands on his shoulders, kissed his chin and then looked up at him. "Running away wasn't the answer, but eloping was."

Laughing, he kissed her. "Yes, it was." Moving toward the door, he said, "We need to leave before I take you back to bed."

She giggled because she wouldn't mind that at all, but she did want him to meet her father and Lane. "I like your apartment."

"Our apartment," he said. "It's up to you if we live here or in Chicago."

"I want to live wherever you are. Wherever you want to live. All I truly want, is for you to be happy." It felt so good to say that. To know what she wanted. Helping others, helping them achieve happiness was what she'd always wanted.

"All I truly want is for you to be happy. If living here near your family makes you happy, then that's what we will do."

She considered that, but his happiness was more important to her. His life and business were in Chicago, so that was where they needed to live. As they stepped out into the sunshine, she said, "I would like to visit my family, but I think we should live in Chicago. I miss the cold. The snow. Gus. Elwood. Charlene. Joshua."

He chuckled. "You might not miss them, or the snow, by February, but if that's where you want to live, we will, and we'll fly out here to see your family whenever you want."

"Deal."

"The A and R bought an airplane."

"You did?"

"Joshua and I did, with Grandpa's full approval." He opened the car door. "They are all looking forward to seeing you again."

"I'm looking forward to seeing all of them, too."

He shut her door, walked around the car and climbed in behind the steering wheel. "We

should visit the Rooster's Nest while we're here."
He winked at her. "The site where it all began."

Happiness bubbled inside her. "Yes! Let's!"

He steered the car away from the curb. "And
you can show me how you used to appear and
disappear. I watched you—you never used the
door."

She laughed and then leaned closer to whisper in his ear, "I'll show you, but you can't tell
anyone."

"All right." He hooked her around the shoulders and pulled her toward him. "Get over here
where you belong."

She slid up tight beside him, exactly where
she belonged and the place she didn't ever want
to leave.

They stopped along the way to her parent's
house, and he picked up flowers for her mother
and a box of cigars for her father.

Father was impressed and very talkative, asking David questions about the A and R, his family and home. Mother's cooking was as delicious
as ever, and she too was talkative.

Patsy and Lane, as well as Betty and Henry,
were there, too, and after they ate, Jane showed
everyone the photo album that David had brought
with him from Chicago.

It was late when they all left, but not that late. She stopped her sisters in the driveway. "I need to show David how I used to get to the Rooster's Nest. Anyone care to join us?"

"Sure," Patsy said.

"But we'll meet you there," Lane said. "Get us a table."

"That sounds good," Henry said. "We'll ride with Lane and Patsy. The back door's unlocked."

"Ducky!" Jane said, climbing in David's car.

"Why are we stopping here?" he asked a few minutes later when she had him pull into Betty and Henry's driveway.

"So I can show you." She opened her door and jumped out. "Come on!"

"Whose house is this?" he asked while climbing out of the car.

"Betty and Henry's," she answered. "That's why he said the back door was unlocked."

"But they were ahead—" he pointed toward the street "—of us."

"And they still are. You wanted to see how I got to the Rooster's Nest." She grabbed his arm. "Right this way."

She led him through the back door and into the basement. While lifting the keys off the hook, she thought aloud, "I still have her suitcase."

"Whose?"

"Betty's. It used to sit on that shelf. I stole it the night we ran away—I mean eloped." She unlocked the door and pulled it open. "Oh, grab that flashlight right there."

He picked up the flashlight and then clicked it on as she waved for him to enter the tunnel.

"What is this?" he asked, shining the light through the open door.

"A tunnel. It goes from here to the Rooster's Nest."

He shook his head. "That has to be a good—"

"Ten blocks," she said, giving him a shove through the opening. "Time to start hoofing it."

Shining the flashlight over the walls and ceiling as they walked, he asked, "You walked through this every night?"

"Yes. After Betty married Henry. Before that we'd take the trolley or walk, but I didn't like doing that by myself."

"But you didn't mind this?"

She laughed at the disbelief in his voice, and again at how he stopped when the ceiling trembled and a rumble echoed in the tunnel.

"What the—?"

"It's just a truck driving on the road overhead."

"This was too dangerous for you—"

"No, it wasn't," she insisted, and then explained how the tunnel had come to be, and how Henry had shown it to Betty while he'd been chasing a criminal, and how Patsy had become a reporter after meeting Lane at the Rooster's Nest. She laughed then.

"What's so funny?" he asked.

"I just realized that all three of us girls met our husbands at the Rooster's Nest. My idea really panned out."

"Your idea?"

"Yes, it was my idea to start sneaking out at night."

He laughed. "Why does that not surprise me?"

She laughed and then put a finger to her lips. "We are here," she whispered, "and have to be quiet so I can check if the coast is clear."

He frowned, but didn't say a word as she climbed the short set of steps and unlocked the door. She peeked into the room and then pushed the shelf all the way open and waved for him to follow her. Quickly she shut the door behind him, pushed the shelf in place and then grabbed his hand to run through the storage room. Again, at that door, she peeked to make sure the coast was clear and then pulled him out of the storage room.

At the edge of the curtain, she once again made sure the coast was clear and then walked out from behind the curtain. "Look, they are sitting at our table."

He looked at her with such awe she frowned. "What?"

"I would not have believed that if I hadn't seen it with my own eyes," he said.

She laughed and slid her arms around his neck. "Do you know what the best thing about being married is?"

"I can think of a few."

Laughing again, she changed her question to, "One of the best things?"

"What?"

She kissed him, a long, slow kiss, and then whispered, "I get to kiss you whenever I want." Then she kissed him again, just because she could, and because she wanted to.

Epilogue

Jane leaped onto David's back for him to carry her to the house, not because her boots were full of snow, simply because she wanted to. And it was fun. Every day of her life was fun. Today was extra special because her family was here, in Chicago. Her parents and sisters and their husbands. David had invited them all to fly to Chicago for Thanksgiving before they had left to come home last week, and they had! To her utter delight they had all arrived yesterday.

Therefore, today, she showed them one of her favorite things to do. Have a snowball fight!

David climbed the steps and she released her hold on him so he could put her down on the porch before they spun around, so they could watch the rest of the group walking up the steps.

"I think the men won," Joshua said, letting Charlene down from his back.

"No, they didn't," Patsy said as Lane lowered her down.

Jane laughed, she hadn't realized they'd all copied her in that, too. Even Betty, who Henry was carrying up the steps.

"Yes, I'm sure the men won," Joshua said, looking at David. "Don't you?"

"I—" David stopped and ducked.

Jane had already ducked because she saw it coming. The snowball hit Joshua on the shoulder.

"There!" Patsy said. "Now the women won for sure."

"I guess I was wrong," Joshua said, laughing.

"I was going to warn you to not say that," David said, slapping Joshua's other shoulder. "The Dryer women are not only stubborn, they are competitive."

"We are not," Jane said.

"You're not beautiful, either," David said teasingly.

They were all laughing when Elwood opened the door. "Hot chocolate is being served in the main living room."

"Thank you, Elwood," Jane said. Then, flashing a look of mock shock, she told Elwood, "My husband just said I was homely. Can you believe that?"

"No, I can't. Would you like me to call the doctor? Have his eyes, and head, examined?" Elwood asked.

She kissed the butler's cheek. "I shall let you know."

David grabbed her waist and picked her up, carried her into the house. "The rest of us are freezing while you're chitchatting!"

They all removed their outer clothing and then walked to the doorway of the living room, where her parents and Gus, who got along tremendously, were already drinking hot chocolate.

"I haven't seen you girls play like that for years," Mother said. "And the snowman you made is adorable."

"Yes, he is—" Jane squealed as David caught her waist again.

"Hurry up. Once she gets in the room, the hot chocolate will be all gone," he told the others.

Laughing, she spun around and hugged him. "Brat!"

"Kiss me and I'll give you some of my hot chocolate," he said.

She stretched onto her toes, brought her lips close to his and whispered, "I don't have to kiss you. Elwood will bring me my own pot."

"I see how it is."

"But I'll still kiss you, just because I can."

She did, and then hurried over to make sure there was plenty of hot chocolate for everyone.

Once everyone had been served, Gus stood and held up his cup. "I'd like to propose a toast. To Jane. The woman who brought our families together, in more ways than one."

"Hear, hear!" everyone shouted.

Her cheeks flushed, but she nodded and took a drink of her hot chocolate.

"I would like to make a toast to Jane, too," Joshua said. He held up his cup and, looking at her, he added, "Actually, it's more of a thank-you. A heartfelt thank-you."

That might be the most touching thing she'd ever heard. She had to blink at the tears that formed in her eyes because she knew he was being sincere, and she knew exactly why he was toasting her. "Thank you, Joshua."

David kissed her temple and she leaned against him. Happy. So happy.

"We were going to wait until tomorrow to tell everyone, but now seems like the perfect time." Joshua pulled Charlene closer to his side. "We've decided to adopt, and if all works out, we'll have a baby by Christmas."

Gasps and cheers of delight, as well as congratulations, filled the room. So did hugs.

"We are scared," Charlene said. "And just learning the process, but also excited."

"You'll be wonderful parents," Betty said, hugging her husband's arm. "Henry was adopted."

"We know," Charlene said. "Jane told us, and that's why we decided to look into it. I'm looking forward to your parents arriving and I'm hoping your mother won't mind if I ask her a few questions."

"She'll be delighted," Henry said.

Jane had told Charlene that already. Henry's parents were adorable and would be arriving later in the day. When Henry had said that his parents were flying to California to spend Thanksgiving with him and Betty, David had invited them to Chicago, as well. Jane loved how he'd included everyone, and she loved having them all here. He and Joshua had decided to build an airport in Chicago, for which she was very grateful because it meant she'd be able to see her family more often; however, she'd made David promise they would drive to California sometimes, too. And that she'd like to take the train a time or two, too.

"If we are talking about babies," Patsy said,

resting a hand on her stomach. "Lane and I will have one by the end of the summer."

Another round of cheers, congratulations and hugs filled the room.

"Don't look at us," Henry said as the room quieted. Patting Betty's stomach, he added, "It's obvious we are having one."

Betty was barely showing, but was forever caressing her stomach. Jane knew Betty would be the best mother ever. So would Patsy. And Charlene.

As the laughter quieted, all eyes settled on her and David. Jane laughed. "No, not yet." She looked up at David and then laid her head on his shoulder. "Someday, when I'm ready to share him."

"Oh, darling," Mother said. "You don't share your love when a child is born, you multiply it. Just like it's multiplied here. In this room."

"Hear, hear!" Gus said.

Once again, her mother was right. Jane was still in awe at how wise her mother was in so many things, especially when it came to assuming things. So much had changed the past few weeks. For the good. For all of them. It now felt like they were a real family. One that had made mistakes, but also loved one another. Made apologies for their actions, for their lessons learned, and looked for ways to make things better. Just like David and Joshua had. They now got along very well.

"My wife does have something to share with all of you, though," David said as he stood. "Bring your cups."

Jane was nervous but excited, and once everyone was in the music room, she sat down next to him at the piano.

"Ready?" he asked.

"Yes."

At his nod, she laid her fingers on the keys and then began tapping out the notes of the popular tune.

"It's 'We All Scream for Ice Cream'!" Patsy said. "I love this song!"

"I know!" Jane replied, laughing as David joined her in playing the snappy tune. When the song ended, everyone clapped and congratulated her. She accepted their praise, mainly because it truly belonged to her husband.

"Play another!" Father said. "That was wonderful!"

David glanced at her.

She nodded and held a finger over a single key. Although she'd enjoyed leaning to play a song, she loved merely tapping a key while he played more.

They were still playing songs and the others were singing when Henry's family arrived, his parents and Uncle Nate.

By the time she and David entered their suite that night, Jane truly didn't think she could be happier. As she put on one of her flannel nightgowns, she giggled because she knew she'd be taking it back off within minutes. She did not need nightgowns with David near. For more than one reason.

He was already in bed when she climbed under the covers, but he sat up as she scooted closer.

Holding out a wrapped box, he said, "I have a gift for you."

She smiled at him. "Why?"

"Just because. Open it."

Curious, she took the gift, untied the red bow and unfolded the paper to reveal the box. Glancing up at him, she lifted the lid. There were two gold rings, just like the wedding bands both he and she wore. He'd asked her if she wanted a different ring, one with diamonds or other jewels, but she'd said no. "What's this?"

"Wedding bands. Exactly like the ones we have." He lifted out the smaller of the two. "But the rings we have are made of cheap metal that will eventually wear out. These are made of gold and will last forever."

He removed the metal one from her finger and replaced it with the gold band. "That's what I want. Forever. I don't want anything between us to ever wear out."

Her heart had been full, but it swelled a bit more inside her chest, making room to love him even more. She took the other ring out of the box, then removed the one he was wearing and replaced it with the new one.

"That's what I want, too. Love that multiplies and never wears out."

* * * * *

LET'S TALK

Romance

For exclusive extracts, competitions
and special offers, find us online: